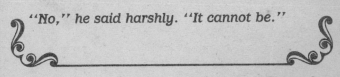

Without even questioning what she was doing, Sarah put her arms around his neck, pressed against him. "Evan?" she begged softly, "Is that what you really want to do? Leave me without a word?"

He moved so swiftly that Sarah was unprepared, and she gasped as he crushed her in his arms. His mouth slanted down over hers, and he kissed her with such hunger, she was almost shocked by it. Still, she responded eagerly as his hands caressed her back and his lips became more demanding. She buried her hands in his thick blond hair, reveling in his touch, the clean warm smell of him—his strength.

"No," he said harshly. "It cannot be."

MONDAY'S CHILD

Barbara Hazard

FAWCETT CREST • NEW YORK

A Fawcett Crest Book
Published by Ballantine Books
Copyright © 1993 by BW Hazard, Ltd.

Library of Congress Catalog Card Number: 93-90189

ISBN 0-449-22207-1

Manufactured in the United States of America

First Edition: August 1993

For Mary Jo Putney
and Cynthia Henry
—Monday's Children

Monday's child is fair of face,
  Tuesday's child is full of grace.
Wednesday's child is full of woe,
  Thursday's child has far to go.
Friday's child is loving and giving,
  Saturday's child works hard for its living.
And the child that is born on the Sabbath day,
  Is fair and wise and good and gay.

Quoted by A. E. Bray,
Traditions of Devonshire

Prologue

SARAH, THE DOWAGER Viscountess of Lacey, folded the letter she had just been rereading and, deep in thought, tapped it softly against her cheek. As she did so, a tiny frown creased her brow. The letter had come in the afternoon post, and a most unwelcome one it had been, too.

For I don't want to go home, no, not at all, she admitted to herself as she stared at the cheerful blaze in the fireplace. But if what Father writes is true, I really have no choice. I must go.

It seemed strange that her mother was ill. Sarah could not remember the lady ever spending a sick day in her life. She was so strong and robust, so full of life! And yet, if her father was to be believed, she was now confined to her bed, and had been for some considerable length of time. And what was worse, the doctor could put no name to her malady and therefore could affect no cure.

Perhaps it would do her good to see me again, Sarah told herself, even as she cringed at the necessity for it. But five years was a long time to have been gone. Indeed, so much had happened in the interim, it seemed even longer.

She grimaced then. Five years ago she had been wed against her wishes but at her parents' insistence to the wealthy viscount Roger Lacey, who had been almost thirty years her senior. And since that day, although she had tried to forgive her parents, she had never been to see them again.

Her marriage had transported her from a quiet life in the Kent countryside to the noise and crowds of London, and to balls, soirees—endless parties. And when she and her new husband had not been there, they had traveled here to the viscount's estate in Oxfordshire, or gone to visit others of the nobility at lavish house parties. It had been a busy time, full of gaiety, extravagance, and self-indulgence.

But the Viscountess Lacey had not been happy. Indeed, she had loathed every moment. She only hoped Roger had not known. It was not his fault that she found him distasteful, the life he led meaningless. She did not think he had suspected, for she had done her best to hide her feelings from him. She smiled to herself a little then, for she knew her happiness or lack of it was far from a concern of his. He had been a completely selfish man.

To him, she had been merely his wife, bought with good coin of the realm, to be a lovely object displayed for his friends' admiration. She needed only to be pleasant, smiling, and acquiescent, to please her lord well.

Still and all, she had mourned him dutifully, if not with any great degree of sorrow, when he died in a hunting accident. Much to her regret, they had not had children, for she had felt that a child would give her some purpose in life. But the one time she had mentioned it, the viscount had only laughed at her.

"Don't want any brats! Too old for it. But not to worry, m'dear," he had said, squeezing her waist and giving her a brief salute on the cheek. "M'brother's eldest will do very well for the title when I am gone. And this way I can have your entire attention, don't you see?"

And so she had given him that attention, no matter how it had bored her to do so. They had so little in common. The viscount was a sportsman and a gambler, a man who never considered anything but his own well-being and comfort, his own amusements. How he would have stared if anyone had dared suggest that his young viscountess might have other interests in life!

Neither was he a great thinker, concerned about the problems of the nation, interested in the new inventions, indignant at the inequalities of the system that decreed that station in life was everything. Why should he? He was one of the elite, at the top of the heap. The unfortunates below him were beneath his consideration. Sarah had never seen him with a book, and she had learned how he hated to be alone. A quiet evening at home was nothing but a dead bore to him.

When he had died, Sarah was honest enough to admit that she felt she had been relieved of a great burden, her heart was so much lighter. She had removed to the dower house almost immediately, for her brother-in-law and his son had implied that would be desirable. The new viscount was just her age, and she had seen the hot speculation in his eyes when he met her at the funeral. That speculation had made her all eagerness to leave the Court.

As the months passed, she had had as little contact with him as she could manage, and still be polite. Yet now he had begun to annoy her, for he was constantly on her doorstep. Sarah had foiled too many other gentlemen during her brief marriage to be misled about Henry Lacey's plans for her. His young viscountess was big with child now—her husband was forced to look elsewhere for his satisfac-

3

tion. She could tell he thought a discreet love affair would be just the thing, and so tidy, too, keeping it in the family as it were. And there was no denying she was certainly handy!

She looked at the letter she held again. Here was a perfect way to escape the man. And if she could not look forward to visiting her parents, at least she would be safe there. What she was to do when her mother released her at last, she had no idea, however. She had no desire to live in town, and she certainly had no intention of remaining at her girlhood home. No, never that, she told herself firmly. And it would not be prudent to come back here—not for a very long time. Ah well, she told herself, rubbing her forehead to ease the little ache there, time enough to think of all that later.

A knock on the drawing room door startled her, and she looked up to see her butler standing there and bowing.

"Your pardon, m'lady. The viscount has called and asks for a moment of your time," he said.

Sarah glanced from Petson's expressionless face to the gilded Cartel clock on the mantelpiece, and her brows rose.

"At ten o'clock at night?" she asked.

"Just so, m'lady. Shall I—shall I deny him?"

She thought for a moment. She could tell by Petson's voice that he disapproved of a visit at this hour—well, so did she herself if it came to that!—but she decided she might just as well get the interview over with now, rather than having to face it later.

"You may show the viscount in," she said at last.

As he bowed, she added mischievously, "But stay close, and if you hear the bell, I expect you to come running. None of your usual stately tread, now!"

For a brief moment, the butler's face creased in

4

a smile, a smile that was gone as quickly as it had come.

When he left the room, Sarah put her letter down and rose from the sofa, for she had decided to stand during this confrontation. She intended it to be brief. And now that she had decided to leave the dower house, there was no need to shilly-shally. The new Lord Lacey would find himself on the drive in a matter of minutes.

As he entered, she bowed slightly, but she did not smile. It did not deter him from coming toward her eagerly, hands outstretched.

"My dear Sarah!" he said as he captured hers in his own big ones and squeezed them. Behind them, Petson coughed as he shut the drawing room doors softly.

"Whatever is it, m'lord? Is the viscountess brought to bed with the child?" Sarah asked, still unsmiling. "It is the only thing I can think of that would explain your calling here at this time of night."

Henry Lacey flushed a little, and she pulled her hands away to walk back to the fireplace and the bell that was placed on a table there. She had smelled the brandy on his breath and she steeled herself.

"No. No, Emily's not in childbirth," he admitted, his eyes never leaving her face. He looked around then, as if surprised to find himself still on his feet, and he added, "Aren't you going to ask me to sit down, m'dear? Order me a brandy? It's not very hospitable of you, 'pon my soul, it ain't!"

His face was wreathed in a jovial smile, and sure of himself and his reception, he winked at her.

"There is no need for you to sit or have refreshments, for I do not intend you to remain," Sarah told him. As he started toward her, frowning now, she picked up the bell and showed it to him.

"Stay where you are or I shall ring this bell and have Petson show you out," she threatened. "Now, what is it you want, m'lord?"

"I—I wanted to see you, of course," he said, trying for an air of nonchalance. "Surely it has not escaped your notice how very much I—I *admire* you, my dear?"

"I?" Sarah asked, her voice cold. "Your late uncle's wife? How extraordinary! And while your own wife is carrying your first child, too."

"But that's just it," he admitted, smiling at her again. Sarah could not help shivering at the lust she saw in his eyes, the way his glance roamed over her, inspecting her slowly from head to toe. "It occurred to me that we might share some, hmm, pleasant hours together, Emily being unavailable at this time. And after that old fogy you were married to, I'm sure you must be eager to have a love affair with a younger, more virile man. Indeed, I suspect you've had plenty of them in the past, have you not, my tempting Sarah? No one as lovely and luscious as you are, with that divine figure, could not have! And your red hair gives you away. So—so hot, ain't it?"

Sarah stared at him, speechless with rage, and he threw out his hands and shrugged. "Well, I didn't intend to be so blatant about it, but you would make me stand over here! Now, if you'd only let me kiss you, caress you, all this plain speaking would not have been at all necessary.

"Sarah, these past few months I have felt I was going mad! Mad for you, living so close to me, and yet so unattainable! Come, sweetings, let me show you how wonderful it would be, the two of us together. And unless you're giving your favors to one of the footmen or a groom, surely you must feel a driving need as well. No, no, you must not feel I

6

censure you for it, if you have. After all, it's been a year since the old man died, and—"

The lady remembered the bell then, and she rang it—hard. "I have seldom been so insulted and disgusted," she said through clenched teeth. "I have no intention of having a love affair with you. I don't even like you, if you want the truth, you horrid, lecherous man!

"Ah, there you are, Petson! The viscount is just leaving. Be so kind as to show him out."

For a pregnant moment, Henry Lacey glared at her, and Sarah felt a tremor of unease. He was a tall man, solid and well muscled, and Petson was no match for him. If he decided to make trouble . . .

"Do give my best wishes to your wife. Tell her I will call on her tomorrow for a comfortable coze," she said, hoping to remind him of the scandal that would ensue if he pressed the issue before a servant, the miserable life he would lead if his viscountess discovered what he was up to.

That possibility must have occurred to him then, for he spun around, almost upsetting the butler who stood so close behind him. The frown on his red face and the way he stalked from the room made it clear how angry he was, and Sarah heard the front door slam behind him long before Petson could even reach it. She shook her head and sighed.

All her disinterest in him, all her refusals to see him, talk to him, accept dinner invitations at the Court, had been for nothing. Henry Lacey was just as stubborn a man as his uncle had been, and he wanted his own way in everything. Especially, he wanted her. Perhaps it ran in the family.

Well, she thought as she sank down on the sofa again, it is a good thing I'm leaving the estate, for I have no intention of letting him have me. And I've no doubt he plans force now that I have not only denied him, but insulted him as well.

Men! Sarah thought with a grimace. How impossible they were! How overwhelmingly, thoroughly, *despicably* conceited!

One

IT WAS THE invariable custom of Miss Eloise Withers and Miss Hannah Farnsworth to take tea together at four every Thursday afternoon. Only sickness or the vilest of weather could keep the two elderly ladies apart, as everyone in the village of Sutton Cross, Kent, and indeed in the countryside for miles around, could attest.

The ladies alternated weeks. If tea was to be at Miss Withers's, Miss Farnsworth could be sure of getting watercress or potted hare sandwiches, depending on the season. At Miss Farnsworth's cozy cottage, which faced the green, Miss Withers enjoyed cucumber sandwiches on thin-cut bread in summer, and ones of salmon paste in winter. Only desserts were allowed to be a surprise, angel cake or cream puffs, queen's cake or macaroons. Occasionally a heavy plum cake would be introduced, or perhaps a rich éclair. But whatever the menu, it was served on each lady's best plates, with delicate linen napkins, the India tea being poured from silver services polished to a fare-thee-well, for even though the best of good friends, the ladies were fierce rivals when they entertained each other.

On this particular Thursday, Miss Withers made her way from her home near the stone church and around the green to arrive punctually at Miss Farnsworth's cottage as that church bell struck the hour. Admitted by the little maid, she divested herself of bonnet and gloves before she entered the tiny parlor that overlooked the street. Discreet lace curtains hid the passing scene as the elderly ladies pressed faded cheeks together and inquired of each other's health.

Miss Withers could see that her friend was big with news, and to tease her, she strung out an account of a headache that had bedeviled her the day before, and described in great detail the tisanes and cordials she had tried before it had been vanquished.

As she rang the bell for tea, Hannah Farnsworth listened with only half an ear. Eloise was prone to headaches, and although she was sure it was unfortunate, she did wish her old friend would conclude her recitation so she could relate the momentous news she had gleaned since the last time the two had met after church the previous Sunday.

But when her soliloquy ended, and to Eloise Withers's surprise, Hannah did not immediately rush into speech. Instead she chatted of ordinary things, the weather and the coming church bazaar, until Molly had brought in the tea tray and curtsied herself away.

Accepting a plate containing salmon sandwiches and a piece of nut bread and butter, Miss Withers eyed her friend sharply. She noticed that Hannah's cheeks were flushed, and her eyes sparkled, and for a moment she thought to allow her the victory of being the first with the news. But this generous feeling did not survive, for in gathering news as well as in entertaining, the ladies were competitors.

As she spread her napkin on her lap, she said, "I see that you have something to tell me, my dear. But can it be that you have also heard that the earl is returning to the Hall at last?"

Miss Farnsworth's face fell slightly. "Never tell me you know that!" she exclaimed. "Why, and here I thought to be quite before you, for I heard it from Molly only this very morning. You know her brother is in service at the Hall."

Miss Withers nodded. "But the vicar's wife learned of it from m'lord's agent two days ago. It seems strange, does it not? Why would he come home now? 'Tis only early October, and I did not expect to see him before Christmas. If then," she added darkly, for it was a sore point with her that Jaspar Howland, the young Earl of Castleton, so seldom graced his estate, thus providing her with endless gossip and speculation about his activities and his occasional guests.

"Perhaps he has come to see his sisters and his aunt?" Miss Farnsworth speculated as she poured out the tea.

"It would be lovely indeed if he had any such noble purpose." Miss Withers said. "But since he has left university, he has appeared to prefer the fleshpots of London to quiet Kent."

Miss Farnsworth raised an admonitory hand. "Oh, surely we do not know that he frequents such places, dear," she said. "Whatever they may be, and please don't tell me," she added quickly.

"I cannot imagine him spending his time in church or engaged in any worthwhile pursuit, and if you will but recall what you have known of him all his life, neither could you," Miss Withers said bluntly. She had always prided herself in calling a spade a spade.

"No, I daresay he is only coming on a repairing lease. I have heard tell that young men these days think nothing of whistling away a fortune on their gambling, their extravagances, and their demimondes."

Miss Farnsworth squeaked a little in protest,

turning quite pink as she did so. She was as elderly a virgin as her friend, but unlike her, she still preserved a girlish modesty, and even the mildest oath had her searching for her handkerchief and vinaigrette. "How can you, Eloise?" she asked in reproach. "You know I never mention *that* kind of woman! And to think the earl, and at his tender years, too, would—no, no, I will not think it of him! And surely you are wrong! Why, the nobility are above such things, I'm sure of it! They are too high, too proud, too aware of their exalted titles to soil them by stooping to dally with—oh dear!"

Her friend could see she had become quite upset and she leaned forward to pat her trembling hands. No point in telling Hannah that men were all the same no matter what their station, and not a bit different than they had been when the two of them had been young.

"The sandwiches are delicious, Hannah," she said instead. "So moist this week. Your cook is to be congratulated. No, no," she added as Miss Farnsworth proffered the platter again, looking easier now. "I have had quite enough, I do assure you. But I will not say no to another cup of tea with my cake. So satisfying, tea, is it not?"

Miss Farnsworth nodded as she took her guest's cup and busied herself pouring out again.

"I have heard some news that perhaps you have not," Miss Withers went on, watching her friend carefully as she did so. "The vicar's wife told me only yesterday that Lady Lacey is also returning home."

Not at all disappointed at Miss Farnsworth's start, the way her faded blue eyes widened, she settled back in her chair and tried not to smile at her victory. "Oh, yes, it is true indeed! She returns to attend her ailing mother."

"Poor dear Mrs. Jennings," Miss Farnsworth mourned. "She has not improved then?"

"No, and as we were discussing last week, that is unusual. She is the healthiest-looking woman, and this malady seems to quite confuse Dr. Holmes. The man does not seem to be able to either name her sickness or cure it. If you ask me, Hannah, I think it is all a hum, but for what reason she could be pretending to be ill, I have no idea."

"Well, I am sure we must commend Lady Lacey for her thoughtfulness," Miss Farnsworth said bracingly. "How delightful it will be to see her lovely face again! Why, I cannot remember the last time she was here, can you?"

"Five years ago last spring, it was," Miss Withers reminded her. "She left here immediately after her wedding and has never returned. And remember how strange we thought that? I mean, after her husband died so suddenly last year, we both expected her to come back here to live, to support her dear parents in their declining years, but she did not. The young, Hannah, are a deal too careless in their behavior. Besides which, widow or no, Sarah Lacey in entirely too young to be living by herself."

Miss Farnsworth nodded vigorously. "So much more suitable for her to retire to her parents' home. I quite agree. There is something about a young widow living alone that is not . . . quite . . . nice."

"Well, she must be twenty-six now if she's a day. Hardly a girl. In fact, if she were still unmarried, people would say she was old-cattish, quite on the shelf, in fact."

"Such an indelicate phrase that," Miss Farnsworth murmured in reproach, no doubt thinking of the many decades both she and her friend had been placed there.

"Still," she added, holding out the cake platter again so Miss Withers could select another macaroon, "if she is coming now, perhaps she might be persuaded to make a permanent move. Such a comfort she would be to her parents, for young Mr. Jennings, being a man, is so seldom seen."

Her friend snorted. "Ha! And of what use would he be if he were here? Men! No good at all where sickness is concerned. And, as far as I can see, in few other instances either!"

Miss Farnsworth ignored this familiar complaint. It was a well-known fact that Eloise Withers looked down on the entire male sex, with the possible exception of her long-deceased father and elderly members of the clergy. Even young curates were suspect in her eyes, until they had proved themselves over the years.

And yet she had hinted more than once that she had once loved a man, only to cry off at the last minute when she discovered he was not worthy of her. Miss Farnsworth had sympathized, remembering a young man of her own who had never returned from the revolution of the American colonies years ago. Now she put these faded memories from her mind as she said, "Still and all, I do look forward to seeing Sarah again. It will be good to call on her, find out what is happening in town. Although I do recall hearing that she has spent most of her time in the dower house on the late viscount's estate in Oxfordshire, hasn't she? I'm sure Mrs. Holmes told me so."

Miss Withers sniffed. "I would not depend on Helene Holmes to know anything of the young lady's doings. Tells things to make herself important, that one."

Miss Farnsworth shook her head a little in reproach, the white curls she affected swaying gently as she did so. "You are too harsh, my dear," she scolded in her gentle voice.

Miss Withers smiled, wondering, and not for the

first time, why Hannah had let herself get so old-looking. Now, she herself applied a discreet hair color that kept her thinning locks as ebony as they had been in her girlhood. "Only with you, Hannah," she assured her. "Come now, admit Mrs. Holmes has only been regaling you with tidbits to get herself invited here for tea someday. So often has she remarked our little visits!"

As she tittered, Miss Farnsworth looked distressed again. "Yes, I agree she has been hinting, quite blatantly, too. Do you think that perhaps it would be kind to—"

"On no account," Miss Withers said sternly as she eyed the decanter of sherry that sat discreetly on a table against the wall. Sometimes Hannah suggested a glass, if they had a great deal to discuss. And surely today it would be appropriate, with Jaspar Howland and Sarah Lacey arriving soon. Miss Withers was quite sure they would stir things up a bit, bring a little life to the village through the dreary November days that lay ahead, and she could hardly wait for them.

As if she had read her friend's mind, Miss Farnsworth gestured coyly to the decanter, and Miss Withers nodded and smiled.

In no time at all, the two elderly ladies who were known throughout the area as "Miss Dye and Pry" and "Miss Prim and Proper" were deep in a discussion of possible coming events over a glass of nut-brown sherry.

Not even dreaming that her arrival was awaited with such delight and anticipation by anyone besides her parents, Sarah Lacey stared out of the window of the carriage that was carrying her back to her girlhood home, her face blank of any expression.

The long days of travel had done nothing to ease

the tiredness she felt, for once the decision had been made, she had hurried to put her plan into execution. Indeed, not two days after Henry Lacey's unfortunate call, she had been on the road, all the plethora of details that a lengthy absence entailed, settled. The house had been closed except for the few servants who had been left to see to its care, the viscountess—and of course, her husband—had been informed, the packing had been done, and a letter sent before her to apprise her parents of her arrival.

The Kentish countryside was as lovely as she remembered it, with fields ripe with grain being harvested. The fruit trees were heavy with their crops of apples and pears, and well-cared-for cattle stood knee-deep in thick, green grass, looking complacent under the warm October sun.

After the carriage swept through the village of Wye, Lady Lacey began to see familiar landmarks, and she knew that Sutton Cross, the village that was nearest to Three Oaks, lay only a few miles ahead. Mentally she began to prepare herself for her reunion with her family.

Across from her, her maid wondered why the lady's soft lips tightened so, and why a tiny frown creased her smooth brow. She was a lovely woman, was Lady Lacey, Betsy thought. Wonder what's bothering her, then.

By the time the carriage came up the long drive to her father's manor house, fronted by the massive oaks that gave it its name, Sarah Lacey was ready. She had a warm smile for the butler when he opened the door at her knock.

"Good afternoon, Bradbury," she said, holding out her hand. "How good to see you after all this time!"

Mr. Bradbury grasped her hand for a moment in return, but he was quick to bow as well. "Welcome home, m'lady," he said, beaming down at her. The butler was very tall and thin, his white hair and erect posture lending him dignity.

"Is my father at home?" she asked as she went to the ornate mirror on the wall to remove her bonnet and gloves so she could smooth her hair. She handed the articles to her maid.

"I regret to say that he is not, ma'am," Bradbury told her as the footman came in with the first of her cases. "Take those to milady's old room, Thomas," he said in an aside before he turned and added, "Called away to Tunbridge Wells he was, yesterday. We expect him in time for dinner, however. Of course, your mother is here, for she never leaves her room these days."

"I'll go up to her immediately," Sarah told him. "This is my maid, Betsy Grinnell. Do look after her for me, won't you? Show her where she is to sleep, explain the household routine?"

The butler bowed, and Sarah ran lightly up the stairs. How much the same the old place looked, she thought, smiling a little at the romantic painting of a little girl with some kittens that adorned the upper hall. When she had been younger, Sarah had often stuck out her tongue at her, and she was tempted to do so now. The little girl still looked smug, and she still had the same insipid smirk.

"Mother?" she called out softly as she tapped on that lady's door. "Are you awake?"

For a moment there was only silence. Then a weak voice bade her enter. It was so unlike her mother's usual authoritative tones that Sarah's brows rose.

The room she entered was airless and somehow depressing. But perhaps that was because the draperies were closed over the windows, keeping out the sunlight.

"Daughter Sarah," Mrs. Jennings murmured,

holding up her arms and presenting her cheek. "At last you are here!"

"I came as soon as I could arrange it, Mother," Sarah said as she bent to kiss her and hug her carefully. As she did so, she noticed that her skin was cool. There was no fever then. And she certainly seemed as robust as ever she had. Mrs. Mary Jennings had always been a large woman, and if anything, Sarah thought she had added flesh since she had seen her last.

As she sat down near the bed and took her mother's hand in hers, she also noted that her eyes were bright, and her complexion good. What was going on here? Was she really sick, or had that been a ruse to get her daughter here? But for what reason?

"What does the doctor say about your illness, Mother?" she asked, stroking her hand.

"He does not know what it is," Mrs. Jennings complained. "And each medicine and tonic he gives me tastes worse than the last. But he can bring no improvement. It is too bad!"

"Yes, it is. But how do you feel?" Sarah persisted. "Are you in pain?"

"No, not in pain, precisely. It is more a lassitude I feel. Indeed, sometimes I am so weary, it is all I can do to drag myself to a sitting position to take nourishment. Not that that matters, for I have lost all my appetite. And my head aches all the time."

Ignoring the lady's considerable girth, Sarah made sympathetic noises as her mother went on, "But perhaps I will get better now that you are here at long last. I was so distressed that you did not come to us after Roger died. It would have been so much more appropriate! For even though you are a widow now, you are a very young one. And there has been talk about it in the village; of that you may be sure!"

"I fail to see why. I *am* a widow, not a young girl

who has to be chaperoned anymore," Sarah said firmly. "And I prefer to live in the dower house. I am afraid I have grown used to having things my own way, Mother, issuing orders, arranging meals and my own schedule. Two women in one house never bodes good for either one. I do seem to remember you saying much the same thing when there was a plan afoot to have Grandmother Jennings come and live with us. Do you remember?"

Mrs. Jennings closed her eyes and sighed. "It is not at all the same thing," she said, her voice querulous. "James's mother was a terrible tartar, quarrelsome and bossy to a fault. Whereas we have always got along well! And a mother is not to be compared to a mother-in-law, you know!"

Wisely, Sarah decided not to comment on this irrefutable fact, nor did she try to contradict the lady on her rose-colored version of the past. Had she forgotten the arguments the two of them had had? How often she had bemoaned Sarah's "willfulness" and "disobedience"? Her icy treatment when Sarah displeased her? The difficult tasks she had set to punish her? Obviously she had.

"Well, I am here now for a long visit," she said soothingly instead. As her mother opened her mouth to speak, she went on, "And I won't leave until you are quite well again."

"But tell me, what news of Geoffrey? I have not heard from him this age. Is he still in London? Has he been down to see you?"

As they always did, Mary Jennings's eyes brightened at the thought of her only, beloved son. She even smiled a little. Sarah tried not to remember that she had not smiled at her, not once since her arrival.

"Darling Geoffrey! No, he has not been able to come. He is much too busy," his mother said fondly.

Sarah wanted to ask "Doing what?" but she kept

her mouth closed. From what she had been able to gather, her twenty-four-year-old brother had never done anything since he had abandoned university after only a year but gamble and waste his time in London. Oh, and spend money, of course.

"He is well?" Sarah asked instead, struggling to keep her face expressionless.

"I am happy to be able to tell you he is. And so handsome these days, you would stare! I'm sure there's many a miss who would give her eye teeth if he would but propose. Of course, he is much too young for any such entanglement as yet. My son! Do you remember what a dear baby he was, Sarah?"

"Not really. I was only two when he was born, remember. What I do recall is that he cried at all hours of the day and night. In fact, at that tender age, I considered him a terrible nuisance."

She smiled as she spoke, to show it was a jest, but even so, Mrs. Jennings frowned now. "You were jealous of him," she said coldly. "It was most distressing, for he was such a delicate baby. Not like you. You were such a healthy infant, you never gave anyone a moment's concern. And of course, Geoffrey has remained delicate to this day. I cannot tell you what a worry it has always been to me; the times I despaired of ever raising him to adulthood!"

"Oh, I believe I have always understood your anxiety for Geoffrey, Mother," Sarah said dryly. Then she rose. "Should you like to rest now? I must help my maid with the unpacking; see she gets settled."

"Yes, I am tired again," Mrs. Jennings admitted, her hand picking at her blanket in a fretful way. "But do come back and take tea with me, Sarah. We have so much to discuss!"

"Of course," her daughter agreed easily as she

curtsied. At the door of the room, she turned. "Shall you be able to come down for dinner, ma'am?"

"Oh, no, that is quite beyond my poor powers," Mrs. Jennings mourned, turning down her mouth. "But your father will be back from Tunbridge Wells by then. You need not dine alone."

Sarah smiled and nodded, but the smile disappeared as she went back along the hall to her old room. She had the strangest feeling that something was not right here, and it wasn't only that her mother had such an unusual ailment. For there had been something in her manner, her voice, the way her eyes had slid away from any prolonged contact with her long-gone daughter, that made Sarah suspicious that things were not at all as they seemed. She told herself she must keep up her guard. No doubt it would all be made plain to her in time.

Later, Sarah's reception by her father was much warmer. He had a wide smile for her as he took her in his arms for an encompassing hug. Somehow it made her feel better.

As she went in to dinner on his arm, he patted her hand and chuckled. "How fine you look, my dear! Quite smart! You'll have all the ladies hereabouts deep in envy of your London gowns. But of course, with Roger Lacey's fortune, I'm sure you've grown accustomed to the best, have you not? And that is how it should have been."

As he handed her to her seat beside him, he smiled again. Sarah was wearing one of her new dresses, a pale green muslin with the fashionable low, round neckline and short, puffed sleeves. It was trimmed with delicate lace and knots of darker green ribbons, and with it she wore an emerald pendant on a fine gold chain. It had been such a relief to her to leave off her mourning.

"Oh, I shall not quite overwhelm them, Father,"

she said lightly, nodding as the footman spread her napkin in her lap. "I have brought only my simplest things, for it would not do to be overgrand in the country. Then, too, I expect to spend most of my time nursing Mother."

She frowned a little before she asked, "What do you think can be wrong with her, sir? It is so unlike her to be sick in any way."

James Jennings shook his head sadly. "There's no way to tell. Dr. Holmes is quite at sea. But come, my dear, drink up your soup! I am anxious to hear how you have been, and what you have been doing in Oxfordshire."

"Living very quietly, of course," Sarah told him. "A year of mourning lasts forever, or so it seemed to me."

"Yes, for you are young," Mr. Jennings remarked. "But all that is behind you now, my dear."

As the two progressed through three courses and removes, her father kept Sarah entertained with news of the estate and the surrounding villages, and he asked a great many questions about Lacey Court and the new viscount. Sarah was careful not to let him know the true state of affairs, nor did she malign Henry Lacey's character in any way. He was not important, and it was all in the past now.

Only when the servants had removed the dessert plates, placed a decanter of port before him, and bowed themselves away did Mr. Jennings broach any more personal subjects.

"Do not run away to the drawing room, Sarah," he said with another warm smile. "Not on your first evening home. Five years is a long time to be parted. I feel I have not seen you this age, and I would enjoy your company longer."

Obediently Sarah sat back in her chair, and he went on, "I trust Roger left you well before with the world, daughter? It has been a worry to me, not knowing how things were left."

Sarah was careful to keep her face noncommittal as she said, "Very well before. Of course, the bulk of the estate as well as the title went to his heir. But I was left a most generous portion, and it is safely invested."

"I am relieved. Who is handling these investments for you? A capable man, I hope?"

"The late viscount's own man of business. I trust Mr. Sims explicitly."

She was surprised to see her father frown as he moved his glass of port in aimless circles on the table before him.

"Yes, I'm sure, but somehow I cannot like it," he muttered. "So much more suitable for you to let me handle your affairs, puss! I am your father, and you are barely out of your girlhood. And it is quite a different situation, now that Roger has died and is not overseeing this Sims person himself. What you need is a man's hand on the helm, to steer you through so you will never want."

Sarah laughed merrily, and her father's brows rose. "No, no, sir! You have it all wrong," she said when she could speak. "And after all, Mr. Sims is a man, is he not? He has explained the situation to me; indeed, we have talked at great length about it. I am sure I can manage."

She saw her father was about to speak, and she hurried on, "Besides, I could not in good conscience put such a burden on your head. You have quite enough to handle as it is, although I do thank you, of course, for your generous offer."

"My dear!" Mr. Jennings exclaimed, looking shocked. "It would be no burden, no, none at all. I am your father! It is my duty!"

"But I do not intend to ask you to assume that duty," Sarah said firmly. "Come, Father! I am not

23

an untried girl any longer, no matter my age. And I am perfectly capable of seeing to my own affairs—with Mr. Sims's help, that is. I am a well-to-do woman now. There is no need for you to worry about my future."

Mr. Jennings sipped his port before he replied. Sarah noted his round, jovial face had paled, and she wondered at it.

"I see," he said at last, and then he forced a smile again. "And no doubt you will be marrying again, one of these days. Yes, of course! No one as lovely as you are, my dear, would not. You must be careful, however. There are too many fortune hunters in the world today, and with your wealth, to say nothing of your beauty, you are sure to be preyed on. I beg you allow me to counsel you, give you the benefit of my advice; indeed, I insist on it!"

Sarah hid a smile. "Certainly, if the need arises, sir," she said easily. But she said nothing further, for, for some reason, she did not care to tell her father she had no desire to marry again, and most probably would not. No, not "probably"—most certainly! For she knew very well that if she did marry, she would lose all her newfound and very important freedom. Her husband would acquire her wealth, and she would have nothing to say about it. No, nor about anything else of importance either, without his express permission. It was a situation she had chafed at with Roger, being treated like a simple child, ordered about, and trusted with only a small amount of pin money. And as much as she did not want a husband controlling her, so, too, was she determined her father would not do so either.

Much later, when she went up to bed after spending the evening playing piquet with her father for penny points, she stopped at her mother's room to make sure she didn't need anything. She found her fast asleep, snoring even, and she tiptoed from the room. Her mother's maid, Finney, would take care of her. There was no need for Sarah to spend the night in attendance, and for that she was glad. She was looking forward to a good night's sleep in her own bed. She was so very tired—from the journey, the emotions she had felt at being almost driven from the dower house, and most especially, those she was feeling now that she was home, where she had said she would never come again.

Two

By THE TIME a week had passed, Sarah Lacey found herself settling into a sort of routine. She would spend an hour or so with her mother every morning, listening to her orders for the day before she interviewed the butler and the cook to make sure those orders were followed. Only then was she able to escape.

She had brought her favorite mare with her to Three Oaks, and accompanied by her groom, she rode out every fine day, revisiting old haunts of her childhood. After luncheon she would sit with her mother for a little while, then read or work on her correspondence until Bradbury came to announce the inevitable callers.

In twos and threes they came, all the ladies of the neighborhood and the village. Mrs. Denton and her daughters, Fay and Janet, Miss Withers and Miss Farnsworth, Lady Howland and her young nieces from the Hall, the doctor's wife, Mrs. Holmes—oh, a multitude of ladies, one right after the other! To Sarah it seemed that each day she was forced to answer the same questions, accept the same condolences on her husband's untimely demise, avoid the same delicate prying into her future plans, and discuss her mother's strange illness in endless detail. Still, she was not at all reluctant to do so. It amused her to see these people again whom she had known most of her life, and hear all their news in return.

And every one of them, at some time or other during their visit, mentioned that the Earl of Castleton was due back at any time. Sarah could hear the anticipation in their voices, and more than once she had to swallow a strong desire to laugh at them, even though she knew the earl was the most important personage by far in this part of Kent. She supposed it was no wonder he was so eagerly awaited. Even his aunt, Lady Howland, seemed agog, and as for his sisters, the Ladies Rose and Caroline, they could barely sit still through their aunt's recital.

"You must be anxious to see your brother again, m'ladies," Sarah said at last, smiling at them.

"*Very* anxious!" Lady Rose said. "It is so *boring* at the Hall when he is not there!"

Ignoring Lady Howland's gasp at such boldness and bad manners, she added, "We have not seen him this age, have we, Caroline?"

Her younger, shyer sister only shook her head, her blue eyes wide. Both the Howland young ladies were pretty girls with an abundance of dark, curly hair, oval faces, and cheeks just tinged with wild rose color. Sarah smiled again at the picture they made together. Rose must be all of sixteen now, she thought, and Caroline, perhaps fourteen?

She did not remember them very well, for they had been children at the time of her wedding. As for the earl, he had been away at university, not that he would have acknowledged the daughter of a mere country gentleman. And for some reason their paths had never crossed in London, where, she had learned, he spent most of his time.

Sarah doubted that, even though she was the Dowager Viscountess Lacey now, she would see much of him here, and she chuckled when she realized that she was probably the only female for miles around who didn't care if she did.

27

But one glorious October morning when her father rode out with her instead of her groom, they chanced to meet the long-expected earl himself. The earl was also riding, but he reined in and tipped his hat when Mr. Jennings waved to him jovially.

Sarah inspected the earl as inconspicuously as she could as she and her father rode toward him. Jaspar Howland was certainly a fine-looking young man, she thought. He had broad shoulders and a slim build, with regular features and a crop of thick, dark brown hair, wavy where his sisters' was curly. But it was his eyes that were his most attractive feature, Sarah thought as they came up to him. Blue and dark as the midnight sky, those eyes were deep-set and widely spaced above a pair of high cheekbones. Yet Sarah found she did not admire his mouth. It seemed petulant, as if he were annoyed that he had been accosted and was now forced to do the pretty against his will.

How old was he? she wondered idly. Although a man in years, he still gave the impression of a boy who had not grown into his bones as yet. Neither had his face matured, his jaw firmed. It was like looking at an unfinished sculpture. There was promise there, but the work was in no way perfected.

"Well met, m'lord! Welcome home!" Mr. Jennings said with a broad smile. "Allow me to jog your memory, sir. I'm James Jennings of Three Oaks, your nearest neighbor to the north.

"Give you my daughter, Sarah, the Dowager Viscountess Lacey."

"Lady Lacey," the earl said, bowing a little over his saddle. Sarah gave him a small bow in return. She was a little startled at how closely he was studying her, completely ignoring her father, who was babbling on now about inconsequential things—the weather, village news, the harvest. Sarah thought it impossibly rude, and she raised her chin. Still m'lord continued to stare, his eyes intent on her face, her hair.

As Mr. Jennings stumbled to a halt, looking confused, Sarah took matters into her own hands. "I am delighted to have met you, sir. But surely we should not keep our mounts standing after their run. Therefore, I give you good day, m'lord."

He bowed over his horse's neck again, apparently speechless, and Sarah wheeled her own mare and rode away. Mr. Jennings could do nothing but accompany her.

"I say, Sarah, why did you terminate the meeting with the earl so abruptly?" he asked later after they had left their horses in the stableyard and were strolling up to the house. "It was almost rude of you, my girl. After all, he is the earl, you know, and, well . . ."

"*He* was more than just 'almost rude,' sir!" Sarah retorted. "Staring at me the way he did without a word, and ignoring you as if you weren't even there. And I don't care if he is an earl, the insolent puppy!"

Her father sputtered, and she laughed at him as she took off her riding hat to swing it by its ribbons. "Never mind, Father," she said lightly. "He will survive the slight, believe me. He is young, is he not? Twenty or so? I believe he has only recently finished university."

"He's not that young, and he's mighty high in the instep, or so I've heard tell. You watch what you're about now, Sarah! It wouldn't do for the family to get into his black books, not with my land bordering his."

"I promise I will be as nice as can be should we chance to meet again. Not that I've any expectation of it.

"Excuse me now, sir," she added as Bradbury admitted them to the house. "I haven't had a chance

29

to read today's post as yet, and I would do so before luncheon."

Mr. Jennings waved her away to the morning room she had appropriated for her own. When he went to his library, he was deep in thought.

At luncheon he made no mention of the earl, and Sarah was grateful, although she could not like the way he kept after her to send her carriage back to Oxfordshire.

"Surely there is no need for you to set up your own carriage here, daughter," he said for what Sarah was sure was the tenth time that week. "It's just taking up space in the stables, and your coachman and grooms are doing nothing but eat their heads off! You can always order my carriage if you wish to go visiting, or shopping. Grogan will drive you as he always has."

"I should be happy to pay for the stabling, and for my servants' food, Father," Sarah said evenly. "For I prefer the carriage to remain here. And in a few days or so, I'll have another surprise for you."

"Now, why is it that I've come to suspect you and your 'surprises'?" James Jennings asked, bending a suspicious glance her way as the butler refilled his mug with ale. "Besides, it ain't the expense! It's merely that I hate to see servants with nothing to do!"

"Set them to any chores you like, sir, as long as it's stable work, or driving," Sarah said easily. Then she rose and curtsied. "Dr. Holmes is coming this afternoon. I hope to speak to him so I might ask him some questions about this illness of Mother's."

Mr. Jennings looked glum. "She's no better, is she, Sarah?" he asked in a despairing voice. "If only there was something we could do . . ."

Sarah found herself holding her breath in astonishment. In all her life, she had never heard her father profess any real concern for his wife. Indeed, she had often thought they had a most singular marriage. They seemed content to go their own ways, live their own lives, with little contact between them. Why, there were days when her father did not even bother to see his wife for a few minutes, but relied on his daughter's reports as to her well-being.

And yet just a minute ago, he had sounded so regretful, so anxious! Well, it was none of her concern after all. She would see the doctor and relay everything he said to her father at dinner, for she was aware he had an appointment in Wye that afternoon.

She was none too pleased later, just after the doctor had been taken up to her mother, to receive the message that Miss Withers had called and begged a moment of her time. Sarah was tempted to say she was too busy to see the lady. She was almost positive that Miss Withers had discovered when the doctor was to call, and had come hotfoot on his trail, to discover what she could. But remembering the old lady's joyless life, the little economies she was forced to practice to live genteelly, Sarah could not deny her the advantage of being first with the latest news of the patient. As she nodded to Bradbury and composed her features in a welcoming smile, she only wished it were "Miss Prim and Proper" she had to deal with. Just the hint of anything to do with the *female* condition would be enough to send that lady speedily on her way.

For a few moments, Miss Withers discussed the latest village news: How obvious it was to all that the innkeeper's wife was with child, and for the eleventh time, too. *Tsk, tsk.* Little Perry Akins had been bitten by a dog. What a shame it was that his mother let him run wild! The times he had been spanked for chasing the ducks around the common!

And one of the willows near the brook had come down in the wind last night. Had dear Lady Lacey heard of it?

Then abruptly she changed her tactics, and inquired how Sarah was spending her time now that she was home.

"That is, if you have any spare time, dear girl," she said, tilting a head covered with that incongruous black hair and looking coy. "I know what a blessing you are to your father and mother, indeed, your mother especially in her trouble. And I am sure you spend hours beside her each day."

"If I were to do so, I'm positive she would fall quickly into a decline," Sarah said wryly, the corner of her mouth twisting. "No, I do no such thing. Mother seems to need a great deal of rest. She is always tired. I hope Dr. Holmes can reassure me that this is only a passing malaise. Perhaps it is her age. . . ?"

Eloise Withers nodded and changed the subject. Nothing more needed to be said, for she had gone through the period between womanhood and approaching old age not many years ago herself.

"I saw Earl Castleton this morning," she said as she smoothed her old lilac afternoon gown down over her thin, bony legs. "Such a handsome young man, is he not? And not at all above himself, to my surprise, for he nodded to me quite pleasantly as he passed by on his horse."

How very good of him to be so condescending, Sarah thought. Then she was recalled to her company as Miss Withers went on, "Have you seen him yourself yet, my dear Sarah?"

"Yes, Father and I came upon him this morning when we were out riding. We exchanged a few words. I agree he is handsome enough, although very young, wouldn't you say, for all the responsibilities he has? But perhaps he only appears so to me because I am older than he."

"Surely by not many years!" Miss Withers interjected, sounding horrified. "And what are a few years, after all?"

Her sharp little eyes watched Sarah carefully for any sign of consciousness, but to her disappointment, Sarah only burst into merry laughter.

"Now, now, Miss Withers," she said at last. "No matchmaking, if you please! It would not do. In fact I—"

Later, she was glad that Bradbury had knocked just then, for it had been rash of her to even think of telling the area's premier gossip that she never intended to marry again. Why give the old dear that ammunition, after all? If she had let it slip, it would have been all over Sutton Cross in an hour!

"Your pardon, m'lady," Bradbury said. "The doctor has remained to have a word with you, as you requested."

Sarah nodded and smiled at her guest as she rose. "I am so sorry, Miss Withers," she said, holding out her hand. "I asked Dr. Holmes to stay, and I must not keep him waiting. But perhaps the next time you call, we can have a longer visit?"

Miss Withers was forced to gather her gloves and reticule and take her leave, bowed away by the courteous butler. The doctor had been taken to the library, and it was there Sarah found him.

"Thank you for staying," she said as she shook his hand. She had known Dr. Holmes all her life, and his round, red face and mop of untidy white hair looked just the way they had in her childhood. "Please sit down. May I order you a glass of wine?"

"No, no, do not bother, m'lady." Dr. Holmes beamed at her. "You're looking well, I'm happy to see. Positively blooming, you are!"

He seemed to recall the loss of her husband then,

for he coughed against his fist and looked away from her. "I wish I could say your mother was as well."

"Yes, it is very worrying for all of us," Sarah agreed. "I am afraid I don't understand what can be the matter with her, and I thought you might be able to enlighten me. For there are no symptoms of illness that I can see, except for this weariness she complains of."

The doctor shook his head. "That is so. An unusual case, your mother's. But I am not alarmed as yet. It may be ... that is to say ..."

"You may speak plainly, sir. Do you think this is all caused by her age?"

The doctor looked easier now that the awful truth was out. "Yes, I must think so, for there is no other explanation. In fact, every time I come, I expect to find that she has grown tired of lying in bed, and is up and dressed, issuing her orders, and bustling around as she was wont to do. But don't you dare breathe a word that I said that, mind!" he added, looking alarmed.

"Not even a hint shall pass my lips!" Sarah whispered, and the doctor chuckled as he rose and bowed to her.

"Well, my dear, all I can advise is patience. This will not last forever. If, however, you notice any change in her, or her condition, send a message to the village at once. I don't know everything—no doctor ever does."

"I used to think *you* did," Sarah confided as she walked arm in arm with him to the door. "For whenever something was wrong with me as a child, I knew dear "Dr. Holmesy" would fix it. And so you did."

He patted her hand, looking pleased. But as he put on his hat, he said, "How fortunate that you were only afflicted with the usual childhood complaints! I would so hate to topple off any pedestal you had placed me on, m'lady!"

Sarah was still smiling as she went up to her mother; but a few minutes in that lady's company soon had her sober again. Mrs. Jennings was feeling fractious after the doctor's visit. Perhaps she had taken umbrage at something in his attitude? Sarah wondered. Perhaps he had even intimated there was nothing wrong with her, and that was why she was so cross?

To divert her, she began to question her mother about some household matters. Mrs. Jennings declined to hear her, saying she was too weary to think of such things, and wondering in a querulous voice that Sarah had even bothered her with them, when, as she herself had claimed, she was perfectly competent to handle even a very *large* establishment. And by herself, as well.

Bristling at such sarcasm, Sarah was quick to take her leave before she said something rash, or hateful. And as she went down the stairs, she wondered why it was that she and her mother had never been able to deal together comfortably.

A few minutes later, something occurred that drove her mother and her testiness right from her mind, for she heard her head groom speaking to Bradbury in the hall.

"Leary!" she cried as she came to greet him. "You are here at last!"

The groom tipped his hat, his faded eyes twinkling. "Came as soon as the phaeton was repainted, m'lady," he said easily. "I think you'll be pleased. 'Deed, I'm sure of it, it's that smart now."

"Oh, I must see it at once!" Sarah exclaimed, hurrying to the door. As Bradbury swung it open for her, she gasped and a large smile appeared on her face.

"Now, that is something like!" she said as she

flew down the steps. There, drawn up close, was a shiny black phaeton, with a delicate gold design adorning the sides, and the wheels picked out with gold as well. It was drawn by two matched black horses, their harness gleaming with polish. Even the little dust that had accumulated during the trip from Oxfordshire could not hide the smartness of the rig.

"I cannot wait to tool it about the countryside!" Sarah exclaimed. "Perhaps I could even do so this very afternoon?"

"But no," she added in regret before the groom could remonstrate with her. "That was a silly idea. The team must be tired after the long journey and in need of a good rest. And you must be tired, as well. Take them around to the stable, Leary. Joe Coachman will show you where to stall them, show you where you are to sleep."

The groom tipped his hat again. "They'll be fresh as daisies come morning, m'lady," he said as he climbed to the seat again. "I brought them over easy stages. If it's a nice day, then?"

"Ten o'clock, and not a moment more," Sarah agreed with her pleasant smile. "It will give me something to look forward to."

Jaspar Howland, Earl Castleton, spent his luncheon in a state of complete bemusement. He neither heard nor cared for his aunt's rambling conversation, or his younger sisters' babbling. And if you had asked him what he had eaten later, he would have been hard-pressed to answer.

Lady Rose frowned as her aunt excused her and her sister, Caroline. She had endeavored in the most subtle, teasing way to obtain Jaspar's promise that he would take her out in his perch phaeton soon—but he had not done so. It was too bad! she thought as she ran after Caroline to the garden.

But she would not despair. There was still teatime, and if he did not take her today, there was always tomorrow. Lady Rose had always been single-minded in pursuit of her goals, and had seldom faced failure in achieving them.

As Lady Howland prepared to follow her nieces, the earl asked if he might have a moment of her time, and obediently she took her seat again.

"I met a Mr. James Jennings this morning, Aunt, while I was riding," he began. "He was accompanied by his daughter, a Lady Lacey. Tell me about the family, if you please. I do not recall Lady Lacey."

"Probably not," his aunt said complacently. "She is a few years older than you are, dear boy, and was the daughter of a local squire until her marriage to Viscount Lacey. You never had anything to do with the locals, if you recall."

"How much older is she than I?" he persisted, never taking his eyes from his aunt's plain, lined face.

Lady Howland stifled the unease she felt at his eagerness and began to count on her fingers. "I believe she is all of twenty-six now. Or is she twenty-seven? And as you are just turned twenty-two, that would make her four or five years your senior."

The earl waved a careless hand and left her without another word. Lady Howland had the irrelevant thought that in doing so, he was trying to brush those years away as if they did not exist. And although she was not a perceptive woman, much given to deep thought, Emma Howland felt vaguely disquieted.

What mischief was Jaspar up to now? she wondered. Sarah Lacey was not some little nobody anymore to be cajoled into an affair to pass the time the earl spent in the country. But how to remind him of that? Jaspar had always been so high, she had hardly dared to reprimand him even as a child, when she knew he was in desperate need of a set-down or some discipline.

It had never occurred to the lady that her negligence in doing so throughout his formative years was the reason he had grown up so arrogant and so careless of anyone's feelings but his own. Handsome as you could stare, bright and forward for his age, he had been petted and kowtowed to by relatives and staff alike. For was he not the next earl? The hope of the house? Great care had always been taken not to upset the child, or cause him to lose what was a truly monumental temper.

Emma Howland sighed as she rose from the table. How very disastrous it had been that her brother and his wife had died of a fever when Jaspar was only eight. She had tried to do the best she could in their stead, but she had always thought it unfortunate that her nephew had come into the earldom at such a young age. And when he was twenty-one, he was freed of his trustees, indeed, any constrictions that might have controlled him and his handling of vast estates. And of his life and how he chose to live it.

She sighed again. She had the most uneasy feeling that they were all of them rushing headlong toward some horrid doom. A doom she had no way of averting. It made her feel queasy with foreboding.

But perhaps that queasiness was only the result of her rashly taking two servings of highly seasoned seafood at luncheon? She did so hope it was that!

Three

A<small>T FIVE MINUTES</small> past ten the following morning, Sarah Lacey was tooling her phaeton down the drive of Three Oaks, her head groom beside her. Leary sat staring straight ahead, his arms crossed over his chest, completely unconcerned at the rapid clip they were traveling behind a pair of fresh, frisky horses. As well he might be, for it was he himself who had taught the viscountess to drive a pair.

Sarah stole a glance at him as she took the corner out of the gates at speed. As she did so, she thought how well he looked in the green and gold livery of the Laceys.

"If you're expecting a compliment, milady, ye'll not get it from me," the groom said brusquely. As Sarah's eyes twinkled, he added, "A very good thing it be that no one was passing the gates jes' then, for ye can't see the road from the drive. We might both o' us be sprawled in the dust, the phaeton ruined, an' the horses screaming with broken legs."

Sarah shook her head as she settled the team into a mile-eating trot. "But I did not need to see, Leary," she explained. "I have ears, after all. And there wasn't a sound of anyone else's passage."

"But a dog or small children would not make much noise, now would they?" he persisted.

Sarah bit her lip. "Point taken," she said, her voice contrite now. "I'll not do so again, I promise!"

The groom nodded, his face expressionless. The Lady Lacey was not headstrong or foolish. He need say no more.

"I intend to drive as far as Wye," Sarah confided. "It would be so tame to merely go to Sutton Cross. And I feel a great need to get away from the house today."

She fell silent then, thinking of what had happened when her father had discovered just before she left that her phaeton had arrived. Such a to-do about nothing! she thought, sniffing a little. As if no female had ever driven a carriage behind a smart team before! Really, Father was so old-fashioned. And to think he had even tried to *forbid* her to do so! She remembered she had had to count slowly to ten before she reminded him, as gently as she could, that she was not under his jurisdiction anymore.

His round face had grown very red at that, his lower lip coming out in a massive pout as he glared at her, and she had gone to him to take his arm and squeeze it.

"There now, sir, give over, do! I assure you many ladies of fashion have their own carriages; why, some of them drive without even a groom in attendance in London. I shall not do so here, of course. Leary goes with me.

"Besides, the viscount thought nothing of it. Why, it was he who suggested I learn. He who bought me the team and phaeton."

She had seen her father was in no way mollified, and she kissed his cheek quickly before she added, "Perhaps you will allow me to drive you out someday soon, so I can show you my skill. But I hear the rig at the door, and I must be off. Do not look for me at luncheon, if you please. I'm for Wye. I've some shopping to do there. If I remember correctly, it is market day. Have you any charges for me, sir? I would be glad to attend to your errands."

But Mr. Jennings had only stalked off abruptly, leaving his daughter to stare after him with narrowed eyes as she smoothed her gloves and took the whip the butler was holding out to her.

Now she remembered how defiant she had felt, how angry herself as she took her seat on the perch. It was not for James Jennings to say aye or nay to her, no, not anymore. That was one of the benefits of being a married lady, after all, not that she could think of many more. It freed you from parental control. And now she was a widow, she would not allow herself to be controlled again. Somehow she must make this clear to both her father and her mother.

But as she took a deep breath of the crisp morning air, admired the changing foliage of the trees as they flashed by, she remembered as well that she had not thought to tell her mother of her plans. She wondered why she had been so reticent. Perhaps she had felt one argument was enough on this glorious day?

Sarah sighed a little. She had been pleasantly surprised at how well she and her father had been getting along. Up to now, that is. He had seemed to be going out of his way to be pleasant, something she could never remember him doing before. Her childhood had not been graced with such warm smiles; in fact, he had treated his daughter coldly. And when she remembered how she had wept as she begged him not to give her hand to Viscount Lacey, gone down on her knees to him, in fact, and his disgusted reaction, his thundering voice ordering her to control herself and accept her fate, she hated him anew.

But that is all past, she reminded herself. Long gone, best forgotten. I must put it from my mind lest it begin to fester there. For he is my father. I owe him respect, even if I cannot love him, no, nor my mother either.

The highbred team covered the miles to Wye without a sign of any lingering weariness from their long journey from Oxfordshire evident. As they got closer to the larger village, Sarah had her hands full, for the road was crowded with all manner of carts and drays, pedestrians, and driven herds of animals making their collective ways to market. Once arrived in the village's main street, she turned the phaeton into the innyard, and Leary jumped down and went to the horses' heads.

As Sarah prepared to get down unassisted, she sensed she was being watched. Oh, not with the stares she had received on the road from scandalized country folk, but more intently by someone who was not looking at a woman driver, but at the woman herself. She looked around and caught the eye of a man she remembered very well, and without thinking of what she was doing, she smiled at him in delight.

Evan Lancaster, a local squire from near Sutton Cross, made his way across the crowded yard and held up his arms. "M'lady," he said, his deep voice steady, although Sarah thought she saw a light dancing in his hazel eyes. "Allow me to assist you."

She put her hands on his shoulders and was swung lightly to the ground. As she straightened her skirts, glad she had worn such a stunning carriage dress, trimmed with gold buttons and braid, she was aware anew of the strength and height of the man.

"Thank you, sir," she said, smiling up at him. "I have not seen you since I arrived home. How delightful to do so now."

"Harvest time keeps every farmer busy," he said, his voice noncommittal. "I knew you had returned, of course. To care for your mother, I believe?"

"Aye," Sarah answered, wishing she did not feel such a prisoner of those clear eyes of his with the sun crinkles at the corners that only showed when he smiled. He was not smiling now.

"Why so solemn, sir?" she asked pertly as she waved her groom away to stable the team. As she did so, she marveled at her daring. She had never spoken lightly to Evan Lancaster. In years past, the few times she had exchanged some words with him, she had been all but tongue-tied. "Can it be that you disapprove of a woman driving, too? I do assure you I have been well taught and am very competent."

"I'm sure you are, m'lady. And many farmers' wives drive, out of necessity, not for sport, of course. I was but thinking of your recent loss. Allow me to extend my condolences on the death of your husband, ma'am."

Sarah did not say anything for a moment, and his blond brows rose slightly. Then she shrugged a little and said, "It is kind of you to do so, but it is not necessary. I was not in the least cast down when the viscount died. There was no love between us."

His brows really rose then, and Sarah wondered why she had thought to tell him that. She had never said such a thing to anyone before! Why did she do so now, and to Evan Lancaster of all people?

A little flustered, she drew away as she prepared to leave him.

"Are you meeting someone here, ma'am?" he asked in his deep, calm voice as he looked around.

"Why, no. I came only to see the market—do some small bits of shopping."

"You will take your groom with you then, of course," he persisted. "Markets often attract unsavory types, intent on filching purses and conducting shady deals. And you look much too rich and fine to be anything but a tempting target. It would not be safe for you."

"Come, come, Mr. Lancaster!" Sarah chided him. "I am not a young girl. I can take care of myself."

To her surprise, he came closer then and took her arm. "Not bloody likely you can," he muttered, before he added in his usual voice, "You must allow me to serve as your escort."

Sarah gasped, then turned her head away as if to hide that one involuntary intake of breath. Staring straight ahead as they left the yard, she said, "I must thank you indeed for your concern for me then, must I not? But surely I am keeping you from your own business this day?"

"Not at all," he said. Sarah peeped up at him, noticing how the top of her head only just reached his solid jaw. "No doubt you've forgotten country ways, ma'am. My business was concluded an hour ago."

"Very well, if you insist. But I must insist in return that you join me for refreshment later."

He looked down at her as they strolled along, and his half-concealed smile brought the crinkles to the corners of his eyes. "Are ye sure that's a good idea, ma'am?" he asked innocently. "Oh, the talk there will be! The Lady Sarah Lacey and a mere country farmer. Tsk, tsk!"

"Don't talk so foolish," she said tartly, even as she noticed how he had shortened his steps to accommodate hers. "I shall eat with whomever I please. Gossip offends me. I never listen to it."

"Even now that you've returned to its very hotbed?" he asked, quizzing her. "How brave of you. Or how foolish. I know not which."

"Ah, here we are at the draper's where I have an errand," Sarah was glad to say, rather than risking a reply. "And then I must call in at the apothecary's for my mother. No doubt you will be sorry you were so *galant*, sir, when you see the amount of shopping I have to do."

"Why do ye use a French word?" he asked, sounding almost cold now. "Isn't the English one good enough for ye anymore?"

"Why, I don't know. It just slipped out," Sarah said. "I meant nothing by it. I have often heard it used. In London."

A small child running toward them dodged around them then. He was dressed in ragged clothes, panting and clutching an apple. Behind him the cry of "Thief!" went up, but Sarah saw that Evan Lancaster made no move to detain the little ragamuffin. Indeed, he managed to foil the farmer's wife who came pounding after him by stepping neatly into her path and then apologizing profusely for his clumsiness.

Before she entered the shop, Sarah paused on the step. Thus elevated, she was almost eye to eye with him as she asked, "Why did you do that? No doubt the boy stole the apple, and he should be punished for it."

"He's hungry," Lancaster said, never taking his eyes from her face. "Any farmer can spare an apple or two without making such a to-do about it.

"Go in now, Lady Lacey. I'll wait for you here."

Thus commanded, Sarah did as she was told. She was somewhat preoccupied during the rest of her errands, seemingly not even seeing the colorful crowds, or noticing the noise and confusion. But later, when the two were seated in the inn's common room, for she could not hire a private room with Mr. Lancaster as her sole escort, she returned to the subject again.

"Am I to take it then, sir, that you do not condemn thievery?" she asked as the hard-pressed barmaid put down two mugs brimming with ale. "But surely you can't approve of it."

45

"There's thievery and then there's thievery," he said easily, before he took a large swallow of his ale and wiped his mouth on the back of his hand. "Ah, that's good, that is," he said with a warm smile. "It's thirsty work, shopping with a lady, I've discovered."

Sarah studied him over the rim of her own mug. She had known Evan Lancaster for all her life. He was a man in his thirties now, and he was just as attractive and masculine as he had always been. When she had been a young girl, she had cherished a *tendre* for him, and tried to make him notice her. To her great distress, he had remained indifferent to her. She smiled wryly to herself. Of course he had! Who would not when faced with a simpering, self-conscious young thing who could hardly bear to meet his eyes, and who blushed at the slightest attention?

But even then she had known it was no use. For suppose he had fallen in love with her, asked her to marry him? There was no way her father would have consented to a union between them. Evan Lancaster, although he had a prosperous farm with considerable acreage, was not for the likes of Sarah Leticia Jennings. No, indeed. And in the end she had been married to a viscount, and thus was elevated above her station.

She had thought she had forgotten her girlhood attraction for the man, but now the sight of his big, tanned hand holding the mug, the back of it covered with fine blond hair, made her swallow and look away. Whatever was the matter with her? she wondered crossly. She was being absurd!

The barmaid brought their plates of mutton and vegetables and slapped them down in front of them.

"Behave yourself, Biddy," Evan Lancaster said sternly.

The barmaid stared at him boldly for a moment,

46

but something she must have seen in his eyes made her color up and look away. Still, she tossed her head and gave him a darkling glance as she flounced away. Sarah wondered what that had all been about. The girl was comely, with her abundant curls and big blue eyes, her buxom figure, but what had she to do with Evan Lancaster?

A sudden suspicion of exactly what she had to do with him crossed Sarah's mind then, and to change the subject, she asked after his family. "I trust they are all well, your mother, your sister and brothers?"

His face darkened a little as he reached for the salt trencher. "Nay, I'm afraid I can't say so. My mother died two winters ago. But my sister has married and lives near Tunbridge Wells. My brothers have gone off to seek their fortune, one in the army, the other at sea."

"But surely you are not alone on the farm?" Sarah said, keeping her eyes firmly on the mutton she was cutting. "Surely you must have married, begun a family of your own?"

"I *must* have?" he asked, his voice full of hidden laughter. "Well, sorry I am to disappoint ye, ma'am, but that I have not done. My aunt Hetty lives with me and keeps the house for me."

"Some bread?" Sarah asked, holding out the plate. She did not know what else to say, and she only hoped he had not thought she was prying into his personal affairs. As he took a slice of the heavy, dark bread, she went on, "How good this tastes! I had forgotten what a fine cook the landlord's wife is."

"Yes, one of the best in Wye," he agreed absently. "But tell me, m'lady, have you come home to stay? You understand the reason I ask is so I can be first with the news. There's a heap of conjecture in Sutton Cross about your plans, you know."

"Yes, I do know," Sarah said with a sigh. "Everyone asks me, over and over. But I do not intend to remain at my parents' home. It is too hard for me, for there I am neither fish nor fowl, not a wife anymore, nor yet a daughter to be ordered around, expected to obey."

As she remembered the angry scene with her father that very morning, her face darkened, a fact that Evan Lancaster was quick to note. He had never cared for James Jennings. The man was opinionated and quick to anger. Furthermore, he was a puffed-up stick, too proud by half.

"Ye could live in the dower house yer husband must surely have left for ye, though," he drawled as he inspected her downcast face.

"Of course I can, and I shall probably do so at some point in the future. But right now there are reasons why it would not be wise. . . ."

Her voice died away, and Evan Lancaster's eyes grew keen. "Ye said there was no love lost between ye and yer husband," he said. "Were ye so unhappy in yer marriage then?"

Her brown eyes flashed fire. "What do you think?" she asked. "He was thirty years older than I, and we had little in common. I disliked the worthless life he led, the gambling and the sport. And he was never still. He would not have liked a quiet evening before the fire while a snowstorm raged outside, a good book, a pleasant talk. While I . . . well, I found out I was made for such quiet, homely pleasures."

Her voice died away, and wisely, he asked no more.

After their meal, he went away to find her groom and tell him the phaeton was required, before he bade her a civil farewell, thanking her again for his dinner.

Sarah found herself wanting to say that she

hoped she would see him soon again, but she swallowed such a revealing remark and only thanked him again for his escort. She was aware she had said too much already. *Much* too much.

By the time she left town, her packages stowed neatly under the seat, she knew Evan Lancaster was long gone, for he had called for his horse and ridden away almost immediately.

She thought of him all the way home, remembering his eyes, the long curve of his mouth, the way the hair grew about his brow. It was a little long in back; he should have visited the barber's while he was in Wye. His wife would have told him to do so, if he had had one, that is, she thought. And then she shrugged and laughed at her fancies. What was Evan Lancaster to her, after all? Less than nothing now. She was Lady Lacey, and he was . . . a farmer. A very appealing, handsome, virile, and successful farmer, but a farmer nevertheless. And she was for no man. Not anymore.

As she drove through Sutton Cross, Sarah smiled and nodded to the people she saw in the street. She almost giggled at Miss Farnsworth's shocked face when she saw her making her way to Miss Withers's for their weekly tea party. Oh dear, Sarah thought as she left the village behind. Now I've scandalized the old dear for sure. No doubt she will be breathless and in need of her salts by the time she reaches her destination. And no doubt Sarah herself would be discussed over the teacups for at least an hour. To think of it! Driving herself in a *sporting* carriage with only a groom in attendance! My dear!

Evan Lancaster stabled his horse before he walked up to his farmhouse, located a few miles west of Sutton Cross. As he did so, he looked at it carefully. To his eyes it was a pleasant place made of rose-colored brick, but then, he admitted he was prejudiced, for this was his home and he had always loved it. It was a rambling building, low-eaved and mullion-windowed, with comfortable chimneys sprouting here and there from the roof. Before the house there was a small garden full of asters and chrysanthemums and a few late daisies. The garden had been his mother's pride, and in her memory he had tried to keep it up, although he knew he did not have her touch.

The front door stood open in the warm October sunlight of late afternoon, and he could hear his aunt in the back of the house as she gave orders to the kitchen maid about the disposal of things he had purchased in Wye that morning, which one of his farmhands had brought back earlier in the cart. There was a tempting smell of soup and fresh-made bread in the air.

As he went into the parlor, Lancaster looked at it as if he were seeing it for the first time. There were many books on the shelves on either side of the fireplace, and a bowl of asters adorned the shining center table where he would be served his supper in a little while. A pair of comfortable armchairs faced each other across the hearth. Next to one of them was a small table that held his pipe and tobacco, a lamp, and the book he had been reading last evening before he sought his bed.

So she enjoyed reading before a fire, did she, Sarah Lacey? Or engaging in pleasant talk? He sat down, staring at the chair opposite. What would it be like, if she were there? he wondered. He was tempted to close his eyes, the better to picture her, looking up from her book to smile at him before she moved a little closer to the fire as the winter wind and snow buffeted the old house.

Then his mouth twisted and he rose to pace the room. What a stupid fool he was, he thought. There wasn't a chance the lovely Lady Lacey would ever find herself here at any season, and most certainly not in the evening!

He reached into his pocket then for the horse chestnut he had picked up on his way back to the house from the stable. As he caressed it, he smiled a little. It was exactly the color of her auburn hair. And her large, expressive brown eyes were flecked with gold and fringed with long auburn lashes that curled upward as if they could not bear to hide the orbs they guarded. And her delicate complexion, as pure as the finest cream, yet somehow translucent. And her mouth, so ripe and inviting, yet so tender. He had longed to trace its outlines with his finger, softly, so softly. And as for her figure—well!—slim-waisted, high-bosomed, with gently rounded hips and a neat ankle. Sarah Jennings had been a pretty girl; now, as Lady Lacey, her beauty had bloomed so, it was enough to take a man's breath away!

"You're back late from Wye, Evan," a deep, abrupt voice said behind him, and he turned to his aunt, putting Sarah Lacey from his mind. "Whatever kept you? Samuel came back so much earlier."

"I met an old friend," he told her as he picked up his pipe and filled it carefully.

His aunt, Hetty Barnes, tipped her gray head to one side as she regarded him. She was a tall woman, heavyset, one who gave off an air of competence and authority. His mother's younger sister, she had never married. Once she had told him she had never wanted to, and since she had inherited a modest sum from her grandmother, had not felt compelled to it. But her nephew knew she was not happy here on the farm with its isolation and lack of company. He was sure she sometimes yearned for her own rooms in Tunbridge Wells, with her friends nearby and all kinds of amusements to interest her. He had told her there was no need for her to stay, that he was well able to take care of himself, but she would not hear of it.

No, for she had promised her sister on her deathbed that she would look after him, and she was not a woman who went back on her word. Still, there were times she had thought it might have been better if she had made herself scarce. Left to see to his own comforts, Evan might well have decided to marry at last. Even more than most men, he seemed reluctant to enter that state.

"We made apple butter today," she said as she sat down at the desk and opened a worn account book to make an entry. "We've had a fine yield this year. We'll be able to dry a great many for winter and still have ample left for your cider."

"Cider first. Dried apples second," he ordered as he lit his pipe.

"Men!" she said in a disgusted voice. "Think I don't know how little of it stays pure? You and your spirits!"

"Nothing tastes better on a cold winter's evening, as you have often remarked yourself. Remember the hot toddies I've made for you?"

His aunt Hetty refused to acknowledge the toddies as she sharpened her quill with a little knife she kept for the purpose in her apron pocket.

Evan went to close the front door as the westering sun ceased to shine on the floor there. As he bent to make up the fire, for the October evenings were growing chill, he said, "I saw Lady Lacey in Wye. She was James Jennings's daughter before her marriage."

"Aye, I remember her," Hetty Barnes agreed, intent on her quill point. "Married an old man, didn't she, some years past? Poor lass!"

"Well, he's dead now. Perhaps she'll have better luck next time."

"Or perhaps she'll not wed at all, having already

52

been treated to the dubious charms of that estate," his aunt said tartly.

When there was no answer, she stole a glance at her nephew. Evan sat next to the fire now, his gaze intent on the burning wood. It was evident he was deep in thought, and her brows rose slightly. As she dipped her quill into the fat inkpot, she wondered if he was thinking of the young widow. Sarah Jennings had been such a beautiful young girl, she wouldn't be at all surprised if he was.

Dutifully, Sarah went immediately to her mother's room on her return to Three Oaks. She had been gone most of the day, and she felt a pang of guilt at her prolonged absence.

"I've brought samples of the damask you requested, ma'am," she said after she had curtsied and taken a seat near the bed. "One is a pretty rose color, the other pale blue. They had none of the gold you wanted."

"Rose, blue, gold—it is of no great matter," Mrs. Jennings said weakly. "No, no, do not show it to me now!" she added as Sarah reached into the large bag she carried. "I am too weary to make decisions, and it will give me a headache."

"I am sorry you are not feeling better," Sarah said carefully. "Have you had your tonic today?"

Her mother nodded, frowning. "What is the use of it, though?" she asked querulously. "It does me no good at all!"

Sarah looked around, trying to find some other topic of conversation. Spying the letters on the counterpane under her mother's hand, she said, "I see you have had some correspondence. Surely it must make you feel better to hear from old friends?"

Her mother stared down at the letters, and a little smile appeared on her petulant face. "Yes, I have had good news," she said in a stronger voice. "Dearest Geoffrey has written to inquire after my health, and he has said that he may be able to come into the country soon. How wonderful that will be! I have not seen him for some months, you know. He is so busy in London."

"Mother, what exactly does Geoffrey *do* in town?" Sarah was unable to keep herself from asking.

"Why, what any young man does," Mrs. Jennings said, looking surprised at the question. "He has his friends to occupy him, his parties to attend, his tailor and boot-maker and vintner and heaven knows who else to see—all his many pursuits. He is very busy."

"I trust he has curbed his unfortunate habit of spending more money than he has to hand?" Sarah asked. "And of gambling?"

She thought her mother stiffened before she said in a voice so tolerant, it surprised her daughter, "It takes a great deal of money to maintain oneself as a gentleman, Sarah. A great deal of money."

"But what is the sense of it?" Sarah persisted, although she knew she should let well enough alone. "In time, Geoffrey will inherit Three Oaks, come back here to see to its care, and that of the farms. He is not to be an idle gentleman, but a country squire."

"I am absolutely astounded to hear you say such a thing!" Mrs. Jennings exclaimed. "There is no man in England more suited to the role than my darling Geoff! Besides, and have you forgotten, daughter, he is now the brother of the Dowager Viscountess Lacey?"

Sarah burst into laughter. "Oh my," she said in a weak voice. "Oh my! To think it is all *my* fault that Geoffrey must appear so grand! I—I *am* sorry."

Mrs. Jennings opened her mouth, thought better of whatever she had been going to say, and after a moment said instead, "It is worrying, though, for it does cost a great deal. Not that your father and I begrudge it for a moment. Geoff will always be our beloved boy. And after all, daughter, you yourself did so well for yourself, marrying a wealthy viscount, that surely you can not resent your brother's living in the forefront of society."

Sarah's anger made her rise more quickly than she had intended. "I shall leave you now, Mother," she said evenly. "I know you must be tired, and to be talking so much cannot be good for you."

Mrs. Jennings looked as if she would like to refute that statement, but she only nodded, and lay back as if exhausted on her pillows. The last thing Sarah heard as she was closing the door was her mother's heartfelt sigh and the crackle of the paper as she picked up her beloved Geoffrey's letter once again.

At dinner that evening, her father appeared to have forgotten the incident of the phaeton, and his daughter's independence. Instead, he inquired of her visit to Wye, chatted for a while about a problem on one of the farms, and told her of an invitation that had been extended by Mrs. Denton when he chanced to meet her in Sutton Cross, to bring his daughter to dinner some evening soon.

"I told her I would have to inquire if you would care for it, Sarah," he added. "Perhaps you would not? The Dentons are, after all, not anyone of note. Why, there's not even an honorable anywhere in their family. And you are used to finer company. I would not be at all displeased if you refused, for you, indeed, all of us, must be aware of your station now and strive to be worthy of it."

"I am not so proud, sir," Sarah told him as she refused a second helping of veal in a lemon sauce. "I have always liked the Dentons. Their young son, Ralph, is such a madcap—or at least he used to be. But I must say I am surprised that Fay and Janet are still unwed. Aren't they almost my age?"

Her father nodded. "Turned their noses up at the only men to offer, from what I hear," he said. "And that's a shame. They're not well-enough-looking to be so particular, either one of them."

"I always thought them pretty with their blond curls and blue eyes," his daughter disagreed as she sipped her wine.

"But not to compare to you, my dear," Mr. Jennings said, toasting her with his own glass. "You are a beauty and cast both of them in the shade."

Sarah kept her expression noncommittal. Stranger and stranger, she thought. Her father had never been given to compliments where she was concerned. Thinking to turn the subject, she said, "I understand Mother has heard from Geoffrey, and there's some plan afoot for him to visit? I am glad of it. The possibility has raised her spirits already, which, alas, my own visit has failed to do."

Her father began to frown. "Yes, it is time the boy came home on a bit of a repairing lease. I cannot tell you the expenses he incurs in London—you would stare to hear of them. But what must be, must be. I am sure it is no different for any young sprig on the town, and I must not quarrel with him about it. Besides, you are right. His stay here will perk Mary up; just you wait and see!"

Sarah went early to bed that night. Her father had joined her in the drawing room to await the tea tray later, but having to endure another conversation about her absent brother and his wondrous qualities was more than she could endure. Pleading tiredness after her long day, she was quick to excuse herself. But as she ran up the stairs, she wondered if it was some fault of her own that made her so cynical where Geoffrey was concerned. They had never been close for a number of reasons, but that was hardly enough cause for her to distrust him so. And she had yet to figure out where she fit into the scheme of things here at Three Oaks; exactly why she had been summoned home. It surely was a puzzlement.

Four

SARAH DID NOT go driving the next day. Instead, she went for a ride, and on her way home later, she stopped in Sutton Cross to pick up a spill of allspice that unaccountably had been left off the cook's shopping list the day before.

As she dismounted and tied her mare before Abner Bower's shop, she was hailed by none other than the Earl of Castleton himself. Her eyes widened when she saw his quick smile, the glow in his midnight blue eyes, and deep inside she felt vaguely uneasy.

"Well met, m'lady," he said as he dismounted and crooked a finger at a young boy to hold his horse. Never glancing back to see that his request had been honored, he came to stand before Sarah and take her hand in both of his. "A lovely day for a ride, is it not, ma'am?"

"Indeed, m'lord," she agreed as she gently freed her hand from his tight clasp and stepped back a little to curtsy to him. She was not at all loath to put some distance between them. The earl seemed overpowering to her this morning, overeager, and overloquacious as well, she thought as he went on and on about the beauty of the weather. Could he possibly be nervous? But why?

"Perhaps we could go out together some morning soon?" he asked next. "There are some fine riding trails on the estate, with pleasant vistas to admire.

Or so I've been told," he added ruefully. "I know it is not my place to puff them off, now, is it?"

Suddenly Sarah smiled at him. When he forgot his consequence, he had an endearing quality about him, and his charming smile was pure magic. Besides, he was no more than a boy. She had nothing to fear from him.

"That would be delightful," she said, and when an even wider grin creased his face, she added, "Perhaps the Ladies Rose and Caroline could join us? I was much taken with them when they came to call on me last week. They are so lovely, your sisters."

"Surely in *your* company they could appear no better than well enough," he said gallantly with a little bow. Sarah saw that he did not seem at all pleased with her suggestion, and she wondered why. Didn't he care for his sisters?

"As for their coming with us, I am afraid they are too busy with their lessons."

Sarah looked around idly as he spoke. It seemed to her that most of the population of Sutton Cross was abroad that morning. And every one of them was noting her conversation with the earl with great interest. Ah well, Sarah thought in resignation, what else do they have to amuse themselves? I shall ignore them.

"I understand you drove a phaeton to Wye yesterday," the earl was saying now, and she made herself look at him again. "How brave of you to dare it in this backwater. But I was pleased to hear of it. You are evidently a woman who takes no heed of the local restrictions on what is done and what is not."

"Yes, I encountered a number of shocked faces," Sarah admitted as lightly as she could. "I refuse to give up driving, however. I enjoy it too much."

"Whyever should you?" he asked, astounded.

"What you do is of no concern to anyone but your-self. You must never bow to the old-fashioned dic-tates of small-village tyrants, ma'am. And you are of the nobility now, above such strictures. What you and I choose to do cannot be questioned."

The young earl sounded haughty again, and Sarah prepared to leave him. But as she turned away slightly, he added, "And to prove I mean what I say, I invite you to ride with me in my perch pha-eton. That will really set the old tabbies of both sexes astir, won't it?"

"You seem to take an unholy delight in upsetting people, sir," Sarah told him, trying not to smile at his eager, teasing look, the way he bent closer as if to force her to agree. "As to a drive, we will have to see. I am tied to my mother's bedside a great deal. She is ill, which is the reason I am here, after all."

"Yes, I know," he said, sounding more petulant that he was to be thwarted than he was regretful about her mother's illness. "Let us hope she recov-ers quickly. I've a mind to show you my team. Per-fectly matched chestnuts with a white blaze, and such sweet goers, you will stare to see them! Why, I have won every race I've entered them in with my friends' cattle, and that includes the Duke of Har-ford's team. As I'm sure you are aware, his grays are famous, but . . ."

Sarah stopped listening. When young men began to discuss their horseflesh, they were inevitably boring, not that they had a clue of the failing. It was only necessary to murmur an occasional "My, my," or "Fancy that!" to assure them they had your complete attention. She began to wonder how she could extricate herself from this conversation gracefully, and when she looked over the earl's broad shoulder and saw the Misses Denton and their brother approaching, she gave them a warm smile.

The earl swung around, his eyes narrowing. Sarah could feel him stiffening. And when she introduced him to the Dentons, his greeting was abrupt and his bow so shallow, it was almost an insult.

Ralph Denton's color rose, although Sarah knew that he was aware that in acknowledging them at all, the earl was conveying a generosity he had never been known for. As for Fay and Janet, they sank into their deepest curtsies, all atwitter at the honor.

"I must leave you now," Jaspar Howland said, speaking to Sarah alone. His eyes never left her face as he added, "Know I shall be in touch soon about our scheme. The next fine day perhaps? Till then."

He bowed to her alone as well, and tossing a coin to the boy who held his horse, he mounted and rode away, looking neither left nor right as he went.

"Oh my, to think the earl would deign to speak to us," Janet Denton said breathlessly, "Just wait till Mama hears!"

"You make too much of it, Janet," her sister, Fay, said as coolly as she could. "He only acknowledged us because Lady Lacey forced him to do so. I doubt he ever does it again, so perhaps we are in your debt, m'lady."

Sarah grinned at her. "Oh, do come down from the boughs, Fay," she said easily. "To tell truth, I was delighted you interrupted our conversation, so you see, I am in your debt instead.

"But how are you, Ralph? I have not seen you this age."

Ralph Denton blushed again, right up to the roots of his ash blond hair. "I am very well, t-t-thank you, ma'am. And delighted that you h-h-have come home. S-S-Sutton Cross and the vicinity has been a d-d-d-desert without you."

His sisters stared at him in amazement, and not because of his stutter. They were quite used to that, for whenever Ralph was under a strain, he was apt to stumble over his words. No, instead they were stunned by his compliment. Fay even wondered if he had been practicing it in the privacy of his room.

"I am sure you exaggerate, sir, but I thank you anyway," Sarah said. Then she turned to his sisters again and added, "Do thank your mother for inviting my father and me to dinner soon. Please tell her to set any day she likes. We are living very quietly because of my mother's illness."

The dinner party was discussed for a few moments, and then a large cart came down the village street. It was driven by Evan Lancaster, with two of his farmhands perched up behind on a number of large sacks that filled the bed of the cart.

Sarah smiled at him, and he tipped his hat to her. Beside her, Fay Denton waved a friendly hand. "Oh, do pull up, Mr. Lancaster," she called. "I have a message for you from my father."

Obediently Lancaster halted the cart and climbed down. He had a few words with his hands, one of whom took his place on the board that served as a bench and drove the cart away.

"Ma'am, ladies, Ralph," Lancaster said politely. "You said there was a message for me, Miss Denton?"

Fay smiled at him. "Indeed there is. Father said to tell you if we met that he would like to purchase six bushels of your apples, if you have any extra. You must know, m'lady, Mr. Lancaster's apples are the best to be had in the area. I think it must be because Lancaster Farm is such a lovely spot. But there are none better for cider, or—or so my father claims."

"I'll see to it this very afternoon, Miss Denton," Evan said. Then his gaze went over her shoulder to where Sarah stood by the grocer's door. "Not driving today, m'lady?" he asked. "Do not tell me you have given it up already, and so are bowing to convention. It would be too tame of you."

"Not at all, sir," Sarah said, keeping her eyes firmly on his rugged face, and ignoring the deeply tanned, heavily muscled arms under his rolled-up white shirt sleeves. He was dressed much more casually today in his working clothes. "I only decided to rest my team after their trip to Wye. And I cannot let my mare languish without exercise. Faery is a favorite of mine."

He glanced at her horse, assessing it. "A fine-looking animal for a lady. Wouldn't be a mite of good behind a plow, of course."

Sarah chuckled. "I rather imagine Faery would object to such treatment," she said. "She was not bred for that kind of work."

"Not many are," he said. Sarah wondered why she had stiffened at his words. He had not insulted either her or her mare. Had he?

"We must be getting along," Fay Denton said, interrupting their conversation in a way that had Sarah despairing of her manners. "We shall look forward to seeing you with those apples, sir. Perhaps you can stay for tea? Lady Lacey? Give you good day."

Curtsies and bows were exchanged, and the three Dentons walked away. Only Ralph Denton looked back over his shoulder, turning scarlet again when he saw he had been observed doing so.

"If I'm not mistaken, you've added another conquest to your long list of them, ma'am," Evan Lancaster drawled.

Sarah shook her head. "I don't look for conquests, sir, because I don't want them."

"Perhaps you do not, but it is not at all necessary for you to 'look'—do anything at all. Men are bound to fall in love with you all unbidden. Surely you are aware of that by now?"

"Of course I am," Sarah said, trying for a cool, disinterested tone. "How very silly they are, men. Oh, I beg your pardon, sir! It is not at all nice of me to be maligning your own sex to you, is it? I apologize."

He chuckled, his eyes crinkling at the corners as he grinned. As Sarah prepared to climb the step to the shop, he offered her his arm. "Shopping again?" he asked, quirking a brow at her as he opened the door. "I shall think you insatiable."

"Not I. Cook forgot a spice in her marketing list yesterday. Thank you, and good day," Sarah said, looking anywhere but into his amused hazel eyes.

He only nodded before he turned away. Firmly Sarah closed the door of the shop behind her with a decisive snap.

The grocer, Abner Bower, had a big smile for her, and he hurried to fetch the allspice, talking all the while he did so. His wife curtsied, but she was not allowed to say a word. Since Sarah was used to Bower's nonstop chatter, which had in the past made strangers think his wife must be dumb, poor woman, she was not disconcerted. For even though he asked her innumerable questions about her mother, Three Oaks, and her plans, he never paused long enough to let her answer them, even if she had been so inclined.

Poor Mrs. Bower, she thought as she left the shop with his voice following her out to the street. I wonder if he talks like that when they are in bed together. This conjured up such a ridiculous picture that she gurgled with laughter as she mounted her horse and prepared to ride home.

Later that afternoon, a large bouquet of flowers

was delivered at Three Oaks. Sarah was passing through the hall when it arrived, and at first she thought it must be for her mother. But the butler bowed to her as he held it out, his old face wreathed in a conspirator's smile.

"For you, m'lady," he said. "Come from the Hall, it did."

Somewhat reluctantly, Sarah took the bouquet. She might have known. No one but the earl with his extensive hothouses would have been able to produce such blooms in October. The pink roses had an especially delicious scent, as did the white lilies. And there was such a multitude of them.

Still, she longed to refuse the gift, although she knew it would be impossibly rude of her to do so. And how her father would carry on when he found out, she thought. No, she must accept the offering with as good a grace as she could. She heard Bradbury cough, and she looked up.

"The groom awaits your reply, m'lady," he said, pointing to the note that was attached to the flowers.

"Very well. Please see that these are placed in water, and take them to the drawing room," Sarah said as she detached the note and went away to read it privately.

It was very short. After hoping she would enjoy the flowers, the earl set a time and place tomorrow morning for the ride he had mentioned to her in the village. Sarah grimaced. He certainly didn't waste any time about it, did he? But she supposed she would have to go. There was no reason she could think of to refuse. But stay! Perhaps she could say her mother needed her then?

She shook her head. That would not work, and it would just delay the inevitable, for she was sure he would invite her again and again until he gained her capitulation. *I might just as well get it over* with, she thought as she sat down to write her reply. But I shall be so cool and disinterested that he will leave me alone hereafter. And if necessary, I shall pretend to be amused by his interest in me, treat him like the boy he so recently had been. That had often worked with the younger society men in town. No doubt the earl thought himself quite the catch, and no doubt he had chosen her to relieve his boredom while he was in the country. He would be swiftly disabused of any notion he had that she would be honored to agree to a liaison, however.

She decided she would take her head groom with her on the morrow. Leary would dampen any romantic ardor the earl might be feeling, and his presence would mean the earl would be forced to hold his tongue as well. She knew such a precaution was unnecessary for a widow, but she did not care. She would not be opportuned!

Her father was clearly pleased when he came in and saw the floral tribute his daughter had received. He rubbed his hands together and smiled broadly, nodding to her and winking so fervently that she had to laugh at him.

"It means nothing, sir," she told him finally. "I have received such gifts before, from equally smitten young men. They are not serious, you know. It is only a game they play."

Her father shook a playful finger at her. "Well, as to that, puss, we shall just have to wait and see, now won't we?" he asked. "But what a feather for your cap, the Earl of Castleton! My, my, I think I will just pop up and tell your mother all about it. I'm sure she will be delighted to hear such news, and it might make her feel better, more herself."

He hurried from the room before Sarah could remonstrate with him. Oh dear, she thought as she sat down and picked up her book. You don't suppose Father is thinking the earl might ask me to marry him, is he? She would have to correct such a ridiculous notion at once.

But somehow she shied away from saying anything more about it. She did not want to reveal her distaste for the married state. Somehow she had the vague feeling that if she were to do so, her life here at Three Oaks would become vastly unpleasant. Surely it was wiser for her to go on as casually as she could, and no doubt in time, when the earl tired of his fruitless pursuit of her, he would leave her alone, or go back to town, or fall in love with another. He was young, and she knew his heart was not engaged. She would just have to be patient.

When Sarah came down to breakfast the next morning, already dressed in her habit for the proposed ride with the earl, the butler met her in the hall. He was frowning a little as he bowed and handed her a sealed note.

"Isn't it early for the post, Bradbury?" Sarah asked as she took it from him.

"Yes, m'lady, but this did not come in the post. Thomas found it on the steps only a few minutes ago."

"How . . . how unusual," she said, turning the note over in her hand. Yes, it was addressed to Lady Lacey; there could be no doubt it was for her. For a moment she wondered if the earl had written to cry off, until she saw that the note had not been written, but printed in a disguised hand. Stranger and stranger, she thought as she took it with her to the breakfast room.

She was glad that her father had already eaten a hearty meal and gone out, for she had had quite enough of his chuckles and smirks at dinner last evening. She allowed Bradbury to serve her before she dismissed him. And she did not open the note until she had finished her breakfast and poured herself another cup of coffee.

The note was very short, and she was not able to restrain a gasp as she read the one line that comprised it. "Why did you come back?" it said. "You are not wanted here."

There was no signature, and Sarah dropped it to the table as if it were a hot coal, even though her fingers felt icy. But who could have written such a thing? she wondered, staring at it in distaste. Who didn't want her at Three Oaks? And although the note did not threaten her outright, she could not help but feel threatened by it. What did it mean— she was not wanted here?

She sat on at the table for a long time. She was hurt, hurt and dismayed and confused. And she could not think of a single soul who might wish her gone, although she wracked her brain considering every one of her acquaintances nearby. Could it be one of the villagers? or an old friend? Perhaps even Evan Lancaster? But that was absurd! Surely this was someone's idea of a sick joke, and she would be best to forget it, burn the note, put it from her mind. Still, when the clock's chiming reminded her of the hour, and her appointment with the earl, she did not destroy the note. Instead, she took it to her room and locked it away with her private papers. And she was still feeling an ache deep inside. She had left no one hostile in Sutton Cross years ago, nor had she ever harmed anyone by word or deed that she could remember. But someone nearby disliked her enough to send that horrid note, nay, perhaps even *hated* her. It was not a pleasant thought.

She was a little late to the rendezvous, and she saw the earl's black look before he replaced it with a glowing smile of welcome. But when he spotted Leary escorting her, the black look returned.

"Surely there is no need for your groom, ma'am,"

he said stiffly, in lieu of greeting. "I do assure you, you are quite safe on *my* land."

"It is a conceit of mine," Sarah said carelessly. "Leary always rides with me."

"He was not with you when first we met."

She raised her brows, looking astonished at his persistence. "He had not arrived at that time. And besides, my father was with me then, or had you forgotten?"

Not waiting for him to answer, she went on, "But come, sir, I believe you promised me some outstanding vistas to admire. Lead on!"

The earl was forced to comply, but for quite a while he sported a pout that made him look about two-and-ten in Sarah's amused eyes. At last he slowed from the canter he had set to a trot, and waited to take his place beside her on the wide trail that wound through the vast parkland.

"How lovely Castleton is," she said, her voice admiring. "I wonder you can bear to leave it at all for dirty, noisy London, sir."

"It grows tedious here after a while, and it is lonely," he replied, his dark eyes intent on her profile.

"I should think having two young sisters about would liven things up a bit," Sarah said with a little sideways smile.

"But they are not congenial companions. They are so young!" he complained. "And Rose especially can be tiresome. She is very single-minded, you see. Now she has taken it in her head that I am to teach her to drive, and in my perch phaeton, mind, behind my chestnuts, no less. Ha!"

Sarah laughed as they came out of the woods and paused for a moment. Before them, a long, sloping field led down to a lake. It was bordered by a grove of trees, and on an island near the far side, Sarah could see a Gothic folly.

"Oh, how splendid," she said in true admiration.

"In springtime that field is filled with daffodils," Jaspar Howland told her. "They make a brave display."

Softly Sarah began to recite:

> " 'I wandered lonely as a cloud
> That floats on high o'er vales and hills,
> When all at once I saw a crowd,
> A host, of golden daffodils;
> Beside the lake, beneath the trees,
> Fluttering and dancing in the breeze.' "

Jaspar Howland stared at her, his brows contracted. "Who penned that?" he asked.

"The great Wordsworth, of course," she told him. "He wrote it at Grasmere a few years ago, although he might just as well have been inspired by the scene here."

"Oh, yes, of course," he said carelessly. "I thought I recognized the lines, but I was hardpressed for a moment to identify the poet."

Sarah turned away so he could not see the amusement in her eyes. Of course you were confused, my fine young liar! she thought. So the earl was not bookish, was he?

"Should you like to investigate the folly, ma'am?" Jaspar Howland asked next. "There is a bridge to it on the other side of the lake."

Sarah heard the anticipation in his voice, and for a moment she was tempted to deny him. But then she remembered that Leary was close by, and so far, at least, the earl had behaved as a gentleman.

"Yes, let's do that," she said, kicking her mare to a trot.

When they had ridden around the lake, Sarah saw a gently arched span to the island, and she motioned to Leary. The earl was before him, however, and as he held up his arms to her, his dark eyes glowed with his delight that he was to have her so close to him.

Sarah shook her head a little as she slid down and quickly stepped away from him.

"We'll not be long, Leary," she called over her shoulder as Jaspar Howland took her arm and urged her toward the bridge.

"What is it to him if you take hours?" he asked, sounding impatient again. "He is only your servant."

"It was simply a kindness. Haven't you found you get better service from your servants if you treat them well? I have."

He stopped and turned her toward him a little. They stood on the highest point of the bridge then, the dark water below them, serene. Sarah saw the earl was sporting his arrogant expression again.

"I have never considered it," he said. "My servants do my bidding no matter my tone. If they do not, I dismiss 'em. I think that you, like so many other women, have too tender a heart, ma'am. And why bother, after all?"

"If you do not understand, I cannot explain it to you," she said. "Shall we go on?"

Silent now, the earl led her from the bridge.

When they reached the folly, Sarah's eyes filled with amusement. Someone had left a large basket there, and flowers in a pretty vase.

"I thought you might care for some refreshment," he said carelessly. "A glass of wine? A biscuit or some fruit perhaps?"

To Sarah he seemed unsure of himself and self-conscious, and although she was not in the least hungry or thirsty, she nodded. She did not want to hurt his feelings after he had gone to so much trouble. Then she remembered he had not done so. He had merely issued a few crisp orders. But as Jaspar

71

Howland bestirred himself, handing her a napkin, opening the wine, he seemed so eager to win her approval, was so transparent about it, in fact, that she could only feel tenderness. How young he was, after all.

As he poured the wine into footed crystal goblets, he asked, "What shall we drink to?"

Handing her a goblet, he sat down beside her on one of the soft cushions that were strewn about the benches that lined the folly. His dark eyes were intent, his expression serious.

"Let us drink to this beautiful day," Sarah suggested, touching his glass with her own. "It will be nice to remember when the winter storms come."

"I would prefer to drink to the most beautiful woman I have ever seen—you," he said. At her little gesture of dislike, he added, "But I can see you do not care for compliments. How unusual. It's been my experience that most females adore 'em."

"I don't. Well, sometimes, perhaps," Sarah told him, wishing he would not sit so close to her. The wine was a pale gold in color, crisp and dry on her tongue.

"How strange it is that we never met in town," the earl mused. "I know I would never have forgotten it if we had. But I was not at all well acquainted with your late husband. I suppose that's the reason."

"It would have been astonishing if you had been," Sarah told him. "He was a great deal older than you, for he was a man in his fifties."

"Why did you marry him?" Jaspar Howland demanded harshly. "Are you going to pretend you loved him?"

"I have no intention of answering that, m'lord," Sarah said in a voice as haughty as his had ever been. "Not only are we not well enough acquainted, I find such a question impertinent."

Her words were no sooner voiced than he knelt quickly at her feet. "Ah, no, do not be cruel," he begged. "You cannot be unaware that I am not indifferent to you. Indifferent, ha! I have thought of nothing but you since we first met. Don't you remember how maladroit I was that day? It was your beauty that struck me dumb."

Sarah leaned back against the railing of the folly as if to escape his eager face, his impassioned words. But before she could frame a reply, he rushed on, "No, it is true you do not know me. Not yet, at any rate. And yes, perhaps my question was impertinent. Forgive me for it, please. It's just that I want to be as close to you as I can, and in the shortest possible time. And to do so, I must learn all about you—what you think, what you like, what you want. . . . Dearest Sarah, you do understand, don't you?"

Sarah pulled the hands he had captured and clasped to his heart away, but she was careful to be gentle about it. The fervent look on his handsome face made her ache for him.

"You go too fast, sir," she said. "And I think we should be returning to the horses now."

He rose then in one swift, agile movement and sat down beside her again, to put his arms around her. Sarah began to struggle, and he said, "No, wait! I mean you no harm; my word on it. But *speak* to me, please. Speak, nothing else!"

"If you will release me, sir," she said, her chin tilted and her brown eyes flashing at the liberty he took.

Sighing, he let her go, but his eyes never left her face as he did so.

"What would you know, m'lord?" she asked, trying for a casual tone. She could see it was up to her to defuse this potentially dangerous situation. Perhaps some prosaic chitchat would accomplish that.

"I have led a simple life. First growing up here at Three Oaks and then marrying m'lord Lacey when I was twenty-one. That was several years ago. When he died, I remained at the dower house until my father summoned me home when my mother fell ill. A simple little story, is it not? And now I insist we leave."

He sighed and ran his hand through his dark, wavy hair. "But what you have told me is only to give me the bare skeleton of your life," he complained. "But I shall not repine. Someday soon you will tell me what I want to know; I am sure of it."

Sarah rose and walked to the steps that led down from the folly. Jaspar Howland was beside her in a moment, to take her arm and press it close to his side.

Without knowing why she did it, Sarah said, "I must warn you, m'lord, I have no intention of indulging in any dalliance with you. I would not wound you, but I feel you should be forewarned. And any campaign you might have in mind will not work. I am adamant on this point."

She heard his hissed breath as he grasped her upper arms hard, turning her toward him so swiftly, she stumbled. As he shook her, he said in a savage voice. "How dare you insult yourself that way? And me, as well? I mean no dalliance, m'lady; far from it! I intend to make you the next Countess of Castleton. Now, what do you think of that?"

Five

"I THINK YOU have lost your mind!" Sarah said, staring at him in astonishment. "Your countess? Yet you have admitted you hardly know me. And no one can 'love' just like that, m'lord. What you are feeling is nothing more than a boy's infatuation for—"

"I am *not* a boy!" he snapped, still in that same harsh voice. Sarah shivered until she remembered Leary was waiting for them with the horses somewhere close by. She could always call for his aid if she had to.

"You are not so very old," she told the earl as kindly as she could. "Come now, this will not do, no, not at all. Let me go."

When he made no move to obey her, she remembered her earlier plan—how to handle him—and she forced a little laugh. "Come, come, sir," she said in a rallying tone. "I am not at all used to such impassioned pleas and theatrics this early in the day. I find them, fatiguing."

He released her abruptly, and she stepped away from him. Ignoring the burning accusation in his eyes, she went on, "I must for home now. My mother may need me."

The earl was forced to follow her as she went to the bridge and crossed it, calling out to her groom as she did so.

While they waited for the horses to be brought

up, Jaspar Howland recovered his voice. "You may treat my feelings lightly, m'lady, but I do assure you I am in deadly earnest. Yes, I am young. I wish I had ten more years in my dish. You would not laugh at me then. But even so, I warn you that I meant every word I said. I do love you, and someday you will be my countess. Remember I told you so."

"If you continue to speak of such things to me, I will refuse to see you again," Sarah told him. To her own ears she sounded like a prosy old governess, but she did not care.

He picked up her hand then and kissed it, completely ignoring Leary's interest as he led the horses forward. In an entirely different voice, the earl said, "On my honor I would do nothing to distress you, nothing you do not like. I only beg you to give me the chance to prove myself to you. Will you allow me to try, anyway?"

Sarah heard Leary's muffled cough, her mare's whinny, and knowing she could not force the issue now, she nodded.

She despaired when she saw the way his face lit up, his broad smile. He threw her into the saddle himself, and all the way back to Castleton's gates, he spoke only of commonplace things. Still, when he bade her good-bye, his gaze was a naked caress on her face, and as she rode away, she knew he continued to watch her until she was lost from his sight.

Oh dear, she thought, what a fix I'm in. I'd no idea he was going to rush his fences that way. Now what am I to do? It would be folly to see him again, yet she had as much as agreed to it. But perhaps she could control him until he recovered from his volatile passion for her, even as she had planned. It would be tiresome, no doubt, but in the end the earl would thank her for it. Someday, anyway.

But the very idea of saying he intended to marry her, and without even inquiring if she would care for it. His arrogance went beyond any she had ever seen before, and his youth could not excuse it. But no matter how exalted his title, no matter how handsome his face and form, she felt nothing for him but a little liking. And she had been made aware today how different they were. Any marriage between them would be doomed from the start, for he was a younger version of Roger Lacey.

Sarah left Leary to take her mare back to the stables when they reached Three Oaks. The groom grinned to himself at her distracted thanks for his help, the way she frowned as she went up the steps. Poor lass, he thought. Hope she don't take that earl, though. He's a haughty barstid if ever I seen one.

Sarah spent some time with her mother after her luncheon. She was distracted, for she was still thinking of the earl's startling announcement. And when she forced her mind from him, the horrid note she had received that morning invaded her thoughts instead. Who had sent it? For what reason?

Mrs. Jennings was much more garrulous today, and her daughter was glad of it. She did not mention the earl, or Sarah's ride with him, although Sarah was sure she had heard of it. But she could only be grateful for the respite. She was sure her father would demand a complete accounting this evening, not that she had any intention of telling him the truth about what had happened.

At length she became aware of the heavy silence in the room, and she looked up from her needle-point in inquiry. Mrs. Jennings sniffed.

"I do not believe you have heard a word I've said, daughter," she scolded. "I might just as well have been speaking to the wall, for all you care."

"Indeed, I am sorry," Sarah apologized. "I—I was

thinking of something else just then. But you were
saying, Mother. . . ?"

Mrs. Jennings sniffed again. "I was just wondering when Geoffrey would come. I know he is eager
to leave London—oh, my dear poor boy! Just between the two of us, he has overextended himself,
although I have not breathed a word of it to your
father. I only wish I had some money of my own, so
that I might give it to him and thus rescue him
from his predicament."

"Perhaps it is just as well you do not," Sarah
said, choosing her words with care. "It might well
encourage him to further expenditure, you know.
And Geoff must learn to be frugal sooner or later,
don't you agree?"

"You are so hard, so unfeeling," Mrs. Jennings
said, wiping a tear from her eyes. "Can't you sym-
pathize with your brother in his trouble? I am sure
it is not his fault the horse was unplaced. For it
might very well have won if it ran, and set him up
in grand style!"

She paused for a moment then, looking shrewdly
at her daughter's composed face as she bent over
her stitches. "Indeed, I wonder it has not occurred
to you to help him yourself," she said airily.

Sarah looked up then, an arrested expression on
her face, and Mrs. Jennings went on, "What would
a little money mean to you, after all? It's common
knowledge that you are as wealthy as you can stare.
And he is your dear brother."

Something in her daughter's face made her sigh
and change her tactics. "Well, I am sure it is your
own business, daughter, and none of mine. But
when I think of the expense it has been on your
poor father, well! And I myself have not had a new
gown in a year. But we do not begrudge any sacrifice for Geoffrey. I wonder you cannot be as loving,

as concerned. After all, Geoffrey is the only brother you will ever have."

Sarah swallowed a quick retort that if she had any more like him, it would be more than she could bear. But before she could think of a suitable reply, her mother changed the subject.

Still, when she went away at last so her mother could rest, Sarah felt uneasy. And she hoped she was not going to be badgered for the rest of her stay, expected to encourage her brother to ever more extravagance by franking him.

It was not that she was selfish or uncaring. If Geoff had been in real need, she would have come to his aid in a moment. But to part with her future security only so he could amuse himself with his wealthy friends, gambling and drinking and pretending he was as well-to-do as they were, in order to impress them, was too much. No. She would not do such a thing.

Sarah was almost glad when Bradbury announced the usual lady callers. Miss Farnsworth had come today with a bottle of her dandelion wine for the invalid, and separately, fat old lady Willoughby, who lived some way out of the village. This lady was accompanied by a young woman she introduced as Miss Davies, her companion, before she proceeded to ignore her for the remainder of her stay. When she saw her visitors, Sarah hid a smile. Lady Willoughby said exactly whatever was on her mind at the moment, no matter the subject or the company. Sarah was glad that Miss Farnsworth had her salts in her hand, and Sarah saw how distraught she was. She gathered Lady Willoughby had fired a few salvos already. Miss Davies sat quietly to one side, her hands in her lap, and a long-suffering expression on her face.

"So you're home at last, are ye, Sarah?" Lady Willoughby began, struggling to her feet to give her a hug. "About time, I'd say. You've scandalized all the old pussies for miles around, ye know, livin' alone as you've been doin'. Not me, o' course. But I imagine you've had a fine time o' it, haven't ye? Lots o' handsome young bucks in Oxfordshire, eh?"

She winked, but Sarah kept her face expressionless, even as she wished she dared to tell Lady Willoughby to behave herself and stop trying to get Miss Farnsworth to fall into a swoon.

"It is delightful to see you again, ma'am." she said instead. "I trust I find you in good health?"

"Course ye do! Don't coddle myself. Never did," Lady Willoughby retorted. "And you are obviously as healthy as a horse. Tell your mother to stop makin' such a to-do about nothin'. It's only her age. Tell her I said to get up, get goin', and stop indulgin' herself."

"Oh, dear," Miss Farnsworth said faintly. "Don't you think that perhaps, dear Lady Willoughby, Dr. Holmes might be the better judge of that?"

Lady Willoughby bent a steely eye on her questioner. "How so?" she barked. "He's a man, ain't he? What does he know of it?"

Miss Farnsworth subsided, pink-cheeked and all atwitter. Sarah thought to offer her guests tea then, but Lady Willoughby refused.

"Take some Madeira if you've any about. Or sherry. Don't care to maudle my insides with bohea all day. And as my first husband, the captain, would have said, the sun's well over the yardarm now. A large glass, dear girl, and don't bother to include Miss Davies. She don't indulge, more fool she!" she bawled after Sarah, who had gone to the drawing room door to give Bradbury the necessary order.

It was an uncomfortable half hour for Sarah and for Miss Prim and Proper, although Lady Willoughby appeared to be having a very good time. Sarah tried on two occasions to speak to Miss Davies, draw her into the conversation, but she was told in no uncertain terms by the lady's employer that it wasn't a bit of use.

"Never has a thing to say for herself, do you, Bettina?" she demanded. "Wonder I keep you about. Companion, ha!"

At last Miss Farnsworth rose, and Lady Willoughby struggled to her feet, offering to take the lady up in her carriage and thereby spare her the long trudge to the village. Sarah couldn't help but be grateful to her. The old lady had a kind heart, although she hid it well under a cloak of acerbic wit.

As they all entered the hall, they saw Bradbury accepting a large basket of fruit. Sarah's heart sank.

"Well, well, what have we here?" Lady Willoughby demanded. "My word, a pineapple! Had to come from the Hall. No one else hereabouts has succession houses. Who's it for?" she demanded of Bradbury, who sent Sarah a pleading glance.

"Most certainly for my mother," Sarah said firmly. "How kind of Lady Howland to remember her."

To her dismay, Lady Willoughby picked up the note that was included in the basket, and read the direction.

"Lady Lacey, just as I thought!" she crowed. "Caught the earl's fancy, have ye, my girl? I've heard about the interestin' notes you've been receivin'. My, my."

Sarah stared at her. What did she mean? How had she known of the note that had come that morning?

Lady Willoughby patted her cheek as she chuckled. "Come and see me soon, child. I've things to discuss with ye—in private."

Sarah nodded and turned away to thank Miss

Farnsworth for the dandelion wine. As she curtsied to the ladies, she surprised Miss Davies staring at her, such a look of dislike and contempt on her quiet face that Sarah was shocked. But that look was gone so quickly that later she wondered if she had only imagined it.

She took the note that had come with the basket to her room, after directing Bradbury to take the fruit to the cook. Sighing, she made herself read it. To her relief, the earl did not press her for any future meeting. He only told her of his love, his devotion, his desire for her to be his wife, until Sarah did not know whether to laugh or cry. Such impassioned sentences, such glowing phrases, such an abundance of adverbs and adjectives, each tumbling over the other in their haste to outdo their fellows. She supposed she should be flattered, but all she could feel was dismay.

It certainly appeared that discouraging the Earl of Castleton was going to be a difficult, time-consuming chore.

Mr. Jennings was just as interested in her meeting with the earl that morning, as Sarah had known he would be, but she managed to parry all his eager questions with cool replies that, although freely given, told him nothing of the matter whatsoever. Yes, they had ridden the parkland. And yes, it was very beautiful. Yes, they had dismounted once so she might inspect a folly on an island in the lake. No, the earl had said nothing to her of any future meeting. Yes, it had been kind of him to send the fruit as well as the flowers, but it meant nothing. He was only a boy, and he had seemed to her to be bored with the country, even lonely here. Perhaps that was why he sought her out?

"Mayhap he'll ask a few of his fine friends to come and stay," Mr. Jennings remarked at this information. "And there'll be dances and receptions and riding parties at the Hall. That'd be prime, daughter, for you are sure to be included. And what a fine thing for Geoffrey when he arrives. He will not have to make do with the ordinary gentry about, but be able to entertain himself with the nobility as he has been wont to do in town."

Sarah continued to make an excellent meal, not looking at her father until she was sure her features were schooled to a polite mask. But *what* nobility was Geoffrey used to? she asked herself silently. And for what reason? He was not one of them, after all.

She admitted she did not know. Somewhat to her surprise, her brother had not come to see her much in London. She had fully expected him to be constantly on the doorstep, begging for money, attention, invitations. But in thinking so, she had wronged him, for he left her very much to her own devices. And naturally, since he did not travel in Roger Lacey's circles, they did not meet except in public on rare occasions. Once, she remembered, she had signaled her coachman to pull up when she saw her brother riding in Rotten Row with three other men. After a brief conversation, Sarah had been delighted when they rode away. Though they were as young as Geoffrey, as faultlessly dressed and scrupulously correct, she could not like his friends. They appeared to have nothing on their minds but the set of their coats, the value of their horseflesh, and their incessant wagers.

As she and her father were finishing dessert, they heard a stir in the hall, and moments later Geoffrey himself strolled in to shake his father's hand and give his sister an elegant bow. Of no more than average height, he was dressed with great care, his clinging buckskins and broadcloth jacket from Weston covered with a driving coat that sported four full capes. As he handed that article of clothing to the footman, Sarah thought he looked thinner, more drawn than the last time she had seen him over a year ago, and she wondered at his slightly feverish conversation after he had flung himself down in a chair at the table and ordered wine.

"No, nothing to eat, sir. I baited earlier on the road," he said in reply to his father's question. "That is why I am so late in arriving. I met an old friend, Lord Faxton, at one of the inns along the way, and nothing would do but for me to join him and his companions."

As Mr. Jennings beamed and murmured, "Lord Faxton, eh? My, my!" Geoffrey turned to his sister.

"You're looking well, Sarah," he said, raising his glass to her in a toast. "Widowhood agrees with you, I see."

"As you say," she replied evenly. "And you are well, too?"

"Top of the trees," he said a little absently. "How strange it seems to be here at last. I'd forgotten how quiet the country is."

"Mother will be glad to see you," Sarah reminded him.

He nodded, carelessly. "Yes, I'll nip up after a bit and look in on the old girl. Still in bed, is she, sir?"

Mr. Jennings frowned. "Yes, there's no improvement. But we're hoping that *your* visit will do wonders for her."

"And my sister's didn't?" he asked innocently, his eyes sliding around to where Sarah sat, a devilish smile full of mischief on his face.

"Sarah has been everything that is good," James Jennings said. "I'm sure no one could have been more attentive, although that may change soon, my, my, yes."

Before his son could question him, he added, chuckling, "She's caught the eye of Jaspar How-

84

land, the Earl of Castleton. Now, what do you think of that, my boy?"

"I didn't realize Jasper was at the Hall," Geoffrey said. Then he looked at his sister with more respect and added, "What a conquest for you, my dear! He's as well-to-do as Golden Ball. Or so they say."

"He is only a boy, and what he feels for me is mere infatuation for an older woman. He'll get over it," Sarah said dismissively.

"Seems to me you'd make mighty sure he don't have the chance to, if you're not a complete ninny," Geoffrey informed her. "What's that old saying— strike while the iron is hot? I suggest you keep it in mind."

Sarah looked from her brother's face to her father's. The indentically interested and avid expressions they wore made her laugh. "Now, now, I'll not be entangling the young man, so don't think I shall," she said as she rose. Her brother was on his feet immediately to hold her chair for her, and she was reminded of his always impeccable manners, his grace. He was a handsome man, she thought as she studied him carefully. His auburn hair was as wavy as her own, and his brown eyes were flecked with the same gold. He had ridiculously long eyelashes, too, which he had loathed as a boy, to the point that he had even cut them off once, much to his mother's distress. Sarah could see no lines of dissipation on his face from late nights and too much wine, but then, she reminded herself, Geoffrey was only twenty-four.

"Do I have a smut on my face, sister?" he asked innocently. "You are looking at me so hard. Or have I changed so much in the years we have spent apart?"

She smiled at him then as he quirked one mobile brow at her. How often he had practiced that gesture until he perfected it, in front of his mother's looking glass.

"No, not at all. You are as handsome as you have ever been," she told him honestly, and she was amused to see how grateful he was for the compliment.

"I'll leave you gentlemen to your wine now," she said as she went to the door. As she opened it, she added, "Don't forget to go up to Mother soon, Geoffrey. She has been pining so for the sight of you."

He waved a careless hand. "There you go," he said in mock long-suffering tones as he pulled down his mouth. "Do you think the time will ever come when you might forget you are the elder, Sarah? After all, we are not children anymore."

She shook her head at him and left him with his father, both of them chuckling.

Six

SARAH RECEIVED ANOTHER strange note the following morning. This time it arrived with her morning chocolate on the tray her maid brought to her in bed, and she eyed it with misgiving as she questioned Betsy.

But the maid knew nothing about it. She said one of the grooms had found it on the path between the stables and the house. As she moved around, opening the curtains and plumping up Sarah's pillows, Betsy stole many a glance at her mistress. Could it be that Lady Lacey had an admirer here? she wondered. She'd give a lot to find out who it was!

Alone in her room, Sarah did not want to open that note. Merely looking at it made her uneasy, for she had recognized the stilted printing of the direction at once. At last she forced herself to pick it up—break the seal. She told herself she was not a coward. No matter what it said, it was only words, and words, although they could certainly wound, could not slay her.

The note was longer this time, and Sarah read it quickly, grimacing as she did so. "I know all about you," it began abruptly. "Looking so sweet and pure! But you are no better than a whore. Married an old man, you did, for his title and money, and now you're nosing around for another man to rut with. You don't fool me. Go back where you came from!"

Sarah could not restrain a little moan. The hatred in the printed words seemed a palpable thing, almost a miasma that oozed from the paper until she felt she could smell it—all dark and evil.

She looked down and was surprised to see she had crushed the note in her hand. She had no recollection of doing so. Carefully she smoothed it out to read again. There was no signature, not that she had expected one. And the printing gave her no clue as to who the writer might be. It could be either a man or a woman.

But no, the more she considered it, the less likely it appeared that a man would stoop to something like this. Men attacked openly, with fists or guns or swords, when they were enraged. The annonymous notes seemed more a woman's method of getting revenge.

But revenge for *what*? Sarah asked herself as she rubbed her forehead. What did I do to deserve this?

There was no answer. The bright sunlight streamed in through the windows, and she could hear a bird in the branches of the old tree outside her bedroom. It was singing as if it didn't have a care in the world. Lucky little bird, she thought as she rang the bell for Betsy and got up to lock the note away with its fellow.

That afternoon she took her brother driving in her phaeton. Geoffrey had seen the carriage in the stables, and nothing would do but that she show him her skill. Still, coming home later, Sarah was glad she had gone out. The fresh air had blown away the little headache she had had all day, and just talking with Geoffrey, thinking about something else, made her feel better.

As they drove through Sutton Cross, she could even smile at the satisfaction Geoffrey got from overwhelming the villagers with his smart London clothes and his handsome good looks. Why, his bow to Miss Farnsworth caused the poor old dear to blush rosy and turn away to hide her confusion.

"Shame on you, Geoff," Sarah scolded lightly. "Slaying Miss Farnsworth with that devilish smile of yours! I wonder if I should have stopped so we could chat with her?"

Geoffrey pretended to shudder with horror. "Thank heavens you did not," he muttered. "We'd have been there an eternity while she gasped out her little nothings, and if I remember correctly, her crony would have hurried to join us as well, to poke and pry. Oh, how can anyone bear living in this horrid rural place? There is nothing to do here, nothing amusing at all!"

"But when you inherit Three Oaks, you'll have to live here," his sister reminded him.

When he did not answer, Sarah glanced sideways in astonishment to see him looking grim.

"It's not so bad," she consoled him. "In fact, I rather like it myself."

"After London? And society? You're all about in your head! As for me, I'll be going back to town as quickly as I can."

"Mother seemed much more cheerful this morning," Sarah told him. "She even said she may try to get up for a bit, sit in a chair in her room. Your coming has been a blessing, for you know how she dotes on you."

"Yes, she always did, didn't she? Good old thing, Ma," he said carelessly, smirking a little.

He spotted a horseman coming toward them then, and he abandoned his lounging posture to sit up straighter. Sarah stifled a sigh when she saw the rider was the Earl of Castleton, but she pulled up obediently when he raised a hand in greeting.

"M'lady," he said, taking off his hat and inclining his head to her. His gelding sidestepped nervously, and his hand tightened on the reins.

Sarah saw he was eyeing her brother with a dark frown, and she was quick to say, "M'lord, may I present my brother, Geoffrey Jennings?"

"No need to do that," Geoffrey said, smiling easily. "I've met the earl in town, although perhaps you do not remember the occasion, m'lord?"

"I can't say I do," Jaspar Howland replied, although he was looking more at ease now.

"It was in Hyde Park several months ago. I was riding with Lord Faxton and a few other friends. I see you still have the gray. I envy you. It's a handsome beast."

"Faxton?" the earl persisted. "I don't believe I know a Lord Faxton."

"Guy Keating, m'lord. Estate in Northumberland," Geoffrey prompted.

Sarah thought the earl looked a little grim as he nodded. "Oh yes. *That* Lord Faxton."

Turning away from her brother then to give her his full attention, he said, "I see you are driving again, Lady Lacey. I have not given up hopes that you will allow me to tool you about in my carriage, as we discussed. Perhaps in a few days time?"

"It will all depend on how my mother goes on—" Sarah began, but Geoffrey interrupted her.

"No, no, sister, there is no need for you to miss such a treat! I'll be glad to sit with Mother while you and the earl are engaged. Good of you to suggest it, m'lord. I was just telling Sarah she must be moped to death down here. I loathe the country myself. Only filial duty could have coaxed me from town."

"Indeed?" Jaspar Howland said. "It is kind of you, sir, to take her place. Lady Lacey? Give you good afternoon."

As soon as they were out of earshot, Sarah rounded on her brother, prepared to give him a piece of her mind. "Why on earth did you do that,

Geoff?" she demanded. "Couldn't you tell I did not care for it?"

"Don't be a fool," he said carelessly. "The man's a real catch. And earls aren't like hackneys, you know."

"Hackneys? Of course they're not like hackneys! Whatever are you talking about?"

"Oh, it's just something Ma used to say. She'd tell me, 'Never mind, son, if you missed that opportunity, for like hackneys, there'll be another one along in a minute.'

"But earls aren't like that, Sarah. There aren't that many of 'em. And this one is young and handsome as well as wealthy; why, I'd think you'd jump at the chance after being married to that old curmudgeon of a viscount of yours."

"Listen to me, Geoffrey," Sarah said earnestly. "I don't want you meddling in this. It is my life—my business—and none of yours. And I wish you would not encourage Father and Mother to hope I might marry the earl. I shall not. And pestering me about it will not help. There! That's plain enough for you, I hope?"

"How vehement you are, my dear. But can it be you doth protest too much?" he asked idly. "You know you must marry again and—"

"Why?" she asked swiftly, stung to honesty. "*Why* must I marry? I didn't care for it the first time, and I don't intend to try it again. And there's no need for it, after all. The viscount left me very well to pass."

Her brother stared at her without speaking and then he whistled softly. "So, lies the wind in that quarter, eh?" he asked softly. "Silly Sarah! Of course you'll wed, eventually; that is, when you tire of being opportuned by every male who comes your way. You're a damned fine-looking woman.

"You know, I symphathize with you, for I've no

liking for wedlock myself. But I have every intention of marrying as well as I can. It won't even matter if my bride has a face like a horse, not if her gold's plentiful enough, and she comes from a good family. No cits for me. It's the nobility or nothing!"

"It sounds so calculating when you put it like that," Sarah said.

He shrugged. "I am forced to be calculating if I want to escape my background," he said. "Marriage to wealth is the only way I can do so. Let me be blunt with you, sister. I've no intention of moldering away down here in Kent all my days, a mere farmer. Not even though I be a *gentleman* farmer. Oh no, I've better things in mind for my future than that."

Sarah made no comment as she slowed the team for the turn in to the drive. She was thinking hard. She had not realized Geoffrey was so ambitious. He had changed since her marriage, and not for the better, either, she thought. He was hard now, cold—careless of another's feelings. She sincerely pitied the rich, noble young lady who might agree to give her hand to him. For what would she get in return? Certainly not love. Only a handsome face. It seemed a very bad bargain.

The evening designated for the Dentons' dinner party came and went. Riding home from it in the carriage with her father and brother, Sarah could not decide why it had been so awkward. True, the guests were a strange mixture of age and occupation, but it had not been that, for with the exception of the new vicar, Mr. Williams, and his wife, Prudence, Sarah was well acquainted with every one of them.

Whatever it was, Sarah had been uneasy, at times even dismayed, and as the carriage traveled over the familiar roads, she sat deep in thought.

"One can only be thankful that *that* ordeal is over," Geoffrey snarled, his handsome face discontent. "Pray do not include me in any more of these rural parties, sir! I do not think I could bear another such evening."

Before her father could speak, Sarah said, "Yes, it was unpleasant, wasn't it? I was just trying to figure out why."

"*You* should have enjoyed yourself if anyone did, dear sister," her brother told her. "I've never seen such fawning and toadying; such 'your ladyshipping,' in all my days."

Sarah sat up straighter, an arrested look on her face. "Why, I do believe you've got it, Geoff. That was why I was so uncomfortable. But why on earth—I mean, these people have known me all my life!"

"Ah, but you are a viscountess now, Sarah," her father said, his voice rich with satisfaction. "And you bestowed quite a distinction on the Dentons by merely coming to their little party. I'm sure it was no wonder everyone was overwhelmed. . . ."

As Geoffrey barked a derisive laugh, Sarah thought back over the evening. Yes, she could see it was as Geoff had said. Mrs. Denton had paid her extravagant compliments and made sure she had the best seat in the parlor, much to Sarah's distress. She knew either Miss Withers or Miss Farnsworth would have been more comfortable there. And she had gone in to dinner on Mr. Denton's arm. Once seated to her host's right in the place of honor, she had looked up to see Evan Lancaster's eyes on her, a smile quivering on his lips as he helped Fay Denton to her chair.

And as she thought of it now, Sarah remembered that it had seemed that every time she spoke, the entire table hushed, to hang on her every word. The dinner itself had been very elaborate, and it had taken forever to consume.

"I do hope neither of you ate the creamed lobster," Geoffrey remarked. "I tried to catch both your eyes, for it had definitely gone off."

"I wonder Mrs. Denton did not serve a Dover sole," Sarah mused.

"Lobster is more costly, and therefore more impressive," Geoffrey told her. "And that wine! It wasn't bad enough that the Dentons' kitchen maid was pressed into service as butler, but she also dribbled a lot of the swill on my sleeve while pouring it."

"Well, we should not be talking of the party like this," Sarah said. "I'm sure Mrs. Denton tried hard. But I wish she had not attempted such formality. I can still remember the wonderful, homey teas we used to eat around her kitchen table when we were children and had been out sledding or skating together. Remember, Geoff? How delicious her scones were?"

"I am trying as hard as I can to forget everything I ever knew of the Dentons," he murmured, and Sarah subsided.

As they drove on, she recalled what had happened after dinner. They had all gathered in the parlor again, to continue in stilted conversation. Evan Lancaster had come to her side for a moment to chat with her. Sarah thought he looked very well with his blond hair neatly arranged. He wore a bottle green coat and neat linen, and his breeches fit his powerful legs like a second skin. Of course, she knew the great Weston would have shuddered at the fit of that coat and its outdated lapels, but to her eyes it was becoming, complementing his hazel eyes as it did.

But Mr. Lancaster was not allowed to monopolize her, much to her regret. After only a few minutes,

Fay Denton and her mother bore him away to talk to the vicar, and Sarah found herself surrounded by Prudence Williams and the two elderly spinsters she knew so well. She remembered that Ralph Denton had brooded as he leaned against the wall where he could watch her face, and she wished he would not be so obvious in his infatuation. Miss Withers had told her to pay him no mind, for he was nothing but a silly chub, and it was to be hoped he would outgrow these airs as he matured. "For to be aspiring to *you*, m'lady, is ludicrous," she finished, tossing her black curls as she did so.

"Oh dear me, yes," Miss Farnsworth had agreed in her gentle voice. "Why, you can have anyone, I daresay. Even a marquess, or perhaps . . . perhaps an earl?"

Sarah had ignored her and her titters, to ask the vicar's wife about the coming church bazaar. Not that that had been a felicitous choice of subject, for Prudence Williams at once had her promise to not only open the bazaar, but work at one of the booths as well.

Sarah was happy to do so, but she could not like the way the three ladies put their heads together to discuss which booth she should honor. Certainly not quilts and pinafores! Miss Withers had exclaimed in disgust. Nor vegetables either, Miss Farnsworth contributed. Perhaps preserves? Baked goods? Sarah ended their speculations by saying she would like to help with the children's games, just as she had done years ago. Before the ladies could protest such a lowly occupation, she excused herself to go and speak to her brother and Janet Denton. Geoffrey appeared to be making heavy weather of conversation with the girl.

And now, as the carriage drew up at Three Oaks, and her brother climbed down to offer her his arm, Sarah wished that things were the way they used to be. Of course, she knew that was impossible, for no one could ever go back to times past, no matter how dear and simple those times might have been.

The next morning brought a note from the earl arranging the drive he had suggested. Sarah was glad he did only that, making no more declarations of love, and so she was able to return a civil acceptance.

Her mother was delighted when she learned of the drive, and since she was now sitting up part of every day, even taking a few steps on Geoffrey's arm, Sarah had hopes she would soon recover. And then what will I do? she wondered. She would stay at Three Oaks until after Christmas, of course, but no longer. Then she could either go to town or visit elsewhere in the country. Some of the people she had met as Lady Lacey had invited her to their estates time and time again, and one of them might provide a temporary refuge until she decided where she wanted to live.

The following afternoon, the earl arrived with a small tiger wearing his livery, clinging to the back of the perch phaeton. The boy ran to hold the team while the earl went to escort Sarah outside. As she prepared to climb to the perch, she found herself picked up in Jaspar Howland's arms and lifted to it, all seemingly without the slightest effort. As she looked back down at him, she saw his triumphant smile, and her own in return did not reveal her amusement at his boyish trick to show off how strong he was.

"Wait for me here," the earl called to his tiger as he sprang to his seat beside her and took up the reins. "Let 'em go!

"You look as lovely as ever," he said, his eyes firmly on the drive. "That deep scarlet you wear is stunning."

"Thank you, m'lord," Sarah said lightly. She noticed the earl took the turn out of the drive at speed, and wondered what Leary would have had to say to him about *that*.

"You are not nervous, are you?" he asked next. "You must not fear. I would never, ever, overturn anyone as precious as you."

Ignoring his caressing compliment, Sarah shook her head. "No, but to tell the truth, even though I have ridden in perch phaetons before, they do make me a little uneasy. We are so far from the ground, and your team goes so swiftly. How beautiful they are, so perfectly matched and well attuned. Everything you said they were indeed."

Just as she had hoped, the earl began another monologue about his chestnuts, and she could relax for a while.

But all good respites must come to an end, and at length, Jaspar Howland asked himself in exasperation, "Now, why am I prosing on and on about my cattle? Especially when you are beside me, darling Sarah?"

Before she could protest this familiarity, he turned a little to grin at her. Sarah had to admit he had a bewitching grin. "No, forgive me," he said ruefully. "I should not have said that. You see, I am determined to be on my best behavior today—give you no cause to be upset with me. I have come to see that you were quite right the other day. I was much too precipitate and I frightened you with my ardor. It will not happen again. Although," he added more softly and slowly, "that is not to imply my *ardor* for you is not as strong as ever it was. Because it is."

"Thank you, you are kind," Sarah said faintly, ignoring the latter part of his statement. They were approaching Sutton Cross now, but Jaspar Howland did not slow his horses. Instead, he swept

97

around a dray without a check so the team could thunder down the village's main street. Sarah saw that everyone who was abroad was staring at them, mouths ajar, and she was glad that for once, Mrs. Akins had a firm grip on her young scamp of a son.

"I wonder if they have any idea how silly they look, gaping at us like that," the earl asked. "But of course, that is why I did it. To give them something to chew over with their tea."

Another boy's trick, showing off, Sarah thought. Although the earl was trying very hard to appear mature, he gave himself away at every turn.

He took the road that led west to Ashford. Sarah had not been this way in some time, and she looked about with interest. She saw the harvest was almost in, for few labored in the fields anymore. In a few days it would be November, and before long, the weather would change, and this delightful hiatus between summer and the winter storms would be over.

She knew to the moment when they reached the first of Evan Lancaster's acres, but although she looked for him, he was nowhere in sight in the well-kept fields and orchards. The farmhouse was set out of sight behind a grove of trees at the top of a slight rise. Sarah could see the smoke from its chimneys, but nothing else.

"Won't you?" she heard the earl asking, and she started.

"I do beg your pardon, sir," she said quickly. "I was thinking how well the countryside looks in the sunlight, and did not hear your question. You were saying. . . ?"

"I was telling you of a surprise I intend in the next few days," he said, sounding disgruntled that he had been ignored. "I am sure you will be pleased. And I was hoping that you would fall in with my plans."

"Ah, but that depends on your plans," she said lightly. "Am I to learn nothing of them before I agree? How rash of me if I were to do so!"

He chuckled then, and she thought to ask him if the Lady Rose had made him teach her to drive as yet.

"No, and I'll be damned if I—I do beg your pardon, ma'am—I'll be hanged if I do," he said, his mouth setting in a stern line. "Rose has become too forward. I have told her that if she does not mend her ways, I'll see she's punished for it."

"But surely it's only high spirits, sir. She is very young, after all."

"All the more reason that she learn how to behave as a lady," he insisted. "My sister Caroline is her complete opposite, so gentle and biddable. But Rose is an imp of Satan, and I'll not have it!"

Before Sarah could comment, they swept around a curve and she gasped. A small mongrel dog was trudging down the middle of the road, and the horses were almost upon him.

She heard Jaspar Howland's muttered curse as he tried to slow the team and avoid the animal, and she grasped the side of the phaeton with both hands, waiting for the worst.

Everything from that moment on seemed to happen very slowly. The team reared up in the traces, and when the earl tried to swing them aside, the phaeton rocked precariously. But there was nowhere for the team to go, for thick hedges lined the road on both sides.

Sarah heard the dog yelping just before she was pitched sideways. And then she was falling, falling for what seemed a very long time, before she landed with a thump deep in the hedge. Gasping for breath, she was aware of the horses neighing and the injured dog's howls, as well as the earl's frenzied shouts and the raucous calls of some rooks as, alarmed, they flew away from a tree nearby.

"Sarah! Are you all right?" Jaspar Howland demanded. "Dear God, answer me!"

"Yes. Yes, I am," she managed to call out as she struggled to free herself. She knew the hedge had saved her from serious injury, but she could not be grateful for it, not now when it scratched at her hands and face, and its thorns seemed determined to keep her smart carriage dress captive as she tried to escape it. Yet even in all her distress, she was aware of how ridiculous she must look, arse over teakettle in an overgrown hedge, and she had to chuckle at the picture she knew she made. Thank heavens there was no one about to witness her plight!

It was several minutes more before she extricated herself from the hedge's clinging embrace, and stood in the road, trying to smooth down her gown and petticoats. Aware that the dog's howling had died away to whimpers, she looked up to see Jaspar Howland still seated in the phaeton, trying to control his high-spirited team as they lunged and snorted. He had lost his hat, and his dark hair tumbled over his brow. His face was as white as his shirt.

"Thank God you are all right," he called, then added, "Whoa, now, *whoa*! Stand, dammit, *stand*! You *are* all right aren't you?"

"Well, you may not have overturned me, m'lord, but you did manage to tip me out," Sarah called, smiling up at him to ease the torture she saw in his face.

"My darling! Oh, do forgive me, dearest Sarah. I never meant to, you know. . . . That damned dog!"

"Oh, the dog," Sarah cried, pushing past the side of the phaeton to go and search for it.

"Do have a care! The chestnuts are still wild,"

the earl warned her. "And it's only a cur, after all."

"But it is injured and in pain," Sarah retorted. "I must see if I can help it."

"It might bite you—*whoa*, there, I say! Sarah, I insist you come away. Leave the animal—*whoa! Steady!*"

Sarah ignored him as she knelt by the side of the road where the dog had been thrown. She spoke to it softly with soothing words as she tried to assess its injuries. One leg was bent in a peculiar way, but it did not appear to be bleeding. She wondered what she was to do as she stared down into its dark, liquid eyes and put a tentative hand on its head to smooth the fur there.

The dog continued to whimper its distress, and Sarah looked around, desperate for help. But although the chestnuts were quieter now, she saw there was no way the earl could get down and leave them unattended. Not that he would have done so for a mongrel, she thought bitterly.

The dog licked her hand then, and she smiled. She saw it was still a puppy, and an emaciated one at that. Its ribs showed clearly, and its fur was matted with burrs and dirt. Poor thing, she thought, I wonder who you belong to?

She stared down the road then when she heard pounding hoofbeats, and smiled in relief when she recognized Evan Lancaster riding toward her.

As he reined in, she cried, "Oh, how glad I am you are here, Mr. Lancaster! Please come and see if you can help me with this dog."

Lancaster glanced at the Earl of Castleton seated in his perch phaeton and nodded to him as he dismounted and tied his horse to the hedge.

"I take it there's been an accident, m'lady?" he asked Sarah as he knelt beside her.

"Do come away now, Sarah!" the earl commanded. "The farmer will see to the animal. There is no need to trouble yourself further."

Again Sarah ignored him. "I think his leg is broken, but I can see no other injuries," she said. "Do you have any idea who owns him?"

"Her," he said absently as he inspected the dog, his hands sure and gentle. The dog, which had trembled at his approach, relaxed. "No, I know of no one. I've not seen the animal before."

"He, er, *she* was walking down the middle of the road when we came around the bend. There was nothing the earl could have done, although he tried his best to avoid the dog," Sarah explained. "And I was tipped into the hedge."

Evan Lancaster's lips quivered. "I'd already surmised you'd had some kind of problem, ma'am," he said.

Sarah looked down at her dusty, snagged gown. One of the sleeves was ripped, and part of the ruching at the hem had come undone and was trailing in the dirt. Obviously she would not be able to wear it ever again.

"Bad place here, with that curve. And I daresay the earl was traveling too fast."

Sarah flushed. "Well, yes, we were going rather rapidly," she admitted.

"Can you climb into the phaeton by yourself?" he asked next. Behind them, Jaspar Howland fumed quietly.

"Yes, of course I can. But the dog . . ."

"I'll take her back to the farm, try to heal that leg."

Sarah gave him a heartfelt smile. "And feed her, too?" she persisted. "She's so thin."

He picked the dog up then, cradling it against his shirt. "And feed her, too," he agreed. "Now, if you'll just untie my horse and hold it for a moment . . ."

Sarah hurried to do his bidding.

When he was mounted, he took the reins up with one hand. "Thank you, Evan," she said, smiling up at him again.

He stared down at her, and although he didn't smile, Sarah was sure he wanted to. "You'd better straighten your bonnet, ma'am," he said. "You don't look in much better shape than the dog."

As he rode past the earl, he nodded to him and added, "Best to have a care on country roads, m'lord. There are so often animals . . . other people . . . teams to be encountered. And this is the public road to Ashford and not your private domain."

Sarah was scrambling to her seat again. As she sat down and straightened her hat, she saw the earl was white again, with fury this time. "Of all the cheek!" he exclaimed as Evan Lancaster rode away. "Did you hear that, Sarah? To think such as he would dare to chastise *me*!"

"He was right to do so, and you know it," she said calmly. "You were driving at a reckless pace. But let's forget it, sir. The dog will recover, and I was not injured, nor were you or the chestnuts. But I think I'd like to be taken home now. I'm sore from my tumble."

Immediately the earl forgot the insolent farmer in his anxiety for her. And by the time they reached Three Oaks again—driving at a more sedate pace this time—Sarah was delighted to dispense with not only Jaspar Howland's constantly voiced concern, but his company as well.

Seven

THE SPELL OF fine weather that the county had been enjoying broke that night, and Sarah Lacey woke the next morning to the sound of rain splattering against the windows and gurgling in the drainpipes. Content to stay warm in bed, she stretched a little and then groaned as her aching body protested the move. She told herself she didn't care if it rained for a week. Besides, she couldn't go anywhere, not with a scratched face and hands.

If was funny, she thought, as she cautiously squirmed into a more comfortable position. Neither her father nor mother had seemed at all concerned by her bedraggled condition when she had returned home. Mr. Jennings had even gone so far as to say that accidents will happen, and he was sure the earl felt terrible about it, poor lad. And Mrs. Jennings in turn had no sympathy to waste on anyone else's problems but her own. But now Sarah remembered her brother Geoffrey's dancing eyes and little smile, and she blushed again. It was obvious that Geoffrey put little credence in the accident, and had his own, much more interesting theory about how she had torn her gown, ruined her hat, and acquired those scratches and bruises. And shame on him, too, for such thoughts, Sarah told herself.

She spent the morning in bed, reading and sipping tea and enjoying her leisure. At eleven a large bouquet arrived from the Hall. The fervent letter that accompanied it begged her pardon so many times that Sarah had to chuckle.

The next day brought a lovely book of flower prints and a slim volume of poetry, and the day after that, a box of chocolates and a basket of oranges. But when the earl came to see her later in the week, Sarah refused to receive him. Her scratches were all but indiscernable now, and her bruises fading, but she rather thought it might do Jaspar Howland good to be denied a little longer.

Mr. Jennings was most upset when he learned the earl had been turned away, and he spent a long time remonstrating with her. "And after all his lovely gifts, too! Where are your manners? And I must tell you, his attentions have been so marked that everyone is talking about it. Best you watch what you're about, missy! It don't do to be too careless with the nobility. He's likely to take a pet and cry off."

"And if he does, I shall be delighted to be free of him," Sarah said calmly. "I've told you before, sir, I prefer to have little or nothing to do with Jaspar Howland, be he the earl or no. He'll get over his infatuation, and when he does, I'll be glad."

Her father's face turned almost purple with fury and he turned away abruptly and stalked to the door, slamming it behind him. Sarah winced, but she picked up her book calmly.

But the story she had been reading had no power to hold her now, and in a short time she put the book aside to wander over to the window to rest her forehead on the cool pane. Why was her father so upset? she wondered idly. What was it to him, after all, whether she married the earl or not? She did not think the earl would be vindictive, take out his disappointment on James Jennings. And even if he wanted to, how could he accomplish such a thing? It was true her father's land marched with his, at

105

least in one tiny corner of the vast estate that was Castleton, but those lands were her father's property. It was a poser.

When the next morning dawned fair again, Sarah sent a message to the stables, asking that her horse be saddled. She was tired of her inactivity, and she had remembered Lady Willoughby had asked her to call to discuss something privately. Now was as good a time as any to find out what that something might be.

She found Lady Willoughby seated in her drawing room. Miss Davies was there as well, but Lady Willoughby was quick to send her away. Sarah was glad she had. She could not like Miss Davies.

"Heard you had an accident, gel," her hostess said as she motioned her to take a seat. All her chins wobbled as she chuckled. "Also heard the earl's been hauntin' your doorstep with his lavish gifts."

"Is there no way to keep anything private in this neighborhood?" Sarah asked in mock despair.

Lady Willoughby shook her head. "Impossible! But tell me what happened. You wouldn't believe the garbled accounts that have been goin' around."

She nodded throughout Sarah's explanation, and when it was done, she looked thoughtful. "Do you remember me sayin' I wanted to speak to you privately?" she asked.

"Indeed I do. That is why I rode over today."

"Well, I wanted to give you some good advice about the earl," Lady Willoughby began. When she saw Sarah's moue of distaste, she shook her finger at her. "Yes, I daresay you've had more than enough on the subject already, but I intend to put in my mite, too, so do take that Friday face away!"

"You see, Sarah, it's plain as the nose on your face that Jaspar Howland is mad for you. And if you have an ounce of common sense, you'll make

106

sure to tie him up all right and tight before he changes his mind. Young men are so volatile. And he's not much more than a boy. It would be a very good thing for you, my gel, becoming a countess. There's a deal of wealth there. And you're a widow now."

"I have wealth of my own," Sarah said, stung into speech as the fat old lady coughed and had to resort to a sip of water. "I neither need nor want any more."

"Ha!" Lady Willoughby snorted. "No one can have enough wealth! Where's your common sense?"

"But I don't want to ensnare the earl," Sarah said patiently. "He doesn't love me, not really. And I don't love him."

Lady Willoughby stared at her, looking puzzled. "What does that have to say about anything?" she demanded. "Marriage is not about love, and you, of all people, should know that. There was no love between you and the viscount, surely."

"Certainly not! That marriage was arranged by my parents, and much against my will."

"I suspected as much. But the earl is no aging Roger Lacey. No, he's a handsome young buck. He'd be a good thing for you, in and out of bed. Surprised you haven't seen that yourself."

Sarah lost her temper. "You must not think I'm ungrateful for your help, ma'am, but I do not intend to marry again. Not ever. Not even to your precious earl. And if I did, I certainly wouldn't do so for wealth and social advancement!"

Lady Willoughby had been shaking her head throughout this impassioned speech. "Oh, child, still an idealist?" she asked. "You disappoint me. I've been married four times, each time for the better. And I did so without a single thought of 'love.' Worked out well, too. And I daresay none of my late husbands felt the slightest bit cheated. We all got what we wanted. So could you and the earl.

"Well, I've said my piece. You go away and think about it."

Sarah rose and curtsied, glad this difficult interview was over. Then, remembering Lady Willoughby's remark about the notes she had received, she thought to ask her what she had meant.

"About your notes? Why, I meant those you've been receivin' from the earl, of course. What else could I have meant?" the old lady asked in some confusion.

"I see," Sarah said, lowering her eyes and smoothing her gloves. "I only wondered, ma'am."

As she went out and mounted her horse, Sarah also wondered why she had not told the old lady about the others she'd received. It would have been a relief to talk to someone about them, get her opinion as to what she should do. But perhaps she had not done so because she had been so annoyed with the lady and her advice about snaring the earl? Or was it because she still could not bear to have anyone know how much she was hated?

The ride home brought her close to Evan Lancaster's farmhouse, and on a whim, she decided to call. It was not as if he were a man living alone, she told herself. There can be no impropriety when his aunt is there. And I have a very good reason, for I want to see if the dog is recovering. Unexceptional, I'm sure. No one could think a thing of it.

But as she dismounted before the old brick farmhouse, admired its comfortable lines and the little garden that fronted it, she knew people would think a great deal about it if they were to find out. And they would talk about it as well. More talk.

Her knock on the door was answered by a wide-eyed little maid who blushed as she bobbed a curtsy before she ran away to fetch her mistress.

Sarah had met Miss Barnes once years ago, so she did not have to introduce herself. She noticed how cool she was, how contained, as she led the way to the parlor and asked her guest to be seated.

"I came to see if the dog that was injured by the earl's phaeton the other day is recovering," Sarah explained. "It was so good of Mr. Lancaster to say he would take care of it."

Miss Barnes had picked up a large workbasket, and now she began to darn the heel of one of her nephew's wool stockings. She snorted a little before she said, "Dirty animal! I was that upset when Evan showed up here with it. It's out in the barn, and as far as I know, it's still alive. But I'll not have it in the house, and so I told him."

"You are not fond of animals?"

Miss Barnes shook her head. "Can't say I am. Bring in a lot of dirt, make messes, and are always underfoot. He'll stay in the barn."

"It's a she," Sarah told her. At Miss Barnes's stern look, she added, "Mr. Lancaster told me so."

"Oh dear, and before we know it, I suppose there'll be puppies. Well, I hope Evan can find the owner, is all I say. I've no mind to have the place overrun with pesky puppies."

She paused for a moment before she said, "Are you planning to remain at Sutton Cross long, m'lady? Seems to me I did hear tell that your mother is improving."

"Yes, at last. It is such a relief to us all. As for my plans, I have no idea at this time."

"Well, just remember it never does any good to try and go back to what you once were," Miss Barnes said comfortably.

She looked up then and saw her nephew in the doorway. "You here, Evan? You're back early from Wye."

Sarah turned on the settee to smile at him. "I

came to see how the dog is, sir," she explained. "Your aunt says she is doing well."

"And how would she know?" he asked. Sarah wondered at the stiffness in his voice as he went on, "Won't have a thing to do with her. But if you'd like to see her before you go, ma'am. . . ?"

"Yes, I would. Thank you," Sarah said as she rose. Miss Barnes got up, too, still holding her darning. "It was nice to see you again, ma'am. Give you good day."

Her hostess curtsied, her face unsmiling. Sarah wondered if she disapproved of her calling here, and her cheeks flushed a little.

As they walked to the barn, Evan Lancaster said, "You're looking better than the last time I saw you, m'lady. I'm glad you came to no harm from the accident."

"I was sore for several days, but it was nothing serious," Sarah told him. "I suppose I should be grateful to that hedge, although at the time I cursed it heartily."

They walked around the end of the house, and before them was a stable yard and several outbuildings. Sarah could see a chicken coop, and in the distance, a pigsty. In the fields beyond, a herd of cows grazed, and there were three neat cottages for the farmhands.

It was such a pleasant day, and she felt so lighthearted, that when one of the pigs made a rude noise, she laughed.

"The farm looks well," she said. "You have had a good season?"

"Aye. Fine yields this year, and the animals are thriving," he told her. Sarah looked sideways at him. He was wearing heavy breeches and a homespun shirt, but his tanned face and the hair that was bleached even blonder by this past summer's sun made her think him attractive even in his working clothes. And he was different from other farmers, too. More educated, better spoken. She had seen the books in his parlor, and the one on the table that held a man's pipe and tobacco.

"I noticed you are reading Scott's *Lay of the Last Minstrel*," she said. "It is one of my favorites. Are you enjoying it?"

"I have read it before, but yes, I am," he said.

"May I ask you something?"

"Of course."

"Then will you tell me where you learned to read? It is not at all usual, I mean . . ."

"For a common farmer?" he asked, his voice cool. Sarah blushed as he went on, "I don't suppose it is. But my father wanted his sons to have a better chance in life than he did, and he paid the vicar to see to our schooling in the winters when we could be spared from the farm. We always kept an extra pig to fatten, and called it the Holy Swine. You see, that was how my father paid the vicar—in hams and pork and bacon."

Sarah chuckled. "It's hard to picture a holy pig," she said. Then she grew serious. "But you stayed on the farm, even though you had an education. Why?"

"I guess farming's in my blood. I like it," he told her, turning to look at her. "Besides, I'm on my own land here, and I'm my own master. That's important to me."

"Of course. I understand," Sarah said, watching the breeze as it stirred in his hair.

"Here we are," he said, indicating the large barn. He held the door back for her so she could go in first. The barn was dim and warm, its loft stuffed to the rafters with hay for the winter. An old horse neighed to her from its stall, and she wished she had thought to bring a sugar cube with her. Then

111

she saw the dog lying on an old blanket, and her eyes widened.

"Why, how much better it looks," she said as she knelt to pat it. The dog gave a few little yelps, its tail going in wild circles as it tried to get up and lick her face.

"It seems to remember you, ma'am," Evan told her.

Sarah noted the neatly splinted leg, the clean brown fur. "You've even given it a bath," she said. "And I didn't suspect that white ruff around the neck."

"How could you when it was so filthy before? You know, it objected to the bath more than it did to my setting the leg, didn't you, girl?"

He went down on his haunches then, to pat the dog's head.

"I imagine she's eating you out of house and home," Sarah said, eyeing the empty dish that was next to another filled with water.

"She's trying to," he told her wryly as he scratched the dog's ears.

"Mr. Lancaster, what will happen to her, I mean, after she gets well?" Sarah asked, frowning now. "Suppose no one claims her."

He smiled. "She's claimed *me*. You're not to worry, m'lady. I'll not turn her out to fend for herself, no matter what my aunt says."

"What will you call her? She has to have a name."

"I've no idea. What would you call her?"

Sarah thought for a moment, her head tipped to one side. Then her eyes lit up. "Why not Ruff?" she asked. "It seems to suit her."

"Yes, she does have that white fur, and she's certainly had a rough life so far," he agreed.

Sarah smiled, but suddenly she was conscious that they were alone in the dim barn; alone together. Evan was crouched close to her, too, so close she could hear his quiet breathing, smell the warm essence of him, all sunlight and sweet hay, feel his muscled arm touching her shoulder. Somehow it was a very intimate moment, and her breath caught in her throat as she watched his big hands playing in the dog's fur. What would it feel like if he touched her? she wondered. His hands were so big and hard. Yet watching him with the injured dog, she knew they could be gentle.

She looked up into his face then and surprised him staring at her, his hazel eyes intent under frowning brows.

Suddenly he rose and held out his hand to help her up. "Best you be getting along now, ma'am," he said, his voice devoid of expression. "It wasn't wise of you to come here, not alone," he added. "There's those who'd have a lot to say about it if they knew."

Sarah's chin came up. "I fail to see why," she argued. "I only came to inquire for the dog. And your aunt lives here with you. She received me. I begin to think people have terrible minds!"

"I see you understand me, and yes, they certainly do. Perhaps for very good reason?" he added grimly.

Sarah stared at him. She was aware he was still holding her hand in his, but she made no move to free herself. Indeed, for one insane moment she wanted to be closer to him still, but Evan shrugged and let her go to walk to the barn door. Reluctantly Sarah followed him. The dog whined behind them, but neither of them noticed.

As Evan opened the door, Sarah saw him start, and she hurried to his side. As they stepped out, blinking in the bright sunlight, she saw Mr. Denton had ridden into the stable yard, and her heart sank. His greeting to them was warm and courteous, but Sarah could tell how astonished he was to find her here alone with Evan Lancaster.

"Do thank your aunt for me, Mr. Lancaster," she said as she held her hand out to him. "And be sure to take care of Ruff. I'll be anxious to know how she goes on."

Evan only nodded as he helped her to mount and untied her horse for her. Sarah said her good-byes with a careless smile before she rode away down the drive. As she did go, she wondered if the two men were watching her. But she did not have to wonder if the news of her call at Lancaster Farm would soon be common knowledge in the area, for she was sure of it. How she wished Mr. Denton had not come along just then! But even if he didn't mention it, she told herself, Miss Barnes or the maid might very well do so.

But no matter how much talk there is, I did nothing wrong, Sarah told herself fiercely. I had to see if the dog was all right, since I was partially responsible for the accident. But even though she had been armed with such a noble purpose, she could not help asking herself now if her visit to Lady Willoughby had been only a ploy all along. Had she intended to stop at Lancaster Farm, hoping to be alone with Evan? Was that why she hadn't taken Leary with her this morning? Of course not! she told herself sternly. No matter Mr. Lancaster was a very nice man, a surprising one, too, so unlike other farmers she knew. Educated, well-spoken. And she liked him. But that was all there was to it.

The next evening Mary Jennings came down to dinner for the first time since she had taken to her bed weeks before. Supported by her son, Geoffrey, she moved slowly, but she was smiling as she took her seat at the table, and graciously accepted her husband's toast on her returning health.

Sarah sipped her wine, wishing she did not feel so depressed. Bradbury had given her another note when she came in from her morning ride, and she had recognized the printing on it at once. Smiling at the old retainer to ease the concern she saw in his eyes, she had sought the privacy of her room before she had read it. It was much shorter than the last, and although it called her no horrid names, it sent a shiver up her spine. "If you don't leave here, you'll be sorry," it read. "Very sorry."

Sarah had spent most of the day wondering anew who would do such a thing, and for what reason, but she was just as confused as ever by the time she came down to dinner. And what a terrible thing to receive on her birthday, she thought, as her father and brother made much of her mother's appearance. To add to her depression, not a one of her family had even remembered, no, not a single one of them. And although she told herself that she was too sophisticated to be upset by such things, as well as too old to be celebrating birthdays anyway, she was still hurt.

Mrs. Jennings reveled in all the attention she was getting while her daughter grew quieter and quieter. As last Geoffrey looked across the table at her and cocked his eyebrow in inquiry.

"You're very withdrawn this evening, sister," he said. "Is anything amiss? No, never mind answering that. I think I know why you are so pensive, for today brought neither a gift, a note, nor a call from Jaspar Howland. Am I not right? Come, confess!"

Stung, Sarah said quickly, "How ridiculous you are, Geoff! I care nothing for the earl, as I have told you before. And if I am pensive, then perhaps it is because today is a rather important one for me, as well as Mother. You see, I am now turned twenty-seven. It is my birthday."

She saw her brother's frown and her father's

astonishment, but her mother showed not a shred of remorse. "Yes, of course it is, daughter," she said, pushing her plate away with a small sigh. "But I wonder you can take us to task for not remembering when we have not had the opportunity to celebrate with you for five long years. If the occasion faded from our memories, I am sure that was only to be expected after your neglect."

Sarah swallowed a sharp retort. It wouldn't do any good, she told herself. Her mother always saw things the way she wanted to, and no other.

"Here, now, Mary, you are too harsh!" Mr. Jennings scolded. "Sarah was married for most of that time, and subject to her husband's whims. Don't you remember the wedding ceremony—'forsaking all others'? It is unreasonable to have expected Sarah to visit us on her birthdays."

Mrs. Jennings did not look pleased to be reprimanded, even as gently as it had been done. She only sniffed a little as she said, "So you are twenty-seven now, are you, Sarah? My, you are getting on, aren't you? And before you know it, you will be old, without a husband to rely on, or children to comfort you in your old age. I do advise you to think most carefully about your future, my girl. And especially with regards to my lord Earl of Castleton. To be throwing such a glorious union aside makes me all out of patience with you."

"He has not asked me to marry him, Mother," Sarah said evenly as she buttered a roll. And that is no lie, she told herself. He had only announced his intention of making her his countess, nothing more. He certainly hadn't asked her if she would care for it.

"Nor will he if you continue this stupid cat-and-mouse game with him," Mrs. Jennings said, leaning closer and looking fierce. "I suggest you be a deal more conciliatory and approachable where that young man is concerned, lest his interest in you all come to naught."

"Because he isn't a hackney?" Sarah murmured, too softly for her mother to hear. But Geoffrey caught the words and chuckled as he raised his wineglass to her.

"Here's to you, lovely Sarah, on the festive occasion of your natal day," he said grandly. "All best wishes to you, my dear."

Mr. Jennings raised his glass as well. "Here, here," he called, smiling broadly. "Come, Mary, drink a toast to your daughter! It is a special night for her."

Mrs. Jennings picked up her glass, her face sour, but Sarah ignored her. How strange it was, she thought as she smiled, not listening to Geoffrey as he recalled some of her more memorable birthdays. Why are Mother and Father so insistent on my marriage to the earl? It will not do them any good financially, for even if the earl felt called on to make a settlement, it would go to her, not them. Not now. Not anymore.

But perhaps they wanted the marriage for Geoffrey's sake, a little imp prompted. Perhaps because the brother of a prominent, wealthy countess was so much more impressive than one who was merely a dowager viscountess. That reasoning sounded so ridiculous that Sarah chuckled. Fortunately Geoffrey was recalling her ninth birthday, how she had climbed to the roof of Three Oaks to announce the day at cockcrow. As everyone laughed, Sarah's private merriment went unremarked.

In his library up at the Hall, Jaspar Howland was spending what he knew would be the last quiet evening for some time. Ten days before, he had sent invitations to a number of friends and acquaintances, asking them to a house party here. He had done so for one reason only: so he might have a legitimate reason to see Sarah Lacey more often.

Deep in his perusal of lists of wines, menus, and entertainments, he was somewhat startled at ten o'clock when the door was flung open, and a voice he knew well exclaimed, "There's no need to announce me, man! To his sorrow, Jaspar knows who I am."

The earl stood up behind his desk, grinning as his cousin Bartholomew Whitaker came in with an impatient stride. Behind him, the butler raised his eyes to heaven as he gently closed the doors and went away, so m'lord's reunion with his cousin could be private.

"Bart! You old dog, what are you doing here a full day early?" Jaspar asked as he clasped his cousin's hand and shook it. "Serve you right if I turned you out until the appointed time."

Whitaker took off his caped driving coat and tossed it to a convenient chair. "Come down from your high horse, cuz," he said in his deep, mellow voice. "No need to do the haughty with me, you know. And if you did turn me out, I'd just amble down to the stables and put up with the lads. Wouldn't be the first time I've slept in one."

"Nor the last, I'm sure, the way you live," the earl said, trying and failing to look severe. "A brandy? Wine?"

"A brandy and water would do me well. Devilish thirsty work, driving."

"But why did you come at night? Whatever for?"

"It's almost the full moon, clear as day. And the roads weren't crowded. In fact, I made it from London in record time. But to tell truth, I came early because I wanted to find out what you're up to."

"Up to?" the earl asked from the table where he was pouring them both a drink. "Why do you think I'm up to something?"

His cousin smiled, a smile that transformed his long face and chiseled lips. As tall as the earl, although nowhere near as handsome, he was five years elder, yet they had always been close. "This house party you're giving, for one thing," he drawled.

"But I've often had my friends to stay at Castleton," Jaspar told him as he handed him a glass. "Cheers."

"Cheers. So you have, my fine young sprout, but you've never included a parcel of females before. Now, why is that? Can it be you are thinking of choosing your countess? I do advise you to rid your mind of the notion at once. You've years before you must marry, and besides, it isn't a bit of fun, although that's only hearsay, of course. You know how I run whenever a church bell tolls anywhere in my vicinity."

Ignoring the latter part of his cousin's speech, the earl asked, "How did *you* know who I'd invited?"

Whitaker shrugged and took a healthy swallow. "Ah, that's good," he said. "As to how I found out, well, your messenger came to me first. I, er, persuaded him to let me see the direction of the other invitations. I've no quarrel with Duke or Alan. No, nor Fen Lincoln, either. But why include his sisters? The youngest just came out this past season, if you recall, and how could you not, since we was all dragooned into standing up with the chit? And then there's Lady Alice, as well as Elizabeth Hawkins. There's something smoky about the whole thing. Come now, confess!"

Jaspar took a seat across from his cousin, and when he did not reply at once, that gentleman's eyes shone keener. He saw the way Jaspar stared down into his glass as if to find an answer there, the slight flush on his cheekbones as he shrugged before he said, "If you must know, they've been invited as a diversion."

"Oh, I'm sure we'll be diverted one way or the other, if we're not bored to death by 'em, but why was it necessary?" Whitaker persisted.

Jaspar hesitated again, then he blurted out, "I've already chosen my countess, and don't you say a word! But I can't invite her to the Hall by herself, and there are no others of the nobility about."

He drew a quick breath and rushed on, "Bart, wait till you see her. I swear she is the most beautiful creature in the world! That chestnut hair, her lovely face and form, and when she smiles, I feel as if everything inside me were melting. And—"

"Who is she?" his cousin asked before he finished his drink with one long swallow. He was more than a little uneasy. Jaspar was only a cub as yet, though he'd slay you if you pointed it out to him, and in no way was he ready for marriage. Not to anyone, no matter what a piece of perfection she was. Bartholomew Whitaker had seen too many young men ruin their lives with hasty marriages. It pained him to think his cousin might go the same way, for he was very fond of him.

"Her name is Sarah. She's the Dowager Viscountess Lacey."

As he spoke, the earl saw his cousin's raised brows and look of astonishment, and he chuckled. "No, no, she's not some middle-aged temptress. You may be calm. She was married to a man many years her senior. He died last year in a hunting accident."

Bart had been thinking hard. "Aha! *That* Lacey. Yes, I've seen his widow. In truth, she is an incomparable. But surely she's just a trifle, oh, the merest trifle, of course, too old for you, cuz?"

"She's only twenty-six!" Jaspar snapped, his dark eyes glinting dangerously. "And what's a few years, after all? I tell you, Bart, I love her, I intend to marry her, and I'll not hear a word against the plan!"

"Of course you won't, not from me," his cousin said easily, even though his brain was working feverishly. Somehow or other he'd have to get Jaspar out of this coil, although how he was to do so, he had no idea. Naturally the Lady Lacey would be of no help to him. She must be continually on her knees thanking God for the boy's infatuation, for what woman would not sell her eye teeth to be the next Countess Castleton? None that he knew of, anyway.

Pray he had not come too late, he thought grimly. For Jaspar must be saved, no, he *would* be saved, no matter what. On that he was determined.

Eight

SARAH LEARNED OF the earl's house party in a long note he sent her the next day. In it he outlined all the wonderful things he had in mind for them to do, picnics and dinners, games and drives, perhaps even a phaeton race? And he intended to conclude the party with a gala ball. Of course, he relied on her to attend each and every event, and he wouldn't take no for an answer. Oh, with her brother, Geoffrey, of course.

Sarah frowned and shook her head. He was really very persistent, this young earl, she told herself, even though she was flattered that he had gone to so much trouble for her. For Sarah had no delusions that the house party was anything but a ruse to get her to the Hall, involved with his friends, and finally, forced to accept his hand. He had hinted broadly enough in his note that that was his purpose.

Still, it did sound like fun, she told herself. And it is such a long time since I had any fun. Surely, sometime during the festivities, she could show him once and for all that she was not interested in marrying him. Just the fact that they would be seeing so much of each other was in her favor. He might well tire of her indifference, or fall in love with one of the other ladies present. And even if he did not, she was sure there would be some occasion that would allow her the chance to give him his congé.

Besides, Geoff would be with her, as well as all the other guests. In this case there was definitely safety in numbers.

Smiling a little, she wrote a short reply, thanking Jaspar Howland for his invitation, and telling him she was looking forward to meeting his friends.

Geoffrey had received his invitation as well, and when the house party was discussed at dinner later, both Mr. and Mrs. Jennings beamed their satisfaction. Since Sarah kept her own counsel about her plans, the family was able to spend the merriest evening at Three Oaks that she could ever remember.

The very next day brought a message that a picnic luncheon was planned at the Gothic folly. The party was to assemble at the steps of the Hall at noon so they could ride to the folly together. Sarah and her brother were the last to arrive, and when he saw them, Jaspar's face lit up in a wonderful smile. Sarah noted the others as he introduced her and Geoffrey. She saw the men were all in their twenties, and the ladies present were very young, with the exception of a tall, thin dowager who was mounted on a rangy bay.

Sarah had met Frances, Lady Lincoln, at some of the parties she had attended with Roger Lacey in London. When she learned she had accompanied her two daughters to the Hall, she smiled.

"Couldn't let them come with only their brother, Fenwick, you see. He's a good boy, but he's not up to snuff as yet," Lady Lincoln confided to Sarah as they rode off side by side, much to the earl's disgust. He had been appalled when the strict elderly lady had arrived with Fen and the girls, but there was nothing he could do but be gracious and welcome her, although he immediately struck an impromptu hop on the terrace under the full moon from his list of entertainments. But perhaps she'll help keep an eye on Rose for me, he told himself, his eyes never leaving Sarah as she rode before him in a scarlet habit.

Beside him, Lady Alice Arne pouted and determined to work even harder to get his attention. She had had great hopes for this house party, but now it appeared that Jaspar was involved with that older woman, and she a widow at that. Well, Lady Alice told herself, I suppose it is as Mama said. All the young men must have their light-o-loves, and I shall not think a thing of it. For of course, when the time came, the earl would marry a virgin bride his own age, not a fading dowager.

But as she looked ahead to where he stared so intently, a little frown appeared on her round brow. Lady Lacey was in profile to her, her head thrown back as she laughed at something Lady Lincoln was saying. With her smooth complexion and lovely face, that glorious hair, there was nothing faded about her; even Lady Alice had to admit that. Indeed, the only words that came to mind to describe the lady were *beautiful* and *vibrant*. Lady Alice's lips tightened, and a determined look came into her china blue eyes.

The island where the picnic was to be held had been transformed into a fairyland for the occasion. There was a tent for the ladies if they cared to retire, and soft cushions were scattered over the grass, some shaded by umbrellas, so the guests could lounge there at their ease. The earl had even provided fishing rods for the men, and an archery target had been set up onshore so the guests could aim at it over the water. There were a number of servants as well, to serve the food and wine and assist the ladies. To Sarah's amusement, a young man had been engaged to play the guitar so they might have music to entertain them.

Jaspar Howland came to her side almost as soon

as she had dismounted, to lead her over the bridge himself.

"No doubt it will seem very different from the last time we were here, dear Sarah," he said softly so only she could hear. He bent closer to add, "How I wish we were alone today as well!"

Sarah gave him a vague smile, and she was quick to move away from him when they stepped from the bridge. Spotting the Lady Rose and her sister, she went to greet them. Rose's eyes were sparkling, and she wore a satisfied smile. She had promised her brother she would behave herself and not beg to come to the dinner table or evening parties if he would allow her to attend the daytime events. With her promise, the earl had relaxed.

Lady Caroline looked uncomfortable with so many strangers, and Sarah spent some time drawing her out. When she saw the men getting ready to have an archery contest, she took the girls with her to watch. Geoffrey joined them, and Sarah introduced him to the earl's sisters. She did not think a thing of it when he took the Lady Rose's arm, since she herself was walking beside Caroline.

Some of the shots were far abroad of the target, and some of them did not even clear the water. There was a lot of good-natured chafing about each archer's skill.

"I wish they would let us try," Caroline said softly.

"Yes, Caro is wonderful with a bow," her sister said. "I'd wager anything you like she could best all the men."

Sarah heard her brother murmur something to the girl, and Lady Rose's giggle, and she stiffened for a moment. But no, she told herself, as she turned to look at them. Lady Rose is only a member of the infantry. Geoff would not try anything there. In fact, it was very good of him to bother with the girl when there were so many other young ladies about.

Lady Alice, for instance, in her pale blue habit and plumed hat, was a very pretty girl, and Miss Elizabeth Hawkins, a stunning brunette. As for the Lincoln girls, once they outgrew their habit of tittering and turning scarlet when anyone spoke to them, they would be attractive, too.

The earl insisted Sarah join him for luncheon in the folly, and he led her to one of the tables himself, beckoning a footman to serve them. Lady Lincoln and his cousin Batholomew Whitaker joined them. As she ate and chatted, Sarah had the oddest feeling that this gentleman didn't like her, and she wondered why. It was not that he wasn't polite, but it seemed to her that he was watching her, coldly and carefully. It was not the treatment she generally received from men, and it puzzled her. But perhaps he is only concerned for his cousin Jaspar, she thought as she took another bite of her salmon. Perhaps he sees his attraction for me and knows how unsuitable such a match would be. That must be it! There was the faintest suggestion of guard dog about him, but he would see there was nothing to worry about.

Sarah looked around, admiring the reflection of the trees and the folly in the dark, still waters of the lake. It was a glorious day, still warm for late October.

"How fortunate you have been with the weather, m'lord," she remarked, shaking her head when the footman would have poured her more wine. "Today it is hard to believe that winter is coming, is it not?"

"I for one shall pray that it holds off for at least two more weeks," the earl said with an intimate smile for her alone.

Lady Lincoln looked from one to the other, her mouth falling open a little in her astonishment. She shook her head as she caught Bartholomew Whitaker's eyes. Then she hurried into speech. "We all

126

hope so, Jaspar. I can imagine nothing more deadly than being cooped up in the Hall with all these young flibbertigibbets to chaperone. At least if they can ride or drive out on excursions, my task will be easier."

"I do beg you to just enjoy yourself, m'lady," Jaspar Howland told her. "My aunt Emma is quite capable of chaperoning any number of young ladies."

"Hasn't done so well with your sister Rose," Lady Lincoln said tartly, her long, thin nose in the air. "Nor is she here today."

Jaspar spared a glance for his sisters. They were seated with Fen Lincoln and Geoffrey Jennings, and Rose was laughing much too loudly at something one of the gentlemen had said to her. He sent her a warning frown.

"My aunt is not here because she dislikes riding," he explained to the starchy dowager. "You must trust me to control Rose, and with ease, too."

After luncheon had been eaten, the guests wandered about the island in little groups of twos and threes, or sat on the cushions to admire the lake or try their hand at watercolors. When Jaspar Howland begged Sarah to come and sit by him while he tried his hand at fishing, she would have liked to refuse, but she saw no way to avoid it. She noticed that his cousin took up a rod only a little distance away, not even out of earshot.

The earl muttered something under his breath when he saw him there, but there was nothing he could do about it. Nor could he say anything to Sarah while Bart was so near. He'd have a word with the man later, he told himself as he flicked his rod and sent the lure spinning over the lake. There was plenty of time. He would have his chance with her soon.

Sarah leaned back against a tree trunk and closed her eyes. How pleasant this is, she thought dreamily, as behind them the guitar player began to strum an old country tune she remembered from her childhood.

The guests returned to the Hall much later that afternoon. The earl would have liked to ride home with Sarah, but there was no need for such gallantry, not when she had her brother's escort. Besides, he had his other guests to consider. But as he climbed the steps with them, helping Lady Alice, who was having difficulties with the train of her habit, he wondered he did not feel more elated. It had been a flawless picnic, and everyone had assured him they had enjoyed it tremendously, but he could not help but be despondent because he had not had a moment alone with Sarah, to talk to her, make love to her, tell her what was in his heart. However, she would be coming to dinner the next evening, and although she had excused herself from a drive to a deserted monastery that he had planned to amuse the ladies, he had hopes she would join them for a long ride about the estate the day after that.

Sarah thought her brother very quiet on their return to Three Oaks, and idly she wondered what was amiss. He had seemed to have a very good time at the picnic among so many of the nobles he aspired to, and there wasn't a girl there who had not smiled at him, admiring his handsome good looks. Such smiles and little sighs generally had Geoff all smiles himself, yet now he was frowning.

"Is there anything wrong, Geoff?" she asked as they dismounted and gave their horses into the grooms' care.

He shook his head. "No, not really. At least not anything I can't take care of myself," he added. Then he began to tease her about her conquest of the earl, and tell her some of the entertaining things he had heard at the picnic, and Sarah forgot his earlier mood.

"Lady Rose is very lovely, isn't she?" Sarah asked as they reached the gardens. "There is a reckless quality about her, though. I imagine she leads her family a merry chase."

He laughed as he held the door for her. "Yes, she's a daredevil, all right, that one," he said easily. "But she's only a baby. No doubt in a few years she'll settle down to be as namby-pamby as any other debutante on her best behavior. I swear, sister, I don't know what there is about come-outs that turns perfectly unaffected girls so insipid, but there you are. I gave up on them long ago."

Sarah was amazed at how relieved she felt. She wanted no trouble with the Howlands, and there would be a great deal of it if Geoff got involved with Lady Rose. But as she went up to her room to change from her habit, she resolved to keep a close eye on him just in case. Somehow she didn't feel she could trust her brother even now.

She spent the next day at home, reading and writing letters. It had turned chilly overnight, and although it did not rain, the gray sky was full of thick clouds. Sarah was delighted she didn't have to walk around a ruined monastery, although she was sure the ominous weather added to the thrill of it for all the young ladies in the party. Perhaps they might even be lucky enough to see a ghost, she thought, chuckling to herself. How perfect that would be!

Sarah wore her pale green muslin and her emerald pendant to the earl's dinner party that evening. Her father did not consider it anywhere near grand enough for the occasion, but Sarah refused to change. She had brought but one elaborate gown into Kent, and she was saving it for the earl's ball. She left Mr. Jennings frustrated and in a rage, and

Geoffrey twitted her about it as they drove to the Hall.

"You do get the old man's back up, don't you, Sarah?" he asked, chuckling and shaking his head. "And Ma's as well."

"I suppose so, although I don't do it deliberately," she replied. "But Father has no say in my life anymore. I cannot tell you what a relief that is to me! Furthermore, to be sweeping in clad in damask or satin would be ridiculous. He knows nothing whatsoever of the nobility, or he wouldn't even suggest such a thing."

"Very true, but then, he is only a provincial," her brother agreed coolly. He himself was looking stunning this evening in his tight breeches and well-cut coat. His plain linen was dazzling, and his cravat tied to a nicety. Sarah hoped the Lady Rose would be nowhere about, lest she succumb to him in an instant.

She need not have worried. Neither Howland girl was present when the butler announced them at the drawing room door. Sarah had never been in the Hall before; she thought it very rich and impressive. The earl himself came across the huge room to greet them, and he took Sarah's arm to lead her to the other guests. She was amused to see how carefully the style of her gown and the quality of her jewels was observed by the feminine guests. For herself, she thought they themselves looked like a bouquet of spring flowers in their simple pastel muslins and silks.

"You were missed yesterday," Jaspar Howland was saying now as he handed her a flute of champagne from the footman's tray. "The ladies had a wonderful time at the monastery."

"Never tell me they saw a ghost," Sarah said smiling up at him with her eyes twinkling.

"How did you know?" he asked, astounded.

She chuckled. "Oh, put a group of impressionable girls in such a location, add threatening skies, and it was inevitable. And of course, the wind moaning through the ruined walls sounded exactly like monks at prayer, did it not?"

He nodded, but his hungry, admiring gaze never left her face.

"Please, m'lord you must not look so," Sarah said gently. Poor boy, she thought in spite of her exasperation. "It will not do, and it is embarrassing me. You must excuse me now. I would speak to Lady Howland."

She curtsied and left him, but his eyes followed her as she went and took a seat beside his aunt.

Over by the fireplace, the elegant Mr. Marmaduke Ainsworth's brows rose. "I say, Bart, what's to do with Jaspar?" he drawled, raising his pincenez for a closer look.

Bartholomew Whitaker frowned. "But surely you can tell, Duke," he said in an undertone. "The silly cub thinks he's in love, and with the Dowager Viscountess Lacey at that! Was anything more ridiculous?"

"I say!" Mr. Ainsworth exclaimed. "Won't do, y'know. Bad. Very bad. No matter what she is now, she was only a country squire's daughter before. Definitely not countess material. Besides, she's too old for him."

"*I* know that. Now, if only my cousin did!" his companion said savagely.

"Notice she don't hover about him. No languishing looks either," Mr. Ainsworth observed. "Pr'aps she don't care for him?"

At Mr. Whitaker's snort of disbelief, he nodded sagely. "Quite right," he agreed. "Have to be insane not to. Devilish handsome fellow, Jaspar. Said so before. Often wonder why I like him so much."

"I think she's being very clever, pretending indifference until she gets him to the sticking point. She's playing a deep game, but I'm determined she'll not have him. I intend to stop her."

"How?" Duke asked, as always, coming right to the point.

"If I knew that, she'd be vanquished already," Bart growled. "But I'm determined on it. I don't think I'll fail."

"Could almost feel sorry for the poor woman," Duke murmured as the butler announced dinner. "Know you, Bart. Ruthless, that's the word for you. Wonder what silly chits we'll have to take in tonight. Pray not Margaret Lincoln. Girl's an idiot."

Sarah was nowhere near the earl at the table, and she was grateful for the reprieve. The place of honor on his right went to Lady Lincoln, who was not only older but a marchioness as well. Sarah found herself seated between Lord Lincoln and a gentleman she had not spoken to before, a Mr. Alan Feathers. They were untaxing companions, for they seemed more interested in their meal and the number of partridge they had bagged today than in amusing her. Sarah was content to have it so.

Dinner was elaborate and delicious. There was a footman for every two guests, as well as the butler to oversee them. And Sarah had to admit the dining chamber was not only enormous but elegantly decorated as well, in crimson and gold brocades and velvets. Someday, she thought, glancing to where Jaspar Howland sat at the head of the table, handsome and assured, some very lucky young lady would be mistress here. For the earl's sake, however, she hoped his bride would marry him for himself and not for his title and wealth. She herself might not love him, but she admitted she was fond of him. Yet even as she enjoyed a perfect meal in perfect surroundings, Sarah found her mind straying to the Dentons' kitchen at teatime when she had been a child. So full of laughter, it had been, and good fellowship, that warm farmhouse kitchen! This was not the first time she had thought of it with longing.

The ladies adjourned to the drawing room at last, and Lady Alice went to the piano to play for them. Very often her eyes sought the doors, as if she were impatient for the gentlemen to finish their port. Sarah thought her a most accomplished pianist. The two Lincoln girls sat somewhat apart, whispering and giggling together, and she was not at all reluctant to leave them to their girlish secrets to join their mother and Lady Howland.

When the gentlemen came in, the earl hurried to her side. Sarah saw both the elder ladies wore identical worried frowns, and she wished she might reassure them.

"You must permit me to steal Lady Lacey away for a moment, ma'ams," Jaspar said, holding out his hand to her. "There is something of importance I must speak to her about."

Sarah could do nothing but rise and let him take her a little apart from the others. Lady Alice sent her a scathing look, which fortunately she did not see.

"Really, m'lord, this will not do," she admonished him as soon as they were out of earshot. "And if you do not stop it, I shall not come to the Hall again."

"No, really, I do have something important to say, darling Sarah," he insisted.

"Well?" she asked coolly.

"It's, er, well, I wondered if you were aware of the company your brother keeps in town," Jaspar Howland said earnestly. "That Lord Faxton he claims as a friend is received nowhere, for he is a rake and a gambler. And two years ago he tried to elope with an heiress to recoup his fortune. They

133

were overtaken on the road to Gretna before any damage was done, er, that is to say, I mean . . .''

"I know what you mean," Sarah said as he came to a halt, confused.

"But it is not only Faxton. His whole crowd is suspect. Your brother does himself no good being seen in their company. I thought you should know, for of course, being a woman, you are not aware of the danger, whereas I, as a man, know it only too well. Would you like me to speak to Mr. Jennings, give him the hint, you know? I would be glad to be of service; handle this for you."

Sarah didn't know whether she wanted to laugh or cry. The earl was trying so hard to show he was in command—worldly—as a way of proving his maturity.

"It is kind of you to offer, but no," she said when she had command of her voice. "Geoff might take offense, for he is older than you are. I am sorry to hear about Lord Faxton. I met him only that once when he and Geoff were riding in Rotton Row, and I did not care for him myself. But I have nothing to say about Geoff's choice of friends, and would never think of giving him advice. It would not be received kindly, you see. My brother goes his own way, as I go mine, and we seldom see each other. We have never been close."

"I see," he said, stroking his chin and looking earnest. "That is fortunate, for I shall not like him as a brother-in-law. But if, as you say, you are not close, there is no need to encourage the connection, now is there?"

"M'lord, I have told you before that—"

He shook a playful finger at her. "Come now, no argle-bargle, if you please, ma'am! I am a most determined fellow, as you shall discover. But my aunt is looking daggers at me for some reason, and I must see what she wants."

As they went to rejoin the others, he added, "You must come here early tomorrow. I am giving all my guests a tour of the Hall before luncheon. And even if I do say myself, it is an impressive place. Later I plan a horse race for the men. Of course, I hope to wear *your* colors, dearest Sarah. You will cheer me on, won't you?"

"I'm afraid that is impossible," Sarah was happy to be able to tell him. "Tomorrow is the day set for the church bazaar in Sutton Cross, and I am pledged to open it, as well as help."

"You would give up a day of pleasure for a church affair?" he asked, astounded. He had not even noticed that they had arrived at Lady Howland's chair.

"What's that you say, Jaspar?" his aunt asked sharply. "The bazaar? How could I have forgotten! Naturally we must put in an appearance."

"There, you see, m'lady?" the earl said, turning eagerly to Sarah. "We'll all go, but surely a few minutes is all that is necessary for any of us to spend there."

"I fear that is not the case," Sarah said firmly. "I have made a promise, and I would honor it."

"A village festival?" Lady Alice asked as she came to stand close to Jaspar Howland and smile up at him. "Oh, do say we may all go, m'lord! It will be so amusing watching the peasants!"

Sarah gave her a look of dislike, but the earl smiled and patted the hand that lay softly on his sleeve.

"Of course, we shall do the pretty for a few minutes, Lady Alice," he promised. "And I suppose it is my duty to support the bazaar."

"And everyone shall buy something," Lady Alice proclaimed. "No matter that we throw it away later. My mother always does so at home. She claims her patronage encourages gratitude and hard work among the lowly."

Jaspar Howland looked amazed that the duchess would bother to do such a thing, but he only nodded.

When he turned back to speak to Lady Lacey, however, to beg her to change her mind, he discovered she had gone quietly to take a seat beside Miss Hawkins and Mr. Ainsworth, to chat with them.

He found no other opportunity to speak privately to her again, and when the carriage to take her and her brother home was announced, his cousin insisted on escorting the lady to it himself. The earl glowered at his retreating back.

He promised himself he'd have another word with Bart later. Quite a few words, in fact. And this time he'd be much more plain with him.

Nine

THE NEXT DAY dawned sunny, and although there was a slight chill in the air, it promised to be a pleasant day. Sarah was relieved. On her last trip to the village, she had seen the booths being erected, the tables set up, and the bunting hung, and she knew how disappointed everyone would have been if the bazaar had had to be postponed or canceled.

She put on one of her oldest muslin gowns, for by the time she reached home again after supervising the children's games, it would be in a sorry state. She debated for a long time on her choice of hat. It would have been more suitable to wear a simple straw, but she sensed the villagers might be offended if she did so. And perhaps they would even think she was being condescending? Sarah sighed, and to be on the safe side, donned one of her more fashionable bonnets.

The vicar was full of compliments for her when she stepped from her carriage just before ten in the morning, and his wife, Prudence, beamed. A goodly crowd had assembled, and everyone bowed and curtsied as Lady Lacey took her place on the steps of the church. She opened the bazaar with only a short speech, which seemed to disappoint Mr. Williams, who, she knew by now, was never at a loss for words, especially in the pulpit. The villagers and farmers and their families seemed to approve of her brevity, however, for they gave her a hearty round of applause.

For a little while, Sarah strolled around the various booths. She saw Miss Withers was in charge of needlework, while a flustered Miss Farnsworth supervised two women at the bakery table. There were brisk sales of gingerbread men and sugar cookies to the children, and already a cask of cider had been broached by the men. Sarah stopped to chat with Mrs. Denton to thank her again for her dinner party. That goodwife was so delighted, she gave Sarah a hug. Then she looked askance, as if she might have offended by her familiarity, but Sarah only laughed at her and hugged her back even harder. She had always loved Mrs. Denton.

When Evan Lancaster and his aunt came over to speak to her, Sarah saw Fay Denton frowning at her, and she wondered at it. In no time at all, Fay had joined the group, careful to stand close to Evan Lancaster's side. Sarah was struck by a sudden thought. Was Fay in love with Mr. Lancaster? she wondered. Had she hopes he would marry her? And was it possible that it was *she* who had been sending those horrid notes, simply because she had heard of their meeting in Wye, and her father had told her Sarah had gone to Lancaster Farm? Was she *jealous*?

"How is Ruff, Mr. Lancaster?" she asked, determined to put such terrible suspicions from her mind. Really, she told herself, I am becoming unsettled to be thinking any such thing! Fay has always been friendly, and she is a good, pleasant girl. There is no malice in her. It was the outside of enough to even imagine her capable of it.

"She's very well, m'lady," Evan told her now with a twinkle in his eye. "Even managing to get around a bit now, although she can put no weight on the leg as yet. I've had to resort to penning her up, lest she try and follow me everywhere."

His aunt looked gloomy. "Yes, and when you do, the animal howls until you return. There's no bearing it," she said in a long-suffering voice.

"Well, but when the leg is healed, Ruff will be able to follow your nephew, and then there will be quiet again," Sarah said. Then she added, "Except for those pigs."

Everyone laughed, and suddenly Sarah felt light-hearted as she had not for a very long time. How pleasant it was to be here with old friends, she thought. How delightful not to have to listen to a lot of pompous fustian, always bearing in mind protocol and manners. Not that the farmers and their families were rude. She knew they had their own code of conduct, and woebetide anyone who broke that code! But it was an easygoing one that only required common courtesy and consideration of one's fellows. Do unto others, she thought. Not at all a bad way to live.

She excused herself then, for she had promised her mother she would buy some new aprons for the maids, and she wanted to do so before the selection was all picked over. Mrs. Akins sewed a fine neat stitch. Her aprons and doilies were always the first to be sold.

To her surprise, Fay Denton came with her. She even watched while Sarah made her choices, paid for them, and gave them to her groom to put away in the carriage.

"How good of you to patronize the bazaar," Fay said.

Sarah listened hard, but she could detect no sneer in the girl's voice. Indeed, it had been all but colorless.

"Whatever do you mean?" she asked. "You know I have always come to the bazaar."

Fay shrugged. "That is so," she said. "But it is different now, isn't it? I mean, you being a *lady* and all?"

Before Sarah could comment, she went on, "I do hope someone will buy Janet's embroidered handkerchiefs. She has been working so hard on them!"

"Which ones are they?" Sarah asked, looking at the profusion that was spread out on the table.

"Oh, I couldn't tell you that," Fay said mischievously. "You might be tempted to purchase them as a kindness, and I do assure you, m'lady, they are not at all the kind of thing *you* would care to flourish. Unfortunately, Janet is not a good needlewoman, not that any of us would tell her that."

Sarah smiled as Ralph Denton arrived, slightly out of breath, at her elbow. "May I carry your parcels, m'lady?" he asked eagerly, holding out his hands as he did so.

"I don't have any, Ralph," Sarah pointed out, although she was careful to smile at him as she did so.

"Well, when you buy something then?" he persisted.

Beside him, his sister sighed audibly, and he flushed. "Or would y-y-you l-l-like something to eat? A c-c-cookie or a scone? Perhaps a m-m-mug of cider?"

"Not right now, but thank you, kind sir, for the thought," Sarah said. When she looked around, she saw the children gathering on the common, and she excused herself.

Quickly Sarah organized the children into groups by age, the youngest first. There were four toddlers, and she gave each one of them a pewter spoon with an egg on it.

"Now, listen, children," she said. "When I say 'go,' you must all carry the egg on the spoon down the common to the pump and then come back here.

But don't drop your egg or you'll lose. Don't worry, though, everyone gets a prize. Are you ready? Get set then! Go!"

The four little ones started out slowly as the older ones urged them on. One little girl was so busy staring down at her egg that she set off in quite the wrong direction. Sarah ran after her to turn her around before she stumbled into the duck pond. A little boy who was trying to hurry dropped his egg and burst into tears. Sarah was quickly at his side to kiss him and give him a piece of candy from her large bag. There was candy for them all, and for the winner, a red ball.

As the next group of children assembled, she gave out more spoons and eggs and started them on their way. Halfway through the race, she clapped her hands and called for them to stop where they were. She had seen one of the bigger boys trying to push a girl who was keeping up with him, hoping to make her drop her egg. Sarah explained that anyone who touched another player would be out of the race. She was glad when the girl won, and she gave her a pretty satin hair ribbon for a reward.

And so it went for most of the morning. Three-legged races, ring toss, blindman's buff, and musical chairs, for which Sarah persuaded the church organist to sing with his back turned to the children. At last she called a halt. She was warm now, and thirsty and she needed a rest, although the children clamored for more.

"Later, later! Run along now," she said, shooing them away. As she turned to buy some cider, she saw Evan Lancaster bringing a large mug to her.

"You read my mind, sir," she said as she lifted it and took a long swallow. "Ah, that's good. Is it your cider?"

"Yes," he said, but he did not smile. "Come, let

141

me find you a seat. You've been busy enough this morning and you need a rest."

Sarah nodded. As they strolled away, she saw Fay Denton's little frown, and once again those horrid suspicions she had had earlier resurfaced.

As they sat down under a large elm tree, Evan said, "However, you did seem to enjoy yourself. You must like children, m'lady."

"Oh, I do," Sarah told him. "They are such fun to be with, so open and honest. And they can be so amusing, although they don't mean to be. Some of the things they say put me in whoops."

Suddenly she was aware that the village had grown very quiet except for the children, and she looked around to see the earl's carriage arriving. It was followed by two others. As he and his guests alit, people curtsied and bowed.

"I wondered when he'd show up," Lancaster remarked, busy chewing a blade of grass. "It has never been his custom, but somehow I was sure he would come this year."

"Why?" Sarah asked, carefully not looking at him.

"Because you are here," he said evenly. As Sarah swung around to stare at him, he added, "He's mad for you. Anyone can see that."

Sarah could only shake her head. She wanted badly to tell him how tiresome the earl was becoming, but somehow she did not dare. Instead, she watched as the noble group strolled around the bazaar, escorted by an obsequious vicar. Lady Alice was certainly giving everyone a thrill, she thought. In her pale pink silk gown and the elaborate London hat trimmed with ribbons and flowers, she looked as odd in this company of homespun, cotton, and straw as a bird of paradise. Sarah could see her making much of a rather homely quilt, which she purchased and then begged the earl to carry for her.

Sarah noticed he was quick to hand it to a groom. And how incongruous the lady looked, munching a gingerbread man and washing it down with cider.

She also saw her brother sneering at the scene, the Ladies Rose and Caroline on his arms.

The Lincoln girls giggled almost continually, and when any of the others whispered a comment, they dissolved in fresh crescendos of laughter. Suddenly Sarah was very angry. Even without hearing what they said, she knew the earl's guests were making fun of the bazaar and the good people here, quick to point out a misshapen straw hat, or an old, faded gown that was too short for its owner, and she wanted to rail at them for their arrogance.

"Why are you so angry?" Evan Lancaster murmured beside her. As she turned quickly, he added, "Yes, they're making fun of us. Do you think anyone cares? I do assure you, ma'am, they will be mocked tonight in many cottages and farmhouses. Except for the earl, of course. He is *their* earl and he can do no wrong.

"And they will be imitated, too. That gentleman, for instance, the short, slight one in the pale blue coat? See how he minces along? Already there are those who are aching to practice his walk."

"Why, you're right," Sarah agreed, smiling now. "I had not noticed Mr. Feathers's failing till now."

"His name is Feathers? But of course, how appropriate," Lancaster said with a chuckle. "But here comes the earl. Best I make myself scarce. He's not fond of me, you know, not after I scolded him about his reckless driving the day he tipped you out of his carriage. And," he added as he got to his feet and stared down at her, hands on hips, "I can't say I'm overly fond of him, either."

Sarah rose quickly, determined to avoid the earl if she could, as well as Miss Hawkins and Lady Alice, who were trailing in his wake. She was not feeling at all in charity with the arrogant party from the Hall. "You remind me, sir, I've been neglecting the children, and I must get back to them. I'll come along with you, if you don't mind."

She glanced up to see him smiling down at her a little. For a moment she thought he was going to say something personal, and she found herself holding her breath. But he only shook his head ruefully as he extended his arm.

"It will be my pleasure, ma'am," he said formally. "But best we be quick about it!"

Sarah grinned at him as they walked away, leaving Jaspar Howland, who was still some distance away, glaring after them.

A few minutes later, the carriages from the Hall drove away. No doubt they felt they had done enough of their "duty" toward the peasants this day, Sarah thought. She saw the earl's dark frown, and it made her smile to herself, even as she called Perry Akins to order for pinching the boy next to him in line.

It was much later before the bazaar showed any signs of closing. Some of the children had been carried away by their mothers, sleepy from all the activity and excitement, and some had gone on to other pursuits. Sarah picked up the reticule she had dropped on the grass earlier, when all the candy and prizes were long gone.

As she did so, the reticule made a crackling noise, and perplexed, she reached inside. And then her eyes widened as she drew out another note. It was printed in the same crude hand, and there was no mistaking what it was. As she opened it, the sounds of the bazaar faded away.

"This is your last chance," it read. "If you do not leave soon, something bad will happen to you. Do you want to be injured? Scarred perhaps?"

Blindly Sarah stuffed the note back in the bag.

As she did so, she looked around with a lost, hurt look on her face. Someone had put that note in her bag today. Someone who had been here at the bazaar. It could have been anyone, for she had put the bag down many times.

"What is it?" she heard Evan Lancaster's voice ask roughly. "What has upset you so?"

She turned to him, but her throat was so full of tears, she could do nothing but shake her head.

"Something—somebody has hurt you," he insisted. "Tell me! What has happened? Let me help you."

"I—I can't. Not now," Sarah managed to get out. Then as she stared into his rugged, concerned face, those frowning hazel eyes, she reached out to grasp his sleeve. "Mr. Lancaster, would you do me a kindness?" she whispered.

"Of course. Anything," he said, still frowning as he searched her face.

Sarah took a deep breath. "Then please meet me somewhere tomorrow morning. I have something I would like to discuss with you in private. And don't tell anyone about our meeting. It—it is important no one learn of it."

"Is nine o'clock too early?" he asked, bending closer. As she shook her head, he said, "Then let us meet in the glade near Billings Brook. Is that all right?"

"Yes, and thank you. I'll be there," Sarah said. She saw his aunt, Miss Barnes, was approaching, and she made herself wave to her as she walked off in the opposite direction, toward the carriage that would take her back to the safety of Three Oaks. For Sarah Lacey was suddenly—desperately—afraid.

As she rode to her rendezvous with Evan Lancaster early the next morning, Sarah's mind whirled like a pinwheel.

145

She had not slept well, in spite of being tired after her busy day with the children. And she dreamed, strange dreams that made no sense to her when she woke suddenly, her heart pounding. And even when she just lay awake in bed and thought, nothing made any sense to her either. Was it Fay Denton after all who was writing those notes, making those threats? It still seemed impossible to believe it of her. Could it be Miss Davies, Lady Willoughby's companion? But why would she do such a thing? Perhaps she doesn't like me, but she doesn't even know me, Sarah told herself.

Or could it be the earl's cousin, Batholomew Whitaker? Or the Lady Alice? They did not want her to marry the earl, each for different reasons. But no, it could not be them, Sarah told herself as she turned over and tried to find a more comfortable position. They had only appeared on the scene long after the notes had started coming; therefore, no one else at the Hall could be suspected either. Except for Lady Howland, she reminded herself. It was clear she was terrified her nephew might propose to a onetime commoner, one who was older than he, to boot. But somehow Sarah could not see that august dame sneaking about leaving notes on the steps and paths of Three Oaks. No, not ever. But that meant it had to be Fay, unless it was someone she had never even considered.

Now as she rode, she went over the same arguments again, not that an answer came to her even in the clear light of day. At last she allowed herself to wonder why she had asked for Evan's help. She had had no intention of doing such a thing, and had been amazed when she heard the words that came from her mouth. But perhaps it was because he had been so concerned for her yesterday. And it had been such a very long time since anyone had cared what happened to her. Maybe no one ever has, she told herself gloomily. She had grown up in Geoffrey's sickly shadow, even though he was the younger, all but ignored by her parents until Viscount Lacey had seen her on a visit of his to Lady Willoughby, was struck by her beauty, and married her with her parents' beaming approval. And Sarah could hardly claim her late husband had ever cared about her, for he had cared for no one but himself. No, he had *wanted* her. That was a different matter altogether.

When she reached the glade at last, Sarah saw Evan was before her. He had tied his horse to a branch, and now he rose from the rock he was sitting on beside the brook, to help her dismount.

"You look tired," he said, frowning down at her. "You did not sleep well?"

"No, not well," she admitted. "Thank you for meeting me. I have been wondering why I asked you to, but I think it was because there is no one else for me, and I—I am afraid."

"Of what?" he asked. As she hesitated, he said, "Come now, tell me. I cannot help you if I don't know what this is all about."

She nodded, took a deep breath, and began, "Ever since my return here, I have been receiving notes. They are printed in a disguised hand and there is no signature. And every one of them tells me to go away, or I will be sorry. The reason I looked the way I did yesterday was because, just as I was leaving the village, I found another one in my reticule. I put the bag down many times during the day, and when the prizes and candy were all gone, I forgot about it for quite a long time. But someone who was at the bazaar put that note in it for me to find. And this time the note threatened me with injury. Scarring."

Her voice had died away to a whisper, and Lancaster had to come closer, bend over her, to hear her soft words.

"Do you have those notes with you, ma'am?" he asked.

Sarah stared at him. She had never heard such rough anger in anyone's voice before, and she gasped when she saw the fury written plain on his face.

Nodding, she drew all the notes from the pocket of her habit. "This came first," she said as she handed it to him. "And then this one."

She turned away as he read those horrid words calling her a whore, promiscuous and scheming, but she heard his muttered curse.

"Here is the third, and here, the one I found yesterday," she said.

When he had finished the last note, he looked up at her, frowning in concentration. "How were the others delivered?" he asked. "Not by post, for there is no direction, only your name."

"No, they were all left at Three Oaks. Once on the front steps, once on the garden path . . ."

"Do you have any suspicions about who might have done this rotten thing?" he asked her next.

She shook her head. "No, not really," she said. "It seems impossible, for I did not think I had ever hurt anyone here to the point that . . . And I never imagined that someone could hate me enough to—to . . ."

Suddenly, and to her great dismay, Sarah burst into tears. At once Evan stepped closer and took her in his arms to hold her and rock her against him. "Shhh, shhh," he murmured as he stroked her back with his big hands. They were as gentle as she had known they would be.

Sarah cried for a long time. She did not seem to be able to stop, no matter how she tried. She could feel her tears soaking the front of his shirt, the fabric of it rough against her cheek. And she could hear his steady heartbeat, feel the muscles of his chest and the strong arms that held her so close as he murmured soothing words to her, told her it would be all right. She felt safe with him. She realized it had been a long time since she had felt safe.

When her sobs died away and there were no more tears to be shed, Sarah tried to lift her head, but Evan would not let her go.

"No, a moment more," he said. Sarah wondered at the edge to his voice, the constricted way he spoke. It was almost as if he were experiencing some deep emotion. "This has been a terrible burden for you, Sarah. Relax. Rest."

She closed her eyes again and took a deep, shaky breath. And still he held her against the long, hard length of him, still he stroked her back with sure, slow motions that seemed to loosen the hard knot she had carried inside alone for such a very long time. And as he did so, she realized he had called her by her name. She wondered it had sounded so sweet to her, spoken in his deep, concerned voice. She had always thought the name Sarah plain, undistinguished, but it had not sounded like that a moment ago.

At last she sighed, and as she put her hands against his chest, she realized she had been clutching him around the waist, and she swallowed. He let her go reluctantly. But he took her hand and led her to the broad rock he had been sitting on earlier. When she stumbled a little, his arm came around her quickly to steady her.

"Here, let's sit down and talk about this," he said.

Sarah was feeling breathless, and it was hard to meet his eye. She wondered she could feel so shy with him.

"You must have some idea," he said after a long moment. "Some suspicions. Perhaps someone has said something to you? Looked at you a certain way?"

Sarah stared at the little brook that ran through the glade. "I have gone over and over everyone in the vicinity, but I am no closer to the truth now than I was when I began," she admitted.

"Do you think it is someone who has noticed the earl's attraction for you and hopes to scare you off?" he asked.

"I did consider that. But I cannot imagine anyone at the Hall stooping to such a thing."

"Nor anyone else either. Of course, it has to be someone who can write. That eliminates a lot of people."

"For some reason, I am sure a woman did this," Sarah told him. "Men are not likely to write anonymous letters. It is more a woman's device."

He nodded before he said, "I'll be damned if I can think of a single soul. No one that I know of here dislikes you. In fact, you have always been admired, loved even. But stay! Perhaps it is someone who is jealous of you?"

Fay, she thought. Was it Fay then? But she could not say the name to him. It would open too many doors that perhaps were better left closed.

"But that would mean every woman for miles around," he added wryly. "You are so beautiful."

Sarah ignored the way her heart leapt at his words. "I did think of jealousy, yes. Perhaps even jealousy that I married so well, bettered my station, or so they must think." She snorted. "Little does anyone know the life I have led. I would have done anything I could to avoid it, if that had been possible."

He studied the notes again, one after the other. "In essence they all say the same thing," he murmured almost to himself. "Go away. But why would anyone want you to do that?"

She held out her hands, palms up. "What frightens me is that I'm afraid I'll never be able to find out who wrote them. And if I don't, I won't know who to be wary of. And even now, I don't trust anyone."

"You trusted me," he reminded her.

For the first time since she had collapsed against him in tears, Sarah looked right at him. "Yes, I trust you," she said, her throat tight. "I—I don't know why I'm so sure I can, but I do."

They sat staring at each other for a moment. Evan thought her lovely, even with her tear-streaked face.

"You can always trust me, Sarah," he said quietly.

Then, as if the silence that followed threatened to turn into something he feared, he added, "Have you spoken to your mother about these notes? Your father, perhaps?"

"No, no one but you. I am not close to my parents. I have not felt any love for them since they forced me to my marriage. Besides, if my father learned of this, he would use it as an excuse to get control of me again. I certainly don't want that!"

"I see. So you have been trying to deal with this alone. It was brave of you."

She looked away, concentrated on tearing a twig into little pieces before she threw those pieces into the brook. "But what am I to do?" she asked hopelessly.

"You could always go away, I suppose. You would be safe then," he said, his voice colorless.

"No!" she answered quickly. "I can't do that. Not now."

"Because of the earl?" he demanded.

"Of course not! I care nothing for Jaspar Howland. I have told him I will not marry him, although he refuses to believe me. He is only a careless, arrogant boy. And I want nothing to do with marriage. Not again. Not ever again."

"Your husband must have been a proper bastard," Evan remarked.

Sarah shook her head. "No, he wasn't, not really. He was only proud, and the most selfish person I have ever known. And the life he led was worthless; in my eyes, anyway."

"Then, why, if you don't want the earl, won't you go away?" he persisted. "You have said you don't care for your parents, don't care to live with them."

She rose suddenly. Beside her, Evan Lancaster rose as well, more slowly. "I don't know," she said softly. "Perhaps because I dislike being driven away by a malicious person? Perhaps because I still want to find out who it is? I don't know. I only know I can't leave. Not yet, and maybe . . . not ever," she added, more softy. "I—I don't want to go."

He did not speak for a long time, and she stole a glance at him. He was in profile to her, staring out across the glade. She noticed he had clenched his hands at his sides, and she wondered what he was thinking about.

Then he shook his head as if to clear it, and when he turned to look at her, she caught her breath at the bleakness she saw in his eyes. "Best you be going home now, m'lady," he said sternly.

"You called me Sarah before," she whispered.

"So I did, but it was wrong of me to do so. Wrong to forget even for a moment what a lady of your station deserves."

Sarah wanted to cry out, deny that, but she knew she could not. Instead, she held out her hand to him. "Thank you for meeting me," she said with as much dignity as she could muster. "I feel better just for talking with you about this. I know I do not have to ask you to keep it to yourself."

"I shall not speak of it to anyone," he said as he took her hand for a brief moment before he went to fetch her horse.

After she was mounted, he looked up at her, shading his eyes against the sun. "Be careful," he said. "Don't ride out alone again. It might not be safe."

As she nodded, he went on, "May I keep the notes to study? Good. Be sure I shall be thinking of this. If anything occurs to me, I'll write to you."

"Perhaps we could meet instead?" Sarah asked.

Again there was that little silence. Only the sound of the wind sighing through the trees and the murmur of the brook intruded.

Evan shook his head. He stared at her as he said, "I don't think that would be wise, and after you have had a chance to consider it when you are calmer, I'm sure you'll agree with me.

"I give you good day. Go safely, m'lady."

Ten

*E*VEN THOUGH SARAH never suspected he was there, Evan Lancaster followed her until he was sure she was safe on her father's land. As he kept her in sight, he thought over their meeting at the glade, what had happened there, and what she had told him. And even though he knew his hopes of her would all come to nothing as they had in the past, he lost himself remembering those moments when he had held her in his arms.

He had always been attracted to her, even when she had been a shy young girl who had blushed whenever their eyes met. And he had known she liked him, too. But he had also known that there was no future for them together. James Jennings, pompous and overbearing, had grand expectations of the man his daughter would marry someday. And with her beauty, there was no reason to think he would be disappointed.

Nor had he been, for in time Viscount Roger Lacey had appeared. On Sarah's wedding day, Evan had gone for a long ride about the countryside so he wouldn't have to see her coming out of church on her unsuitable bridegroom's arm. He had been twenty-eight then, not a boy but a man grown. And now he was thirty-four, and widowed or not, the Dowager Viscountess Lacey was just as unattainable as she had ever been.

Yet how pleased he had been to learn she did not

care for the earl, and did not intend to marry him. Evan was glad of that. He did not like Howland, and he did not think he could make Sarah happy.

And she had not told the earl about the notes. No, she had come to him.

He had been proud she would trust him with her secret, anxious for her safety, and startled when she let him hold her. And some of the things she had said . . . Another, less wise man might have suspected she was falling in love with him. He could have kissed her, he knew. He could have suggested they meet again in some secluded place. He could have wooed her as he had always longed to do, and perhaps, just perhaps, he might have won her.

But that would not be fair to Sarah. She had grown far beyond Sutton Cross, become used to grander surroundings than a simple old brick farmhouse. And although he was well enough to do in the world and she would never want, he could not give her the things she had become accustomed to—the jewels and elegant gowns and furs, the carriages and parties and the London season. And his home would be lonely for her. There was no denying it was quite a distance from any other. Why, just look how his aunt fretted! Sarah would be isolated there, with no company but that of the wives of his farmhands. Evan's face was grim. He could not picture the lovely Lady Lacey settling down for an afternoon of gossip with Mrs. Kipp, Mrs. Farley, or Mrs. Hanks.

Yet even as he turned his horse and rode for home, he could not help wondering what it would be like to have her with him, every day, every season of the year. Sitting beside him at table, talking over the day's happenings in the evening, looking up from her sewing to smile at him. And wouldn't it be wonderful if they were to be blessed with children? He had always loved children. Sarah seemed to love them, too. She had been so carefree with them at the bazaar, so happy and smiling and content.

A savage snarl escaped Evan's lips then. You damned fool! he cursed himself. Put it away. Don't think of it anymore. It can't be. Ever.

To escape such daydreaming, he began to wonder about the person who had sent Sarah those hateful notes. She had been so sure they had been written by a woman. That was reasonable, after all, for what male from eight to eighty would ever urge *her* to go away? But if not a man, then *what* woman?

Sarah would have been surprised that Evan's first suspicions matched hers so well, that the anonymous writer was none other than Fay Denton. Of course, he told himself, Fay had to be jealous of Sarah, and he knew she cherished hopes that he would marry her one of these days. She often came with her mother and sister to visit his aunt, spending a long time with her, talking and gossiping. And he could tell her motives from her warm smiles and little attentions. Did she suspect he loved Sarah Lacey? Was she the one who wrote, hoping that if Sarah went away, he would turn to her?

Not that that would ever happen!

But even though she was his prime suspect, Evan found it hard to believe Fay capable of such evil. She was a simple girl, friendly and uncomplicated, and with no great depths. Such deep and devious doings as this letter writing seemed both too subtle and too involved for the Fay Denton he knew. But she *could* write, he reminded himself. He had seen notes she had sent to his aunt.

But if not Fay, then who? There were other girls in the neighborhood, of course. Women, too, who might have thought it exciting to worry the lovely viscountess. Maybe even someone who was thrilled to be unknown, yet so ominous a presence?

Lord, he thought as he reined in at last in his stable yard, next thing you know, I'll be suspecting Miss Prim and Proper, or the vicar's wife.

But as he rubbed down his horse, he hoped Sarah would have a care for herself. The last note had had a vicious edge to it, mentioning scarring as it had. He promised himself that as far as he could, he would keep an eye on Sarah Lacey. And, he admitted, be delighted to do so.

When she reached home, Sarah changed her habit for a simple morning gown before she sat down to read her post. She was glad to see there was no printed note among it. But today she could not seem to interest herself in Lady Mather's long, chatty letter, all about the little season in London, nor even in Mrs. Darling's invitation to spend the winter months with her family in Dorset.

Instead, she found the letters slipping from her hands as she stared out the windows of the morning room and remembered the meeting she had just had with Evan Lancaster. She felt confused—unsettled. Oh, not about the attraction she had always felt for him. That was still there, and she did not question it. But today she had felt more than attraction. When he had held her close, comforted her, she had had the wild thought that if she could spend the rest of her life with him, she would die content. And that, of course, was ridiculous.

She did not intend to marry again, and that was that. But oh, how wonderful it had been, how comforting and . . . and right, secure in the haven of his strong arms.

And yet he had put her away from him; told her he did not think another meeting wise. Why had he done that? Sarah had sensed how much he had wanted to kiss her, sensed that, as well as comfort, his hands and body had offered passion and love. If that was true, why would he deny those feelings? For what reason?

A tap on the door recalled her to her surroundings, and as Geoff came in to lounge in a chair across from her, she collected her scattered post and put it away.

"There was something you wanted to talk to me about, Geoff?" she asked.

Her brother yawned and stretched. "No, I'm just so bored this morning. It is tedious here, don't you agree? And since we are not summoned to the Hall until dinnertime, I find I have nothing to do."

The sound of his mother's voice came faintly through the door then, and he winced. Mrs. Jennings had recovered her health at last, and she had lost no time taking up the reins of her household again, harrying the maids, finding fault with the footman, and making her opinions and orders known in the loud, abusive voice she always used to underlings.

"Perhaps now that Mother is well again, you'll be thinking of leaving?" Sarah asked.

Geoffrey shook his head. "I can't. Not for ages yet. The dibs, my dear sister, are not in tune for me at present. And since Pa has said he'll not give me an advance on my allowance, I am forced to rusticate until quarter day.

"I say, you wouldn't by any chance be good for a loan, would you?" he asked, leaning forward eagerly. "I know you're well before with the world, and you never seem to spend a groat. And it would be such a great favor for me, dear, *dearest* Sarah! Lord Faxton has asked me to his estate, but he dips deep, and the gambling is such that without a sizable stake, I dare not venture there."

"No," Sarah said firmly. "I'll not waste my portion franking you, Geoff, for I know I would never see it again."

She saw the flash of anger in his eyes, but she ignored it as she went on, "Don't you think it past time that you began to live within your means? I know Father gives you a goodly amount, yet what do you do with it? Gamble, or fritter it away on new clothes or a new horse. You could live very comfortably if you chose to, you know."

For a moment there was only silence, but at last Geoffrey said so meekly, it startled his sister, "Perhaps you are right. I shall have to consider it."

Seeing he was in such an amiable mood, Sarah ventured to warn him about his closest companions. "The earl was telling me the other day that Lord Faxton has such a terrible reputation, he is nowhere received. Nor are any of his friends. Surely hanging on his sleeve can do you no good, Geoff."

Her brother rose to pace the room, running a hand through his hair as he did so. "I know what he's like, but he's demned amusing for all that. And besides, most of the other nobility will have nothing to do with me.

"But why should they? I've neither wealth nor standing in the world. And even when I became the brother of Viscountess Lacey, it did me no good at all. That demned husband of yours! It was all his fault!"

"Whatever do you mean?" Sarah asked, confused.

"I went to call on him in town right after your marriage. At the time I was only hoping he would help me into society, but he told me straight out he'd not sponsor me, that the only member of the Jennings family he wanted anything to do with was you. And he thanked me to make myself scarce. In fact, he ordered me not to call on you, or ask you for money. Said he'd instruct his butler I was always to be denied. And he told me he didn't care if I ended up in Newgate or had to flee the country for debt someday, for he'd do nothing to save me. Bastard! Mean-hearted bastard!"

Sarah had known nothing of this, but she could well believe it of her late husband. So that was why Geoff had never come to see her in London, why she had never been asked for money. Roger, not wanting to get embroiled with him, had seen to his banishment coldly and competently.

"So of course, it is Lord Faxton for me," Geoffrey went on. "Until I can find my heiress, that is. I have been thinking a lot about that lately. Perhaps it is time I settled to the business with more purpose. It's true I'm only twenty-four, and I hadn't intended to marry till I was thirty or so, but needs must when the devil drives, you know."

"Geoff, I wish you wouldn't do that," Sarah began. "It is the most cold-blooded thing I have ever heard of, and not at all fair to—"

He had walked to the door, and now he raised his hand. "No more lecturing, *dear* Sarah. You feathered your nest in very convincing style. Surely you cannot quibble because I want to do the same thing. How two-faced of you that would be, sitting as you are on all those bags of gold. And with the Earl of Castleton just about to make you his countess, too. Oh, why do *you* have all the luck? It isn't fair!"

On that cry he was gone, slamming the door behind him. Sarah frowned and then she sighed. She wished she could like her brother more, but she realized anew there was nothing admirable about him.

She rose to pace in turn. Perhaps she should go away, as Evan had suggested, she thought. Mother didn't need her anymore, and she did dislike living here with her family. They were petty and greedy and proud. Yet proud of what? she asked herself. Truth be told, Father is only a farmer. What is it that makes him think he is above all the others?

Even Evan? And what makes Geoff think the world owes him a life of noble leisure?

As Sarah Lacey pondered her undesirable family, the Earl of Castleton was engaged in a stroll with his cousin, Bartholomew Whitaker. What the rest of his party were doing, he neither knew nor cared. He had played the host all morning, entertained them at a lavish luncheon, and then excused himself, motioning his cousin to follow him. In doing so, he did not notice Miss Hawkins's face fall, nor Lady Alice's pout, the way she tossed her head at his defection.

No, for he was too deeply engrossed with a problem of his own. His campaign to win Lady Lacey was not going well, no, not well at all. Every time he tried to see her alone, she managed to slip away from him, or Lady Alice interrupted, or his aunt sent him on some fool's errand. The earl had decided to ask his cousin what he should do. After all, Bart was five years older than he, a contemporary of the lady—perhaps he would know.

For, Jaspar thought as he strode through the desolate gardens, switching off the tops of some flowers that had succumbed to the first frost last night, if I do not get her promise soon, hold her, kiss her, I'm apt to go mad!

"Am I correct in assuming there is something serious on your mind, dear boy?" Bart inquired, an amused little grin on his long face. "Do stop mutilating those poor dead chrysanthemums, and confess."

Jaspar turned to him, the dark scowl still on his face. But when his cousin made a dreadful face back at him in reply, he was forced to laugh. Throwing the switch away, he put an arm around his companion's shoulder.

"Good old Bart! Know me like a brother, don't you?"

"Rather better, I think," his cousin said coolly. "If I'd been your brother, I'd have been the earl and you'd never have confided in me lest I stop you doing whatever unsuitable thing you were intent on."

Jaspar's handsome face settled into a frown again. "Surely you know what the trouble is," he said. "It's Sarah! I had such hopes I could get her to agree to marry me sometime during the house party, but she continues to be elusive. And when I tell her, time and again, that I intend to make her my countess, she always says she won't be. There, did you ever hear of such a thing?"

His cousin's brows had risen during this speech. "You've—you've asked her to marry you, have you?" he said. "Already?"

"Ages ago! In fact, I told her she'd be my countess the second time I saw her. She refused, but at the time I only thought it was because she didn't know me well enough. And I knew I could convince her. But—but it isn't working.

"Of course, that might be because I never seem to get her alone for more than a minute or two. Either someone interrupts or she eludes me. Whatever am I to do, Bart? I must have her! I *will* have her!"

Feeling guilty that he had vastly maligned Lady Lacey's character in his previous opinion of her, Bart pretended to be thinking hard. So the lovely Sarah was not interested in becoming Jaspar's bride, was she? He wondered why not, even as he said a quick prayer of thanks.

"Well?" Jaspar asked, his temper rising.

"I haven't the vaguest idea," Bart admitted, throwing out his hands in defeat. "But if she don't want you, she don't want you."

"Why wouldn't she?" Jaspar demanded, stopping short and clutching his cousin's lapel.

That gentleman removed his hand at once. "Have a care, dear boy. Weston, you know.

"Now, as to the ladies, who can tell about them?" he went on. "Take little notions in their heads all the time, and little pets as well. There's no understanding 'em at all, and better men than you and I have tried it. But surely it is not your rank, or your wealth, nor your handsome face and physique that makes her so cold. Could it be she loves another? It is the only thing I can think of."

"*What* other?" Jaspar demanded through gritted teeth.

Bart shrugged. "Be reasonable. How would I know that?" he asked patiently. "But perhaps that is the crux of the matter. Has she ever mentioned anyone? Even in passing?"

"No, never. And she wouldn't talk to me about her husband, the only time I brought him up. But she can't still be mourning *him*. He's been dead over a year, and he was ancient!"

"He does sound an unlikely prospect," his cousin agreed, although he would never have called a man in his fifties, in perfect health, "ancient." As they began to walk again, he went on, "Tell you what. You can't ask her right out, but I can. Would you like me to find out? Subtly, of course."

Jaspar hugged him close for a moment. "Bart, you're a trump! That would be marvelous! And you will do it soon, won't you? I must have this all resolved quickly lest I lose my sanity. Besides, Lady Alice is making me nervous."

"Yes, I've noticed her closing in on you. Be careful not to be alone with her for any reason. I could have told you she'd be a problem in the intimacy of a house party, if only you'd asked me before you invited her. Saw that in London last season. The

Lady Alice has decided you are worthy of a duke's daughter, and she is determined to make you propose."

Jaspar Howland shuddered. "I've decided, after almost two weeks with the lady, that that is all I can stand," he said. "The thought of spending a lifetime with her boggles the mind."

Returning to his primary concern, he added, "Perhaps you will have a chance to talk to Sarah tonight after dinner? I'll keep clear, even if it means engaging Fen's sisters in endless conversation."

"No, no, such a sacrifice is too noble," his cousin protested. "But perhaps Miss Hawkins would serve? It would set the dear girl up so, too, for she also cherishes dreams, dear boy. I'd be most remiss if I didn't warn you about them as well."

"I'll hover about Lady Lincoln instead," Jaspar said grimly, and his cousin laughed at him, feeling much more lighthearted than he had since his arrival at Castleton Hall.

Bartholomew Whitaker made his way to Lady Lacey's side that evening the moment the gentlemen rejoined the ladies after dinner. Sarah had had no intention of sharing a tête-à-tête with him, but by a method she could only admire silently, he disengaged her from Miss Hawkins and Lady Howland and took her somewhat apart where their conversation could not be overheard.

As he did so, Sarah stole a glance at Jaspar Howland. To her surprise, the earl was not looking black as he was wont to do whenever his cousin or one of the other gentlemen paid her any attention, and she wondered at it. Perhaps he was reconsidering his devotion? Had come to see that they would not suit? How wonderful if it were to be so! But Mr. Whitaker's first words disabused her of any such notion.

"As I am aware you know, m'lady, my cousin is enamored of you," he began without preamble. "But he has told me you have denied him, and I must admit I am intrigued as to why you would do such a thing. After all, Jaspar is young, handsome, wealthy, and titled. And he has no horrible character failings that I know of, and I do know him rather well. So, I asked myself, what can it be that makes the lovely Lady Lacey so cool?"

He paused for a moment, but when Sarah did not reply, he went on, "The only thing I can think of that would explain it is that you are in love with another. Is that your reason, ma'am?"

Sarah knew she could refuse to answer such an impertinent question, but the twinkle she saw in Bartholomew Whitaker's eyes made her smile a little in response.

"You do not want me to marry your cousin, do you, Mr. Whitaker?" she asked. As he shook his head, looking rueful, she went on, "It must have been a great relief to you to learn I had no intention of doing any such thing. When you and I first met, I did wonder at your instant antipathy for me, but I came to see it was because you considered me unsuitable for the post of Countess Castleton. And I *am* unsuitable, if only he would recognize that fact. I am a widow, twenty-seven now, five years older than he, although I feel years older still. He is such a boy! What he feels for me, as you and I are both aware, is only infatuation for a pretty face."

Bart held up his hand. "Never that, ma'am," he said earnestly. "Pretty? 'Pon my soul, you insult yourself. You are beautiful."

Sarah nodded coolly. "So I am," she agreed. "But that's a ridiculous reason to marry someone, isn't it?"

He nodded as he leaned closer. "What you say is

all very well and good, ma'am, but it has not answered my question. *Do* you love another?"

Sarah considered. Her first reaction to deny any such thing seemed to stick in her throat as Evan Lancaster's handsome, rugged face came to mind. Because it would be a lie? she asked herself. Because she suddenly knew how much she loved Evan still?

She was aware that Mr. Whitaker was waiting for her answer, and she made herself laugh lightly. "You may say so if you wish when you report back to the earl on the outcome of this conversation," she said. "It is as good a reason as any, and I have become desperate trying to think of something that would serve. Your cousin is so stubborn! But he has many years yet before he must marry, and when he does, although, of course, he should do so for love, he should also do what is correct.

"Yes, tell him that I am enarmored of another, older man. But try not to wound him, if you please! I like him very much, and I wish him well. But I will never marry him."

Mr. Whitaker took her hand and raised it to kiss. "You are a most remarkable woman, m'lady," he said softly. "It is a privilege to have known you."

Sarah smiled and moved away to one of the windows that overlooked the terrace. It was a lovely night, starlit and not too cold. Suddenly she gasped and leaned closer, and Bartholomew Whitaker was quick to join her.

Sarah's hand had crept to her lips when she saw her brother, Geoffrey, standing close to the earl's sister Rose on the terrace. He had his arm around the girl, and they were deep in conversation. Sarah wondered at it, for as usual, the Lady Rose had not been present at dinner. What was she doing out there with Geoff alone? Had the two of them made an assignation? It was most improper. And when

Sarah remembered Geoff's conversation that morning, how he had said he intended to look for an heiress soon, she felt a deep sense of dread.

"You must excuse me, sir," she said in a constricted voice. "I would seek my brother without delay."

To her surprise, Mr. Whitaker's hand closed around her wrist to prevent her from leaving. "No, no, ma'am, there is no need to trouble yourself," he said. "I am an expert in these matters, and any rebuke that comes from me will not cause the resentment you might have to face. I insist you permit me to serve as your emissary."

"Thank you," Sarah whispered as he offered his arm to lead her back to the others.

Seated beside a silently seething Lady Alice, Sarah watched Mr. Whitaker stroll to the doors of the drawing room and disappear. She wondered what he would say to Geoff, and how her brother would react. It was really too bad of him, trying to seduce an impressionable sixteen-year-old, she thought as she turned her attention to Lady Alice, to compliment her on her gown and amethyst necklace.

When Batholomew Whitaker's voice spoke from the darkness, Lady Rose squeaked, and her hands went to her heart. Mr. Jennings had just been about to kiss her, and she was dying to know what a man's kiss would be like. He was so handsome, so sophisticated! She had been thrilled when she discovered some days ago that she had the power to attract such a polished, older man. Of course, she knew what she was doing was wrong, but she did not care. It was all Jaspar's fault anyway, she had told herself as she stole from her room and made her way down a back stairway to the terrace. If he had not insisted she was too young for evening parties, things would not have come to this pass. No, for then she would have been in the drawing room with the others, smiling and flirting and having a wonderful time.

"Go inside, Rose," her cousin had said as he stepped forward from the shadows. "You are a very naughty girl, but although you should be punished, I will not tell Jaspar if I have your promise that all *clandestine* meetings with this *gentleman* will cease as of now."

The scorn in his voice as he spoke made Geoff color up. He was glad the faint starlight concealed it.

Lady Rose took her cousin's measure, her chin tilted in defiance. What she saw in his face and angry eyes made her lower her own eyes at once. Cousin Bart was *not* amused. In all her life she had never seen such disdain from him, and she hoped she would never see it again. She had always loved Bart, and suddenly she was sorry she had lost his good regard.

"I was doing nothing wrong—" she began, but he interrupted her.

"Yes, you were, so spin me no Banbury tales, my girl," he said. "Give me your promise and run along now, or I will think better about holding my tongue."

"All right, I promise," Rose said, sounding sulky before she whirled and ran from the terrace. Both men stood very still until they heard the door close behind her.

"I do assure you, sir, it was only the most casual, innocent meeting," Geoffrey began. "I came out merely for a breath of air, and found the Lady Rose before me. I think she is feeling left out of the festivities and resenting it, and only came here to peek in the windows at the others—"

"Please do not try either my credulity or my temper, Mr. Jennings," Whitaker said harshly. "I do not believe a word you say, and I have no compunction in telling you so. You, sir, are not a gentleman. To be trying for that infant is infamous! Not that you would have succeeded, you know, for in the end the Lady Rose would have scorned you, even if I had not chanced to glance from the window and spotted you here. She is a minx and she has been playing with fire, no more. When she marries, it will be to a gentleman of her own rank. I do assure you, the girl knows her worth and reveres her name. So in spite of your handsome face, smooth words, and teasing ways, she would not have succumbed to such as *you*."

"You are sure of that?" Geoff snarled, stung into speech by the contempt he heard so plain in the other's voice.

Bartholomew Whitaker nodded. "Very sure. That you are a commoner is nothing in comparison to the fact that you are an unprincipled, opportunistic blackguard."

As Geoff hissed under his breath and balled his fists, Whitaker added, "I do think it would be wise for you to take your leave now. Of course, I shall relay your excuses to your host, tell the others of a sudden indisposition. And I think it would be wise for you to remain indisposed for the duration of the house party. If you do not, I shall have to take steps. Steps, Mr. Jennings, that I can assure you, you would not care for. I have made myself plain enough, sir? Ah, good, I see you understand me."

Geoffrey was seething, but there was nothing he could do. The earl's cousin was a big man, strong and in good condition, and Geoff had never been much with his fists. Whitaker could beat him unconscious without even breathing hard, and he knew it.

Bowing in defeat, he said, "As an honorable man,

I resent your implications, sir, but I will not quarrel with you."

"Much better not," Whitaker murmured, sounding amused now. As Geoffrey moved to the terrace steps, he added, "You need not concern yourself for your lovely sister. It shall be my honor to see Lady Lacey safely home myself."

Eleven

THE TIME BEFORE the ball that would mark the end of the earl's house party passed slowly for Sarah. She could tell Mr. Whitaker had spoken to Jaspar Howland, for he looked despondent the next time they met at a riding party, and brooding and aloof as well. She wished she could refuse the invitations that still came so regularly from the Hall, but she did not know how such a thing could be accomplished without giving offense. Well, she told herself, it was only a few more days.

She had no need to question her brother about why he did not accompany her anymore, although Mrs. Jennings was quick to do so. They were all three having tea late one afternoon when she did, and to Sarah, Geoffrey looked most uncomfortable. "I've grown bored with the company there, I suppose," he had said, yawning a little as he did so. "And it is true I am not feeling quite the thing. Perhaps it is the change in the weather."

Sarah had looked out the window. A few gentle flakes of snow were falling, and although she knew they would not amount to anything, they were enough to remind her that winter had arrived. As her mother began to prate of tonics and restoratives, she let her mind wander, wondering when she would see Evan Lancaster again. She had had no word from him, so obviously he had not solved the mystery of her anonymous letters, not that she had expected him to do so. Nor was she any closer to a solution herself. Still, she had received no more since their meeting. That was something.

She was recalled to her company when Geoff slammed down his teacup and rushed from the room. His mother looked concerned and then she shrugged. "Darling Geoffy is so sensitive," she said as she took another cream puff. "He has always been so, even as a small boy. But I shall procure some of that special tonic I was telling him about, and I'm sure it will perk him up wonderfully. It is too bad he must miss all the fancy doings up at the Hall, and the company of the nobility he is used to."

Sarah sipped her tea, her face noncommittal. A few days ago her mother had pressed her again for money for Geoff, much more plainly this time, but Sarah had been unyielding. Since that time, Mrs. Jennings had ignored her whenever possible. If she had realized what a relief that had been to her daughter, she would not have employed the tactic.

Sarah had decided she would not attend the final ball. What was the use of it? she asked herself. I do not care for most of the earl's guests, and I have seen them endlessly. And perhaps her refusal to make one of the party would convince the earl that she cared nothing for him and had no intention of becoming his countess.

She knew such a decision would anger her mother, her father especially, but she did not care. They were ridiculous with their aspirations for yet another, higher title for their daughter, and the social prestige it would bring.

However, she was in no way prepared for the storm that erupted when her father asked her what she planned to wear to the ball, and she told the family she was not going to attend.

"What?" Mr. Jennings roared, glaring at her. "Not go? Are you *mad*?"

They were all at dinner at the time, and Sarah looked from one to the other. Her brother, Geoffrey, seemed sardonically amused, her father livid, and her mother was so frustrated and indignant, she looked like a plump, angry hen, ruffling its feathers.

"I do not care to go," she said as carelessly as she could. "I've spent enough time with the earl and his guests. They begin to weary me.

"No," she went on, raising her hand when she saw her father was determined to speak, "there is nothing you can say to change my mind, and I beg you will not attempt it. Besides, I have already written to Lady Howland, making my excuses."

James Jennings's face was purple with fury. "Unnatural creature!" he bellowed. "Don't have the sense of a goose, you don't! There'll be few chances like this for you to better your position in life! Or was you thinking, so conceited as you are, that with your looks, you might snare a *duke*? A bird in the hand, missy, a bird in the hand!"

Sarah stifled a sigh and put down her fork, all her appetite gone. "I don't care to discuss it, sir," she said as evenly as she could. "I am not going. Indeed, I don't intend to see the earl again for any reason, and nothing you can say will change my mind. Jaspar Howland is only an arrogant boy, and completely uninteresting to me.

"Come now, let us forget him and enjoy this excellent dinner. Cook should be congratulated. I've never tasted a better wine sauce."

Dinner concluded in a cold silence, broken only by the sounds of the silver on china, her father's heightened breathing, and her mother's infuriated sniffs. Sarah excused herself as soon as she could. As she went up to her room, she shook her head, wondering if her original plan to remain with her family until after Christmas was feasible anymore. And as she did so, she wondered again at her brother's considering eyes this evening, the close way he had studied her, as if she were some strange being he had never seen before. Somehow his gaze had made her very uneasy, much more so than her father's blustering and her mother's cold fury had done.

She did not leave Three Oaks again until she was sure the house party at the Hall had dispersed, although she had been disappointed to learn from Miss Withers that the earl himself remained. James Jennings grew more cheerful, however, for he considered it a very good sign, and so he told his wife and son one evening when Sarah had gone early to bed.

Most days after that, Sarah, finding it still unpleasant to remain at home, took to riding out again, although she was careful to do so only in her groom's company.

Leary wondered what was the matter with the lass. She had always been a favorite of his, and he did not like to see her looking so depressed and withdrawn. He even wondered one crisp morning, as they rode together to Sutton Cross, why the lady did not pack her bags, order her carriage, and leave Kent. He could tell she was not fond of her family, and from what he had seen of them—heard, too—she had good reason. But she did not go, and it puzzled him.

Sarah was puzzled, too, although she began to understand that the reason she was held here had nothing to do with family, friends, or old familiar places. No, she knew she stayed because of Evan. This confused her, for he had never told her he loved her and wanted her. Still she suspected he did. And she knew that somehow she was fascinated with

174

him. She told herself it was not love, as she had once supposed. What was love to her, after all? She had decided she would never marry again, hadn't she? Never give her life into another's keeping? Best she leave while she still could. But she made no plans to do so. It was as if she were waiting—waiting for what, she did not know.

She was coming out of Abner Bower's shop later when she saw Evan at last. He was tying his horse to the rail there, and as he raised his head, they stared at each other. For Sarah, all the noise of the village died away, and she could not move. For a moment the two of them remained perfectly still, and Leary, who was lounging near the horses, looked at them with narrowed eyes.

Sarah recovered first, and she smiled as she came down the steps. "Good morning, Mr. Lancaster," she said.

He nodded to her, bowing a little. When she was abreast of him, he touched her arm. "You have had no further notes?" he asked in a low voice.

Sarah felt as if she could not draw enough air to reply without giving herself away, but she managed to say, "No, thank heavens, not a one. And you? Have you discovered anything?"

He shook his head. "Nothing. The writing is disguised, and the paper, the kind sold in Abner's shop. As for the seal, it is a common one.

"I understand the earl's guests have left," he said next. Sarah stole a glance at him, and her heart jumped. "But he himself remains," he added slowly. "Unusual, wouldn't you say? He has never been one to endure the country for long periods of time."

"I do not see the earl anymore," Sarah told him. "I have no idea why he remains."

He only nodded, but she thought his serious expression seemed to lighten a little.

175

"I see you have brought your groom this morning," he said.

"Yes, I go nowhere without him, as you suggested. And I do feel safer with Leary nearby somehow."

There was a pregnant pause, and frantically she wondered what else she might say to keep him with her. Her disappointment when he lifted his hat and bade her good-bye was acute. She nodded, but she did not speak. Nor did she all the way home, and when she left the groom at the stable, she said not a word.

She went immediately to her room, as was her custom now. That way she could avoid her mother's cold sniffs, her father's hectoring lectures, and her brother Geoff's company. She still caught him staring at her on occasion, speculation in his eyes, and it continued to make her uneasy, even though she told herself he could do nothing to her.

She would have been even more uneasy if she had known that at that very moment, Geoff was giving his card to the earl's butler and requesting a moment of his time on a matter of some importance.

Jaspar Howland had no desire to see Sarah's brother. He had not heard of his assignation with Rose on the terrace, for his cousin Bart, true to his word, had not mentioned it. Except for a slight relief that Jennings had stopped coming to the Hall, the earl gave him very little thought. Nor did he now, for all his mind was on his disappointment that Sarah had not come to the ball, and would not see him anymore. Bart had told him he would get over her in time, but the earl could not believe him. The pain was still too great. And so he had refused to travel to London with his cousin as Bart had urged. What was in London for him now? At least here he was close to her, in proximity if not in person.

Still, when he read Geoffrey's card, he nodded curtly to his butler. It would do no harm to see what Jennings wanted, he told himself, and he might even find out how Sarah was faring.

He ordered wine for his guest and they talked of desultory things until the butler had served them and bowed himself away.

"There was some special reason you wished to see me, Mr. Jennings?" Jaspar asked as the doors closed behind that worthy.

Geoffrey nodded, his face serious. "Forgive me for saying so, m'lord, but you do not look well," he began. "I trust you are not ailing?"

"Not from anything physical," the earl admitted with a grimace.

"Ah, I see. I think I know what is troubling you. That is why I am here—to help you."

The earl swallowed his wine with one gulp and laughed, a harsh, grating laugh. "I doubt very much that there is anything you can do, sir," he said shortly.

"On the contrary, I can!" Geoffrey exclaimed, all smiles. "If, that is, I am not mistaken in the source of your troubles. Tell me, m'lord, has this all to do with my sister, Lady Lacey? I know she refused your offer, for she told me so. And I gather you are disappointed? Well, why wouldn't you be? Sarah's a lovely creature. But—but she is just a woman, with all a woman's failings.

"And, as I am sure you will agree, m'lord, women so seldom know their own minds. Haven't you found that to be so? That is why men are so important. It takes a man to show a woman what is best for her, know what will make her happy."

"You begin to interest me, Mr. Jennings," Jaspar said slowly. "Interest me greatly, in fact."

"I was sure I would," his guest said easily. "Now, in thinking of your dilemma, it occurred to me that if only you could spend some time alone with Sarah, you could convince her quickly that being your wife is what she was meant for all this time. You see, I do not think she is happy, either. She spends most of every day secluded in her room, and she is very uncommunicative. Why would she seek solitude, remain silent, if she were not miserable? Perhaps she is even, shall we say, regretting a certain hasty decision? Perhaps wishing she might change it?"

"Do you think so? Really?" the earl asked, leaning forward and speaking with more animation than he had shown before.

Geoffrey nodded, lowering his eyes to his wineglass to hide the triumph he felt. "Perhaps if you were to be more *forceful*, m'lord—carpe diem, as they say—she would be overjoyed to have this matter decided for her. And women do love a forceful man."

The earl rose to pace the library, frowning in thought. As last he turned back to his guest and said, "Let us be plain with each other, sir. What is it that you are suggesting? And *why* are you suggesting it?"

"For my sister's future happiness, of course," Geoffrey said. "And I will admit to you freely, for my own good as well. It will be quite a cachet for me, becoming the Earl of Castleton's brother-in-law. There are some debts. . . ."

The earl smiled grimly. "I see," he said, and in those two little words was such a wealth of scorn that Geoffrey flushed.

"No, no, m'lord, I ask no payment for my help! You misunderstand me," he hastened to say. "It is only that my creditors will cease badgering me when they learn of my sister's marriage to you.

178

That is all I require. A few months to settle my accounts, and all will be well with me again."

"How do you suggest I go about being 'forceful'?" Jaspar asked next as he poured them both another glass of wine.

Geoffrey threw out his hands and shrugged. "Surely there is someplace on your vast acreage where you could take Sarah? Keep her until she agrees to your wishes? Someplace where you could be alone—together? For as long as it takes?"

The earl's face grew thoughtful. He knew of a deserted woodcutter's cottage that was deep in the estate, and far from any habitation. But did he dare? What would Sarah think? And how would he manage? He would have to see to provisioning the place himself with food and blankets and firewood, for he could trust no one on so delicate a business. If it were ever to get out!

Recalled to his company by Geoffrey's little cough, he nodded. "I must thank you for coming, sir, and for your help," he said formally as he rose in dismissal.

"It was nothing," Geoffrey demurred. "If you need any assistance preparing the place, be sure and let me know. It might be easier for me to take care of it than you. And if you will but send me word, I'll make sure Sarah rides out on the day you appoint. I'll go with her, so there'll be no need for her groom. It is the least I can do for her, the foolish girl! And you need not worry, m'lord. I'll see there's no hue and cry after her at home. Leave all in my hands."

"You will be hearing from me. Give you good day," Jaspar said curtly as he sat down at his desk and picked up a paper there. He did not think he could bear to look into the man's smirking face a moment more. But even though he knew what Sarah's brother had just done was dastardly, he would not hesitate to use him and his plan. He was sure it was going to cost him a great deal of money one of these days, no matter what that little worm had claimed, but that was unimportant now. He loved Sarah too much to hesitate. And he *knew* he could convince her, given the time, and the privacy.

But he would not use force, except to capture her. The very thought of such a course of action was repugnant to him, and never mind her own brother had as much as suggested rape. What a terrible creature Geoffrey Jennings was!

Jaspar rose to pace the library then, feeling happier than he had for some time. These days that he had been parted from Sarah had been very hard to bear. More so since his guests had left, for now he was alone with nothing to distract him from his sad thoughts. He smiled then, a sweet smile of satisfaction that lit up his handsome face. He would not be alone much longer.

Twelve

W HEN GEOFFREY SUGGESTED a morning ride to his sister a few days later, Sarah agreed rather listlessly. What did it matter? she asked herself as she sent a message to the stables to tell Leary he would not be required. Geoff would see she came to no harm. And she herself was beginning to wonder if her precautions might not be a little ridiculous anyway. She had had no further notes from her mysterious correspondent; perhaps whoever had sent them had wearied of the game.

It was a gray morning and cold, the sky full of low, scudding clouds that promised sleet or snow later in the day. Full of her own thoughts, at first Sarah did not notice the way Geoff took, and they were well on the road that bordered Castleton to the west before she realized it. Suddenly Geoff reined in and signaled her to halt.

"What is it?" she asked as she came alongside.

Her brother dismounted and tied his horse to a branch. "I'm not sure," he said as he bent to inspect the cinch. "Something doesn't feel right."

Sarah heard the rumble of a cart approaching, and she nudged her mare to the side of the road. "Someone's coming," she said.

To her surprise, her brother grabbed the mare's bridle. "What on earth are you doing?" she asked. "I can manage Faery myself."

"Dismount," he ordered just as the cart came

around the bend. When Sarah saw Jaspar Howland was driving it, her eyes widened. "Loose that bridle, Geoff!" she ordered. Her heart was beginning to pound, but until he chose to release her, she was helpless. She saw he made no move to obey her.

Frustrated, she watched the earl pull up the team, get down, and come toward them. And still Geoff held her captive. A terrible suspicion formed in her mind. No, she told herself. They wouldn't do such an infamous thing. Would they?

"Tie her horse with mine, m'lord," her brother said. "I'll take care of Sarah."

"You—you terrible, horrible man!" Sarah cried as he pulled her from the saddle. "I never believed you could be so vile! And as for you, m'lord—"

But she said no more, for just then Geoffrey put a foul-smelling cloth over her face, and she lost consciousness.

"Was that necessary?" the earl asked harshly.

"Very necessary," Geoffrey Jennings said coolly. "We don't want her screaming for help on the high road, now do we, m'lord? This way she won't recover consciousness until you have her safely at the cottage. And then, of course, it is so isolated, she can scream her head off if she wants. For your sake, however, I pray she will not."

He chuckled as he carried his sister to the cart. "I'll hand her up to you. I'm afraid you'll have to support her. But stay! Perhaps I could put her in back with the supplies?"

"No, it will be too uncomfortable for her," Howland argued as he took his seat. Then, after Geoff put Sarah up beside him, he put his arm around her limp form and braced her against him. As he did so, he looked down into her lovely face, relieved when he saw her breathing was normal.

"Best you be on your way, m'lord," Jennings said.

"Anyone might come along, and that would never do."

The earl nodded as he slapped the reins on the team's back.

"Good fortune, sir!" Jennings called after them. "I'll come in two days to see if you need anything. And don't worry! I've a fine story to tell them at home. No one will worry about Sarah."

After half a mile, the earl turned off the road on an overgrown track. It would have been difficult to find for anyone who didn't know what to look for, but Jaspar Howland had come this way several times in the past few days, and he did not hesitate. And he admitted he felt easier now that they had left the main road. If anyone had seen him in a farm cart, a limp Lady Lacey cuddled in his arm, it would have been disastrous to his plan.

The way he traveled was rough with several turnings, and it took almost half an hour of slow going before he reached the yard of the deserted cottage. No smoke issued from its chimney, and he cursed under his breath. He had started a fire earlier, so Sarah would not be cold, but it must have gone out while he was gone.

He slid along the seat with her still held in his arm, and then he braced her with one hand as he climbed down. In only another moment, he had her in his arms and was carrying her to the cottage. He could not resist dropping a kiss on her soft cheek as he did so. It had all come to pass, just as he had planned! he thought exultantly as he shouldered the door open and went in. He placed Sarah down gently on the bed that had been built against one wall of the cottage and covered her with some blankets. Then he turned his attention to the fire. He saw he would need more wood; best he get that while she was still unconscious. He had never realized how much wood was necessary for a good, steady fire. But then, his servants had always taken care of such mundane things before. And he supposed he would have to bring in the rest of the supplies, stable the team in the rough lean-to, water them. So many things to do!

It was some time later before Sarah stirred. The earl was at her side at once. He had been growing anxious, afraid that whatever her brother had drugged her with had been too powerful. But now he heard her little moan, and he closed his eyes for a moment and said a prayer of thanks. If anything had happened to her!

He sat down on the bed beside her and took up her hand to stroke it. Several minutes passed before her eyelids fluttered open.

"You," she breathed. *"You!"*

He smiled down at her, but her next words wiped that smile away as if it had never been. "How could you be so despicable?" she demanded in a croak as she struggled to sit up. "How could you do this to me? And Geoff! How rotten he is—his own sister—I still cannot believe—"

"Now, Sarah, you must be calm," Jaspar Howland said, disturbed by her agitated words. "Rest. Yes, this has been unpleasant, but—"

"Unpleasant?" she asked, her voice full of loathing as she massaged her dry throat. *"That* is an understatement if ever I heard one!"

"Would you like a drink of water?" he asked.

She nodded, disdaining to look at him. Where was she? she wondered. She had never seen this place before. As the earl hurried to a bucket set on a table near the hearth, she glanced around. It was obvious she was in a poor cottage somewhere. Perhaps a farmer's home at one time? There was only this one room to it, and above her head, a half loft with a rickety ladder leading up to it. She could hear scurrying little footsteps up there, and she shuddered. Pray it was only mice, she thought. She did not like rats.

She noticed there was little furniture in the room. Just this bed, a table, and two chairs. In one corner there were a number of boxes, stacked one on top of the other, and a large trunk. And there were no windows, only the door that was opposite the rough stone fireplace.

Sarah rubbed her forehead, her mind working frantically. She did not waste time wondering why she had been brought here; she could guess that well enough. But although she could easily imagine Geoff involved in something as underhanded as this, she had never thought the earl would be a party to abduction.

She took the mug he was holding out to her and drank deep. Ah, that was better. Now, if only her head didn't ache so.

"Darling, why don't you lie down and rest for a while?" the earl asked in the kind of voice one would use with a fretful child. "No doubt you have the headache, and—"

"Yes, I do!" Sarah snapped. "I'll thank you to stand back! And don't talk to me!"

She lay back on the pillows and rolled over on her side away from him to face the wall. Jaspar pulled up the covers she had disarranged, and she grabbed them away from him as if she could not bear to even have him touching something that touched her.

The earl looked bewildered as he went to take a seat near the fireplace. Of course, he had to talk to her! How else was he going to explain, convince her? But perhaps it would be better not to do so now, he told himself. Dearest Sarah seemed very angry still, and she was not feeling well. Perhaps after she had a little nap, things would improve. And he would make a pot of tea for her, try and find something for her to eat, in case she was hungry. And after that, she was sure to be more amenable. At least he hoped she would.

He saw he would need more wood, and he sighed. It was true there was a considerable pile outside the cottage, but it was old wood, and it was beginning to rot. It seemed to burn much more rapidly than any he had seen before. Putting on his driving coat, he went back outside.

Left alone, Sarah thought frantically. Somehow she had to get away from here, make her way home. She wondered what tale Geoff would tell at Three Oaks to explain her absence, but she found just remembering him made her so angry, she could not think clearly. *Horrible* was nowhere near enough a descriptive word for him, the vile creature!

She wondered if she could escape now. Jaspar Howland had gone outside. Perhaps she would have a chance before he returned? Just then she heard him fumbling with the door, and she frowned. But perhaps it's just as well, she told herself. She did have the headache, and she probably wouldn't get far. Besides, she didn't even know which direction to go. Surely this cottage must be very isolated. He would not risk taking her anywhere else. And it had to be on his own property, not that that helped much. Castleton comprised thousands of acres. She could wander about in it for days, lost and cold, and never find the way. She'd have to trick him into telling her where they were. Later, she told herself as the wood he had brought in slipped from his grasp and crashed to the floor. As he cursed under his breath, a little smile curled her lips. Of course! She knew what she was going to do now, and oh, how she looked forward to it! The Earl of Castleton was going to learn a very hard, very humbling lesson, and she would be delighted to be the one teaching it to him.

Soothed by the unholy plan she had concocted, she began to doze.

Sarah managed to sleep for almost an hour, and when she woke, she felt much better. The headache she had suffered as a result of her brother's drugging was gone, and she no longer felt dizzy when she sat up. From where he was seated before the fire, Jaspar Howland's face brightened when he saw she was awake.

"You are feeling better, I hope?" he asked, rising to come to her.

Sarah nodded curtly as she swung her legs over the side of the bed. Then she looked around, as if for the first time.

"Where have you brought me?" she demanded.

He grinned at her, but she did not respond. "Why, this is a woodcutter's deserted cottage to the west of Castleton," he said.

"One can only pity the woodcutter. No wonder he is no longer here," Sarah said in a scornful voice.

"Well, I realize it is not much, but it will suffice. Er, would you like a cup of tea, ma'am?"

She nodded again, but when he turned away, she said, "I would wash first. Some hot water and a towel. And I would retire, too."

"Retire?" he asked, looking perplexed.

"Yes, *retire*," she said icily. "I assume there is someplace I can go, be private—take care of my needs?"

"Oh. Oh, yes. Over there."

Sarah looked where he pointed. Someone had draped a large linen sheet across the far corner of the room. She sniffed in disdain.

"I know it is not at all what you are used to," the earl hurried to say. "Not what I'm used to either. But it is the best I could do."

Sarah rose to her feet, twitching her arm away

187

when he reached out to steady her. "Don't touch me!" she ordered. "I am quite able to walk there myself. But I must ask you to leave the cottage while I am . . . busy. The hot water?"

He hurried to the kettle that was slung on a hook over the fire. As he touched it, he yelped and withdrew his hand. Sarah could have warned him the handle could be hot. Gingerly Jaspar Howland picked the kettle up with a towel to protect his hand, poured some water into a basin, and carried that to the table. He left the towel next to it.

"Where is the soap?" Sarah demanded.

"S-Soap?"

"One can hardly wash without soap!" she snapped.

"Er, no, of course not, but to tell the truth, I forgot to supply any," he said, running a hand through his hair. Sarah was delighted to see he was beginning to look harried.

"How charming. Well, are you going to leave, or not? If you continue to hang about here, the water will grow cold."

"Oh, yes, of course," he said as he grabbed his driving coat from a peg near the door. "I'll be just outside. Call me when you are through."

He opened the door then and stared in dismay at the sleet that was falling steadily. "Sarah, do hurry! It's freezing out here," he begged as he went out and closed the door behind him.

Sarah did not hurry in the slightest. She used the chamber pot set behind the temporary curtain, and lingered over the basin of water. Then she inspected her quarters slowly. She saw the boxes contained a great amount of food and wine, and when she lifted the lid of the trunk, she noted Jaspar Howland had provided himself with an extensive wardrobe. Her lip curled. What had he thought she was to wear during a lengthy stay?

When she called him at last, he rushed inside rubbing his hands together as he made straight for the fire. "Turned very nasty," he said. "Cold, too. Perhaps we'll have snow before long."

"I do not care to talk to you," Sarah said as she sat down at the table, facing away from him. "I believe you mentioned tea?"

"Oh, yes, certainly. It will be ready in a minute," he said, going to hang up his coat before he rummaged through the boxes for a teapot, a cup and saucer, and a caddy.

"Remove this dirty basin at once!" she ordered as he set his booty down. Looking even more harassed, Jaspar took it and threw its contents out the cottage door. Coming back to the table, he put a couple of pinches of tea in the pot and went to fetch the kettle again. When he poured it, the water was not really boiling, and Sarah had all she could do not to chuckle, he was so inept. But of course, she reminded herself, he has been waited on hand and foot from the moment he was born. What would he know about making tea? Or anything else domestic? She had been counting on that.

"Are you hungry?" he asked eagerly. "There's bread and cheese, some fruit."

She nodded, still staring at the fire. It would need more wood shortly, she saw with satisfaction.

He brought the food to the table and placed it in front of her, and then he poured her a cup of tea. Sarah saw his frown as he looked at it, and she did not wonder. It was barely tinged with color.

"I'm afraid this doesn't look much like tea," he said as he put the cup down in front of her. "But perhaps I'll get the hang of making it soon."

Sarah took a tiny sip, made a face, and put the cup down. "One can only hope so," she said disdainfully. "I believe I'll have water instead."

He flushed and went to fill a mug for her. As he

sat down across from her, she glared at him, but he was not intimidated. Cutting a slice of cheese for her, and putting it on a plate with an apple and some bread, he gave it to her.

"Now, Sarah," he said, his voice stern. "You may not want to converse with me, but you must. Otherwise we could be here for some weeks."

"You mean to keep me your prisoner?" she asked as if incredulous.

He nodded, his handsome face grim. "For as long as it takes to make you see reason, my darling one. I know I can make you love me—"

"I have no doubt you can force me to it, yes, for you are stronger than I. But I wonder that you would stoop to rape, sir!"

He flushed. "No, no, I don't mean that at all," he said quickly. "I never intended—that is, it is not a question of—I would never force you or use you that way. I only meant—"

"I will never come to you willingly, not even if you keep me here for years, and that you may wager on."

"Now, dearest Sarah, listen—"

"I've a good mind to take you to court for this!" she snapped.

"Sarah, Sarah, you are talking wildly. You would never do such a thing. Why, your reputation would be ruined!"

"And yours as well, m'lord. I do not think that even your exalted title would save you from the scandal. And surely English justice would see that you were punished for such infamy."

As he rose, she pointed her finger at him. "Sit down!" she ordered. As he sank back into his chair, looking confused, she picked up her bread and cheese and ate it. "There are no serviettes?" she asked.

Woefully, he shook his head.

"I can see I am in for a poor sojourn. The fire needs attending," she added.

He rose at once, and when his back was turned to her, Sarah permitted herself a small grin. She told herself it was really too bad of her to be enjoying herself so much, but she could not help it. And it certainly served him right.

Sarah spent the afternoon pacing the cottage, sitting and staring into the fire, and pointedly ignoring the earl, no matter what he said or how he pleaded. At last he want out into the early dusk for enough wood to get them through the night. Sarah was hungry now, but she made no move toward the supplies he had brought. She was his prisoner, was she not? Then he must do everything. She had no intention of helping him.

After the wood he brought in several loads was stacked near the fire, he began to open a bottle of wine and was reminded in a sharp tone to wash his hands first. A long time later he put a plate of ham, more bread and cheese, and two small meat pasties down on the table between them. Sarah saw the pasties were the kind peddlars sold at Wye on market day, and they looked several days old. As he poured the wine into crystal goblets, she said as if to herself, "No soap, no serviettes, but wineglasses. One can only hope he remembered utensils."

Flushing again, a weary Jaspar Howland got up to search the boxes. When he had located a couple of knives and forks, he took his seat again with relief. He was starving, and he was tired. It seemed to him he had made a hundred trips to the woodpile this long day, and his throat was sore not only from the cold sleet, but from pleading with a deaf Lady Lacey whenever he was in the cottage. And his feet were cold, and wet as well. He dug into his meal with gusto, although even as he did so, he could not help wondering what his chef was serving for dinner this evening at the Hall. A large rib roast perhaps? Several hot dishes? A steaming soup? Some puddings? He almost groaned remembering some of Francois's more lavish spreads.

After they had finished their cold meal, he wished he had thought of coffee. But remembering the fiasco he had made of the tea, he decided it was probably just as well he had not.

The wind had picked up. He could hear it whistling around the cottage walls, and any spot in the room not directly before the fire was cold and drafty. A sudden downdraft in the flue swirled black smoke into the room, and he coughed. When he looked up, he saw Sarah was regarding him intently, and he wondered at it. Then he had a sudden inspiration. Had she hoped he would grow weary of the work he was doing, the time he must spend just keeping them even this comfortable? Did she think he would call a halt to her imprisonment soon? Well, she was wrong, he told himself as he swallowed the last little morsel of cheese. As long as it takes, m'lady, and we shall see who has the stronger will in the end, he promised her silently, his mouth set in a grim line.

After their simple supper, he pushed the plate to one side, poured another glass of wine for himself, and said, "Now, let us be sensible, my love. I would have you know I am determined, and I have no intention of failing in this. Indeed, as I have told you over and over this day, I—"

Sarah rose from the table. "I must ask you to leave the cottage, sir. I would prepare for bed."

Slowly he rose as well, never taking his eyes from her contained face.

"Of course," he said politely. "I think there is enough hot water to wash with. . . ."

"I shall attend to it. But then you will need more water to do the dishes."

192

"Wash the dishes?" he asked, as if he had never heard of such a thing before.

Her brows rose. "Of course. Otherwise the mice will have a feast on the crumbs. Surely you have heard them running about in the loft. If you do not put every scrap of food in a safe place, it will be spoiled by morning."

"But . . ."

"The chamber pot will need emptying as well."

Sarah turned on her heel and walked to the curtain, standing there with her back turned until she heard the earl leave the cottage. The cold air that blew in when he opened the door made her nod with satisfaction, and she made sure to use the very last drop of water in the kettle as she rinsed her face and hands.

She did not remove her riding habit before she got into bed. She knew she would need it for extra warmth when the fire died down.

Long minutes later, the door opened cautiously. "Sarah? Are you finished?" the earl asked through chattering teeth. Smiling, Sarah closed her eyes and pretended to be asleep.

It took Jaspar Howland a very long time to clean up and think about going to bed himself. He had not needed her to remind him of the mice, for he had seen enough evidence to know the cottage was overrun with them. Eventually he took all his clothes from the trunk, and packed most of the food inside instead. Then there was the chamber pot to deal with, the dishes to wash after he fetched and heated more water, and . . . and . . . *and*!

He turned down the bedclothes next to her at last. But as he was about to climb into the fresh new featherbed he had had Jennings buy, he heard her outraged voice. "How dare you!" she exclaimed. "Leave this bed at once!"

"Now, Sarah, be reasonable," he argued. "This

193

is the only one in the cottage. I promise I won't touch you until we come to an agreement, but I must sleep somewhere."

She glared at him, her eyes almost golden in the firelight in her indignation. "You may sleep anywhere you like, except with me," she said. "The very idea!"

"But where?" he demanded, trying desperately to hang on to his temper.

"There is the loft, or the chair, or the floor. I don't know and I don't care. Oh, I suppose you must have a pillow and a blanket. Here, take them and go!"

Catching the items she tossed him, the earl backed away, eyeing the featherbed with longing. He had not planned for anything like this. Indeed, he told himself as he tried to get comfortable in the two chairs, he had thought that by this time, the two of them would have been in each other's arms in bed, making love. Groaning a little at the thought of it, he eyed Sarah stretched out there, and he couldn't help resenting her. It was a wide bed. There was plenty of room in it for him, with no danger of contact between them. How could she be so unkind? So selfish?

Eventually the earl gave up on the chairs, and he spent the night on the hard floor before the fire. At least he could lie down there, and it was easier to keep the fire going, for he had only to stretch out his arm to the wood stacked nearby. But he did not sleep well, and the sounds of the mice scurrying about made for a restless night. He woke at dawn, stiff and sore. Muttering curses, he walked about, trying to work out the kinks in his body. When he opened the door to look out, he saw it had stopped sleeting, although it was just as cold, and he tried to be thankful for small blessings.

He set a kettle to heat for porridge, found the sugar, and decided he would have to try his hand at tea making again. The milk he had left outside the door in a jug to keep cool had frozen, and he brought it in to place near the fire. As he threw several large handfuls of porridge into the kettle, he could not help looking daggers at the still-sleeping Lady Lacey.

She looked so comfortable, nestled in the feather-bed, swathed in cozy blankets, her head on a number of downy pillows. If he hadn't known she would make a bolt for it the minute he fell asleep, he would have climbed into that bed the minute she left it, for a good long nap.

The breakfast he produced later could not be said to be a success. True, the tea looked a little more like tea should this time, although it was tepid and strangely bitter. But the porridge was nothing more than a glutinous mass that was difficult to ladle from the kettle. Since he had forgotten to stir it, it had burned on the bottom and now was permeated with an unpleasant scorched aroma.

Sarah eyed the bowl he set before her with distaste. She dipped a spoon into it and held it up, seemingly fascinated as Jaspar Howland watched her. At last she turned the spoon over, but the porridge did not fall back into the bowl. Instead, it clung to the spoon like glue.

"Watery tea, porridge you could use to cement bricks together—you do seem to have a problem with, er . . . *consistency*, don't you, m'lord?" she asked sweetly.

The earl lost his temper. He had just discovered he had forgotten to put the scones intended for breakfast in his trunk, and the mice had had a merry time ruining them for human consumption. They had also gnawed through several boxes he had thought secure, opened the sacks there, and scattered the contents. Now Jaspar Howland rose from the table, picked up Sarah's bowl, and threw it to the floor. She watched him silently as it smashed, splattering porridge in large, thick blobs.

"Enough!" he roared. "I'll not hear another word! I'm doing the best I can, and the least you can do is be a little more appreciative!"

"I?" Sarah asked scornfully. "But I am your prisoner, not a guest here. I shall say whatever I choose until you come to your senses and let me go."

He did not reply, and her brows rose. Instead he sat down at the table and put his head in his hands. Moments later when he looked up, Sarah almost gasped at what she saw in his angry eyes, his hard face. He did not look twenty-two now, and she was a little afraid of him.

Without a word, he went to the corner to rummage through the clothes he had placed there. Taking a couple of yard-long, crisp white cravats, he advanced on her. Before she could protest, he whipped her hands behind her and tied them securely to the rungs of the chairback.

"Whatever are you doing? Are you mad?" she demanded breathlessly as he proceeded to kneel and tie her feet in like manner to the chair legs.

"No, not mad, m'lady," he said. "But I must leave you to your own devices for a while, and I cannot leave you free, or you would run away. I have to go to Ashford. We need supplies. But don't worry. I'll remember the soap and serviettes, along with candles, bread, and milk—everything. Oh, and several tin boxes to thwart those damned mice. But most important of all, I'm getting another featherbed. I have no intention of letting you go, but I refuse to spend one more night as uncomfortable as this past one."

"You are just going to go away and leave me here like this?" she asked in a voice so nervous, he smiled grimly to himself. "But—but what if you have an accident and don't return? I shall be help-less here!"

He moved past her to build up the fire before he turned around and nodded. "You'll do," he said coldly. "I'll return as quickly as I can, and if I should have an accident, your brother will rescue you tomorrow.

"Might I advise you, ma'am, to spend the time I am gone thinking very seriously about your situa-tion? And remembering that I am resolved still to make you my countess?"

Sarah sat speechless, glaring at him as he put on his greatcoat and hat. "You shall not win this bat-tle, m'lady," he said in a hard voice. "Resign your-self to failure. And marriage."

As he opened the door and stepped out, Sarah found her voice. "Bring back a broom, too!" she called. "This floor is filthy!"

His only reply was to slam the door—hard.

Thirteen

EVAN LANCASTER HAD been surprised when Lady Lacey's groom approached him in Sutton Cross the previous afternoon. Although the two of them had exchanged nods on occasion, they had hardly spoken to each other, and when he saw the worried look Leary wore, he was suddenly apprehensive.

"There is something wrong at Three Oaks? Is Sa—er, Lady Lacey all right?"

The groom shook his head. "I don't think she is, sir," he said. "I'm that glad to see you. I've been looking for you, for there was no one else I could think of who might help me."

Lancaster waved an impatient hand. "What has happened?" he demanded, frightened suddenly that the mysterious letter writer might have found a way to do Sarah harm.

"This morning Lady Lacey went for a ride with her brother. I didn't go along, but I thought nothing o' that. But much later, Mr. Jennings returned alone, trailing his sister's mare. He told a story o' how they had come upon the carriage o' one o' Lady Lacey's old society friends, how she had begged m'lady to accompany her to Tunbridge Wells, where she was bound for a short stay. On a whim, Jennings said, his sister had agreed to do so, for the lady promised to share not only her wardrobe, but send her back in her own carriage in a few days time. But—but I don't like the sound o' it, sir! It's not like my mistress to do such a harebrained thing, not like her at all! But I can't question Mr. Jennings, and from what I can gather, her parents are not at all concerned. Only her maid, Betsy Grinnell, agrees with me that there's more here than meets the eye."

Evan had listened to the groom's tale in deep concentration. Only moments ago, Abner Bower had told him that the earl had left Castleton that morning, although no one seemed to know whether he was going to London or somewhere else. And he had not taken his valet with him. Unusual, that. The young man had never been known to travel without his services.

Could it be that he had taken Sarah somewhere, with Geoffrey Jennings's help? It seemed a mad thing to do, but then Evan, like Leary, put little faith in this story of an old society friend and a sudden dash to the spa town.

"Do you have any idea which direction they rode out this morning?" he asked now.

Leary nodded eagerly. "Aye, that I do, sir! Mr. Jennings did say they met the carriage on the road to Ashford."

"I see," Lancaster said thoughtful. "I think I'll just ride that way myself today, see what I can find. That road borders a part of Castleton. It may be that—"

The groom gasped. "You don't think that there earl has got her, do you, sir?" he asked. "I know he's mad for her, but surely he wouldn't do such a thing as that!"

"Maybe not. But he does seem the most likely prospect, for he left the Hall himself this morning at about the same time Sarah went for her ride.

"Go back to Three Oaks now, and don't say a word about this to anyone, do you hear? Not even to her maid. To do so might put the lady in danger.

And listen well. If you hear anything else from that brother of hers, come to my farm and tell me."

Leary tugged his forelock and hurried away to mount his horse. He wished he might go with Lancaster, help him search, but he knew he would be missed if he did. And if Jennings was involved, he might become suspicious. Best he go back, listen hard, and act normal.

Evan mounted as well and set out for the Ashford road. But although he searched the entire route of it, he saw not a sign of Sarah or the earl.

At last the sleet and approaching darkness forced him to ride home. He was absentminded all evening and deep in thought. Somehow he had become convinced that Howland had Sarah tucked away somewhere on his own land, and his mouth tightened at the thought of her at that young cub's mercy. But where on his land? Castleton was huge; he might have her anywhere. But no, he told himself, that was not so. If Jennings had taken the Ashford road, the place had to be on the west side of the estate. They would not have risked transporting her on the high road for any length of time.

He was up early the following morning, eating his breakfast just as dawn was breaking. His aunt seemed surprised to see him there when she came down to the kitchen, and more surprised when he told her he would not be accompanying her to church. She was to go alone with the maids, for he had something else to do.

But before she could question him, he was gone. Miss Barnes frowned and shook her head.

Evan rode more slowly today, often investigating breaks in the trees and bushes on the Castleton side of the road, but to no avail. At last he saw the tracks of a team and cart on an overgrown lane. The sleet that remained from yesterday's storm showed them clearly. Exultant now, he followed the tracks until they led him to a deserted cottage.

As he dismounted, he noticed there was smoke coming from the chimney, and his mouth tightened. If Jaspar Howland had hurt her, he would kill him, he told himself as he banged on the door.

For a moment there was silence, then Sarah's voice called out, "Who is it?"

She sounded frightened, and Evan waited no longer. His eyes narrowed as he pushed the door open and saw her there before the fire, bound hand and foot to a chair.

"Evan! Oh, how glad I am to see you!" she exclaimed, her eyes glowing with relief. "You'll never know how glad!"

He knelt and untied her bonds and helped her to her feet. When she rubbed her wrists and grimaced, Evan frowned. The marks left by the earl's cravats were red against the fairness of her skin.

"Where is he, Sarah?" he asked, and she looked up at him, startled by the rough anger she heard in his voice.

"He—he had to go to Ashford for supplies. But how on earth did you find me? How did you know I was here?"

"There's plenty of time to tell you all that later," Evan said. "Best we be off. We'll have to ride double, but the farm's not far. Come!"

As he helped her to the door, Evan looked around the cottage. When he saw the large featherbed against the wall, he felt such a rush of rage, it was a very good thing Jaspar Howland was nowhere in sight.

"But I still don't understand why you were looking for me," Sarah complained as soon as they were mounted and on their way.

"I didn't believe that you'd gone to Tunbridge Wells with a chance-met old friend yesterday," he said, trying to forget how she felt in his arms. "Leary said your parents did, however."

"Is that what my brother told them? Ha! No, I was kidnapped by my brother and none other than the earl himself. He intended to keep me in the cottage until I agreed to marry him, if you can credit that." Then she added anxiously, "Shouldn't we go faster? He might return at any time, discover me missing, and come after me."

"I doubt that, ma'am," Evan said wryly, still wishing he might have a confrontation with the earl. Later, he told himself. "He's forgotten it's Sunday and the shops aren't open. Not that I doubt he'll be able to persuade someone to open shop for him, with all his gold and arrogance, but it will take him quite a while.

"And," he added slowly, "I doubt very much he'd want this escapade bruited about. Lord, just think what Miss Dye and Pry could do with it! No, he'll slink back to his Hall and brood about lost opportunity. It was lost, wasn't it, Sarah?" he added in a deeper, more serious voice.

Somehow she could only nod, but she felt his arms tighten around her in what she hoped was relief.

"I'm so hungry and dirty," she said after a mile or so of silence. "The earl's such an incompetent lad, he forgot soap, and he couldn't cook a lick."

"You could have helped him," Evan remarked. "I mean . . . you can cook, can't you?"

"Of course I can. I learned years ago, but I wanted him to suffer. Of course, it meant I had to suffer, too—you should have seen the burned porridge he served up this morning, like glue—but it was worth it."

As Evan turned the horse in to the drive leading to his farm, Sarah felt herself relaxing, for in spite of his reassuring words, Evan had not seen how determined Jaspar Howland was. And she had really

202

believed he would come after her in a blaze of temper.

She slid to the ground herself, and after Evan tied the horse to the fence, he took her arm to lead her to the kitchen. "I'll make some tea for you, get out my aunt's scones," he said as he filled a large pitcher with hot water and fetched some soap and a clean towel from the scullery. "Here, I'll show you where you can freshen up in one of the spare rooms. Get you a comb, too."

When she came back downstairs, Sarah looked a great deal better, and she smiled at him as she took a seat at the large deal table.

It was very quiet in the house, and she sat silently as he handed her a plate of scones, put out the butter and peach jam, and poured her a perfect cup of tea. "How good that smells," she said as she buttered a scone and took a large bite of it. "Mmmm. Delicious.

"But where is everyone? Your aunt? The maids?"

"Gone to church in the village," he said evenly as he took a seat across from her where he could see her best.

Sarah looked at him, and for a moment there was no sound but the ticking of the old clock on the wall. "I see," she said at last. "Perhaps that's just as well. I've no mind to bear scandal, and scandal there would certainly be if any of this got out."

She finished her tea and ate another scone, then Evan rose. "I'll saddle my aunt's horse for you," he said, heading for the door.

Sarah nodded as she got up to put the food away, wash the few dishes.

But when he would have cupped his hands for her to mount later, she put her own hands on his arms. "Evan, I can't thank you enough," she said seriously. "I don't know why you're so good to me."

"Don't you?" he asked, staring down at her intently.

"I know what I'd like to think was the reason," Sarah whispered. "How happy it would make me, if it were true."

He searched her face, and she watched his expression grow colder as he made a move to step away from her.

Without even questioning what she was doing, Sarah put her arms around his neck, pressed against him. "Evan?" she begged softly. "Is that what you really want to do? Leave me without a word?"

He moved so swiftly then, Sarah was unprepared, and she gasped as he crushed her in his arms. His mouth slanted down over hers and he kissed her with such hunger, she was almost shocked by it. Still, she responded eagerly as his hands caressed her back, and his lips became more demanding. She buried her hands in his thick blond hair, reveling in his touch, the clean, warm smell of him—his strength.

For a long, glorious time they clung together, lost in their embrace. At last Evan raised his head a few inches to look down at her. How beautiful she is, he thought bleakly, watching the way her eyelashes fluttered on cheeks that were now flushed with feeling. Her soft, pink mouth trembled, and he had all he could do not to kiss her again. But he knew that would not be right. What he had just done was bad enough; he must not make it worse. But he had not been able to resist her invitation, not after all the years he had loved her . . . missed her . . . wanted her.

"Best we be on our way," he made himself say roughly.

Her eyes flew open to search his face, and when she saw the coldness there, she shook her head a little. "You cannot wish that kiss we shared away, just like that, my dear," she told him.

"I know that," he said as he removed her hands from around his neck. "I wouldn't want to, for I shall like to keep the memory of it always."

He turned away as she demanded, "But why must it just be a memory? I would be happy to give you as many kisses as you want—a whole lifetime of them, in fact."

"No," he said harshly. "It cannot be. You are Lady Lacey, and—"

"I was only Sarah Jennings before that!" she retorted. "A farmer's daughter."

"A farmer's *beautiful* daughter. Yes, you were, but you have gone far beyond me now, Sarah—become used to a grander life than I can give you."

He saw she was about to protest, and he held up his hand. "No, no more! Come, mount. We must make haste lest you be seen by all the churchgoers making their way home from service."

Sarah saw he was adamant, and feeling more rejected than she ever had in her life, she accepted his lift to the saddle. Her eyes were prickling with tears, but she blinked them away as they trotted down the drive, determined he would not see them.

They were almost to Three Oaks before she was able to put her thoughts of Evan and his decision aside so she could consider what she was to say to her brother and her parents. How I look forward to this confrontation, she thought. How good it will be to tell Geoffrey exactly what I think of him.

When she and Evan arrived at the front of the house, she dismounted so he could take his aunt's horse back with him. And, she told herself as he left her with only a tip of his hat and a last searching glance, she would have time after her interview to decide what she was to do about the stubborn Mr. Lancaster. What she was to do about herself as well. How she was to resolve this entire impossible situation.

She marched up the steps and banged the door knocker. When no one opened the door quickly, she did so herself, to step into the hall. She could hear a murmur of voices coming from the dining room, and as Thomas hurried back to the hall, she realized her family was at Sunday dinner. Good, she thought, nodding to the dumbstruck footman. If they are all there, I can get this over with that much sooner.

As she entered the dining room, Bradbury looked up at her from the sideboard where he was carving a roast, and he gaped. But Sarah had no eyes for him. She looked at Geoffrey first, then her gaze swept her mother and father. To her surprise, they all seemed identically stunned, and, more important, identically disappointed. So Geoff had told them what he had done, had he? And they had approved the scheme? Sarah's anger turned to rage, and she took a deep breath to steady herself before she said, "Bradbury, if you would excuse us, please?"

No one else spoke as the butler bowed and left the room, carefully closing the door behind him.

Sarah walked forward. "So," she said. "I see you are not pleased to see me? Especially *you*, brother? I am sure you did not expect me for some days yet, did you? But it is obvious to me you have told our parents the whole story. I wonder they did not protest such underhanded dealings that involved their only daughter. Sent out a search party to find me in their concern."

She gave her parents a scornful look, and Mr. Jennings had the grace to color up. Her mother, she saw, had set her jaw and was looking militant. She would never admit to wrongdoing, and Sarah knew it.

She took the vacant seat facing her brother and said evenly, "I have never liked you much, Geoffrey, although I could not have told you why. Now I know why. You are not to be trusted. Furthermore, you are vile and despicable. To think you would go so far as to pander me to the earl denotes a character so evil, it revolts me!"

Geoffrey sat back in his chair watching her, and a little smile played over his handsome mouth. But Sarah saw the hot anger in his eyes at her assessment of him.

"How dare you speak to your brother that way?" Mrs. Jennings cried. "He was only doing what was best for you, which you, you foolish creature, should realize.

"And it serves you right, too! So hard-hearted and penny-pinching you are, refusing to help the dear boy in his troubles, give him some of your inheritance. And furthermore—"

"Be quiet," Sarah ordered. "I'll hear no more from you.

"Why did you do it, Geoff?" she asked in a steadier voice as Mrs. Jennings subsided, stunned into silence at her daughter's awful command. "What was the *real* reason?"

He considered her for a moment before he shrugged. "Oh, because Jaspar Howland is so rich, I suppose. And because it would have done me a great deal of good to have an earl for my brother-in-law. I would never have had to worry about money or standing again. By the way, how did you escape Howland?"

"That is not important. Tell me, did you make this decision to sell me to the earl after your plan to seduce Lady Rose failed?"

"So you know about that, do you?" he asked, cocking an eyebrow at her. He seemed so calm, so

207

cool, Sarah wanted to rage at him, but she knew losing her temper would not serve her here.

"Yes, I saw you embracing her from the window overlooking the terrace, the night Mr. Whitaker took you to task," she said.

"It's just as well it came to nothing," her brother said calmly. "The Lady Rose has no money unless she marries with her brother's approval, or, failing that, until she reaches twenty-one. It would have been a long wait. Then, too, this way was much more agreeable to me. . . ."

"To *you*, perhaps," Sarah said swiftly. "Had you no thought for *me*? No, of course you didn't. What a stupid thing for me to ask!"

"Now, Sarah," Mr. Jennings began, sounding as placating as was possible for him, "I can see you are upset, yes, and I admit you have some reason, from your point of view anyway. But what Geoffrey did was not only for your own good, but for the family's as well. I will admit freely that I would like nothing better than to be related to the earl. Quite a step up for me, it would be. And no doubt the lad would have put me in the way of some advantages—land, investments, the like. And you could have lived like the queen. So when Geoff told us what had transpired, we were quite content, Mary and I. Everyone would benefit; you, the most. We did not begrudge it to you, you know.

"I must say I do not understand your attitude; why you take this so hard. For, after you have spent the night with Howland, you are bound to marry him, and there's the happy ending we all sought."

Sarah saw her mother sit up straighter, her attention arrested—the eager look that came over her face—and she laughed.

"This was the reason you invited me to come home, wasn't it?" she asked when she could speak again. "Mother did not really need me, nor was she that ill. No, it was all a ploy to get me under your roof again, and, you hoped, under your control so that you could take over the handling of my money. The earl's arrival and his instant infatuation must have seemed like manna from heaven, did it not?"

No one answered, and she went on, "As for my having to marry the earl, you are wrong, sir. I am a widow, not a maid. And in society many married ladies have any number of love affairs. I do assure you, no one thinks a thing of it. So you may put all thoughts of a hurried bridal from your minds. You made me marry once against my wishes. You will never do so again, for I am happy to remind you, you have no authority over me anymore. Thank heavens for that!"

"Unnatural creature!" Mrs. Jennings muttered. "To scorn her father's and mother's guiding hands . . ."

"They have done such wonders for me, haven't they, those hands?" Sarah asked. "Always put me second to my wastrel brother, forced me to a loveless marriage with a worthless man—oh, how can you doubt my relief that I have escaped them?

"Furthermore, I shall choose my own husband now. And the man I have chosen is not the Earl of Castleton."

Sarah paused for a moment. What am I saying? she thought wildly. Then Evan's beloved face came to mind, and she nodded, resolved. She saw her family was looking at her, incredulous, and she went on, "I am going to marry Evan Lancaster."

"What?" "Good heavens!" "Never!" her parents and Geoff cried out in unison.

"Yes, I am, and there is nothing any of you can do to stop me," Sarah said firmly.

She saw her brother start to get up, his face pale and his hands already forming fists, and she said quickly, "Stay where you are, Geoff. If you offer me violence, I shall call out. By my orders, my groom, Leary, is just outside the door."

She relaxed as Geoff took his seat again, glad he had not called her bluff.

"But—but Sarah, you cannot have thought," James Jennings said in an agitated voice. "Lancaster is *no* one! He's only a farmer!"

"As you yourself are, Father," she agreed, nodding to him.

"But—but if you marry him, *you* will be no one! You won't even be the Dowager Lady Lacey anymore. You'll be a mere missus!"

"So I will. How I look forward to it," she replied.

Her father moaned and covered his eyes with his hands, his shoulders slumping. Sarah saw her mother staring at her with such a look of horror and disbelief that she had to look away quickly, lest she laugh at her. And as for Geoffrey, his steady gaze was so full of poisonous hatred, she was stunned. But of course, she reminded herself, such rich, noble friends as he had were sure to take objection to the brother of a farmer's wife.

How important her title was to these three, she realized. Much more important than she was herself. It was a lowering thought.

"If you persist in this terrible thing, you will cease to be our daughter from this day on," Mary Jennings got out in an awful tone. "Be warned, for we shall never acknowledge you again."

Sarah turned to her, and there was a faint look of regret in her eyes as she said, "I do not think I have ever been your daughter, ma'am. I was only the child who was born before your beloved son. The girl you have always used for *his* advantage, as well as your own. And now it is more than time all that ended. I must thank you for throwing me off. Your decision has set me free."

She rose then and took a deep breath. "I shall

leave Three Oaks tomorrow latest. I would go to-day, but I fear there is too much to do to make that possible."

She turned to leave the silent group, and then turned back. Coolly she took up a plate and filled it with the various dishes set on the table. As she walked to the sideboard to get some beef, she said, "This will be the last food I will ever eat at Three Oaks. You see, I could not be sure that any food brought to me from now on might not have been, er, *tampered* with, shall we say? I would put nothing past the lot of you!"

She shut the door of the dining room behind her and beckoned to the waiting footman. "Take this plate to my room, Thomas. And, Bradbury, please send a message to the stables. Tell Joe Coachman and Leary that the carriages are to be ready to travel tomorrow. I am quitting Three Oaks."

The old butler nodded, but he looked miserable. "We'll miss you, lass. All of us here will miss you," he said.

Sarah did not speak lest she begin to cry. How kind it had been of him to say that, she thought. He was a good man.

As she went up the stairs, holding on to the banister in her weariness, she told herself she must remember that there were many good men in the world. And as soon as she could manage it, she was going to marry the best one of them all.

Fourteen

SARAH LACEY DID not climb into her traveling carriage early the following morning as she had originally planned to do. Instead, she ordered her mare brought up to the house, and told Leary he was to accompany her on a ride.

She had had a long time to think late yesterday afternoon and evening. At first she had only eaten her dinner before she fell into bed exhausted, to sleep for several hours. But when she woke, she began to turn the problem that was Evan Lancaster over and over in her mind.

Somehow it seemed too brazen to just appear at his farm, with all her trunks piled high on the carriage, her phaeton coming behind, and a groom trailing her mare. What would Evan think of such a parade of wealth? And what might his aunt think, to say nothing of the servants?

Sarah fully intended to show Evan the error of his ways in regard to their future together, but she did not care to bludgeon him over the head with it, as if it were a fait accompli. And after all, she had so little to go on—just a few of his words . . . certain looks he had given her . . . how he had held her in the glade and comforted her . . . that one passionate kiss they had shared.

Maybe . . . maybe she was wrong? But no, she told herself, her eyes shining. She knew she was not. He loved her, all right.

Eventually she decided to ride to the farm first and seek an interview with him alone. Then she would confess her love, tell him how many years she had felt this way, and how she always would. And she would tell him as well how little she had ever cared for the life he thought she would be sacrificing to marry him. How no gown or jewel or London party could ever hold a candle to the love they could share together with their children around them. Just thinking about it made her feel warm all over.

A wide-eyed Betsy had brought her a breakfast tray early that morning, assuring her that cook had prepared it herself and allowed no one else to come near it, so m'lady might be easy. Sarah had smiled and eaten everything provided. It seemed she had some champions in this house after all.

By eight-thirty she was trotting up the drive of Lancaster Farm. She had wondered at Leary's smiles, how he hummed to himself all the way there, but she assumed it was because he—as they all were—was so glad to be leaving Three Oaks at last.

The same little maid answered her knock, but when Sarah asked for Mr. Lancaster, the girl shook her head.

"He is not here?" Sarah asked, aghast. She had never thought that he would not be. What was she to do now?

"I see," she made herself say with an easy smile. "Be so good as to ask Miss Barnes if she would receive me then."

The maid hurried away, and Sarah had time to think of what she was going to say. Hetty Barnes was a formidable-looking woman, and Sarah had sensed she took more than a passing interest in her nephew and his well-being. What could she say to convince the woman that she felt the same way? How explain what she was doing here?

It is past time for dithering, my girl, she told herself as she straightened her shoulders. And the Lord helps those who help themselves.

"There was something you wanted to see me about, Lady Lacey?" Hetty Barnes asked in a stiff, cold voice.

"Miss Barnes, good morning. Yes, I do have something I wish to say. I am sorry your nephew is not here, but I would explain myself to you in his absence, if I may?"

She paused then, a little startled that the woman had not asked her to step in, take a seat in the parlor.

As if suddenly reminded of her manners, her reluctant hostess held the door wider and gestured.

"Thank you. So kind," Sarah went on, wondering if she was to bear the entire brunt of this conversation. No matter. She would not be put off.

As she sat down, and Miss Barnes took a seat facing her across the hearth, she drew a steadying breath. "This is not easy for me to say, ma'am," she began. "And I can only pray you do not think me forward. But I am in love with your nephew, and I'm sure he's in love with me."

She paused again, but Miss Barnes only stared at her.

"I know Evan wants to marry me, but he has said he will not. He told me that I have grown accustomed to a grander life than he can give me, and . . . and so he is willing to put our love aside.

"But I will not have it so! I care nothing for the things he thinks I would miss. I never have. And I loathed my first marriage to the viscount, and everything that comprised it."

"You did?" Hetty Barnes asked, her voice incredulous as she spoke for the first time.

214

Sarah nodded, relieved her monologue was over. "I did indeed. My parents forced me to that marriage, and no amount of my pleading could sway them from their purpose. Which was, of course, for me to gain a title so they would all be elevated. Such pride! It is ridiculous! Lately they have been trying to force me to accept Earl Castleton. He is only an infatuated boy, and his rank and wealth do not interest me either. But I could not stay at Three Oaks once I denied him. I am leaving it forever, for my parents have disowned me."

Miss Barnes was losing her skeptical look. Now she clucked her tongue in disgust, and the homely sounds made it easier for Sarah to go on. "I could not leave the area until I had had a chance to see Evan—explain. Will he be gone for long today?"

"For longer than that," his aunt said, and Sarah looked concerned. "When I returned from church yesterday, I found him packing his saddlebags. He said he had some business to take care of here first, and my, he did look that grim when he said it! Then he was going on to Ashford, perhaps beyond. He was so angry, so aloof, I could not question him. But I—I knew that somehow it all had to do with you."

"You did? But how?" Sarah demanded, leaning forward a little in her eagerness.

"I have known my nephew loved you for many years, ma'am," Miss Barnes said slowly. "Aye, many years. Yesterday I hoped Evan would go and stay away for a long time; hoped he would forget you at last, or if he could not do that, become resigned to losing you again."

"Why would you feel like that?" Sarah asked, bewildered. "I have done nothing to hurt you, have I? Been unkind somehow?"

Her hostess shook her head before she looked down at her clasped hands and began to rock in her chair a little as she bit her lower lip in thought. Sarah watched her, perplexed.

"You truly do love my nephew?" she asked at last.

"With all my heart. I have loved him since I was sixteen," Sarah said honestly.

"Even so, I do not see how this marriage could ever succeed," Miss Barnes said, almost to herself. She looked worried now. "Evan needs someone like Fay Denton, a farmer's daughter. One who would help him around the place, cook for him, darn his hose, bear his children. And you, well . . ."

"I would remind you, ma'am, I was not always a viscountess," Sarah said. "When I was younger, I tagged after my father's agent, even helped with the farm chores. And our cook taught me well in the kitchen. Maybe someday we can have a contest as to whose muffins are lightest?

"And I do assure you I can darn and sew and knit. As for children, well, we will have to see. But I love children as much as I think Evan does. I hope to have a whole quiver full of them."

Miss Barnes did not smile. "There's still your money. Evan is proud. I know he'll never take it."

"Then we will set it aside for our children, to give them a good start in life," Sarah said firmly. "I'd not force it on him, although I do think that eventually, when he sees what a good wife I intend to be, he'll agree to use it to buy more land, hire more farmhands, experiment with new crops."

She reached out then and took Hetty Barnes's clasped hands in hers. As she did so, she was surprised at how tense they were. "Do say you will help me, ma'am," she coaxed. "Say you approve?"

To her dismay, the older woman began to cry. She made no sound. Only her wet cheeks and shaking shoulders showed her distress. Uneasily Sarah dropped her hands and sat back in her chair, to give her time to recover.

Hetty Barnes wiped her eyes at last on a corner of her apron. "How wrong I have been," she muttered. "But I did not know. . . . There was no way to tell, and . . ."

Wisely, Sarah held her tongue.

"I pray you can find it in your heart to forgive me, ma'am. But I wouldn't blame you a bit if you couldn't. Just try to remember that what I did, I did for Evan's sake."

"And what was that?" Sarah asked, no more enlightened than she had been moments ago.

"I'm—I'm the one that's been sending you those notes," Miss Barnes admitted at last, her voice gruff.

"*You?*" Sarah gasped. "But why would you do such a terrible thing? If you knew how frightened I have been, how upset . . ."

Her voice died away when she saw Miss Barnes's agonized expression. "I do know. I saw your face when you opened the last one at the church bazaar. The others, of course, I had just dropped off during my rides through the countryside, and I had no idea how they were affecting you. But that one . . . I saw it all too clear. It was then I decided I would write no more. That what I had been doing was so bad that even my love for Evan, and my promise to my sister, could not excuse it."

"But I still don't understand *why* you did it," Sarah persisted. Miss Barnes! she thought. Evan's *aunt* wrote those horrid things? Dear God!

Her hostess rose and walked to the window to hold the curtain aside so she could look out. With her back turned, she said, "I was here when my sister died. She begged me to watch over Evan, her firstborn, best-loved child. And she told me how much he loved you, how, on the day you were mar-

217

ried, he left the farm at dawn and did not return until late that night. Even how he looked when he came home at last. She said he changed that day from a carefree young man to an embittered one. And I promised her before she died that I would take care of him always, do whatever was necessary for his happiness, so she could go content.

"When you came back here, I knew from his face, when he told of meeting you in Wye, that he had not forgotten you as I had hoped. Oh, of course I had suspected that all along, for he would have nothing to do with Fay Denton, or any of the other girls around."

She paused then and added with a touch of pride, "Evan is a real catch, you know, and so handsome!"

"I do know," Sarah whispered. "I think he is, too."

"I was bitter then," Miss Barnes went on, still half turned away, as if she could not bear to look Sarah in the eye. "I have never been happy here on the farm, no matter how much I cared for Evan. I hated the isolation—the loneliness—and I longed for my own rooms, my own friends, in Tunbridge Wells. I thought if you would just go away again, Evan might get over you at last, marry Fay, and set me free. It was . . . it was selfish of me."

"No, only human," Sarah assured her softly.

As if she had not heard her, Miss Barnes went on, "So I devised a plan to frighten you. I thought you would leave quickly. I never imagined you would stay as long as you did.

"Of course, when I heard the gossip, saw the earl's attraction for you, I was sure you stayed for him, and when you agreed to marry him, Evan would see your quality at last. But you did not choose Jaspar Howland. Yet still you stayed. I did not understand why."

"I stayed because I love Evan, of course," Sarah told her.

The older woman nodded as she dropped the curtain and turned to face the girl she had tortured these past weeks. "I know I can't hope you'll forgive me. What I did was terrible. But—but what upsets me most is that when Evan learns what I have done, *he* will hate me. And I can't bear to think of that! He and his sister and brothers are the only family I have left."

Her words ended in a wail, and she threw her apron to her face and began to sob again. "I have been wicked, and I must be punished for it," she mourned.

Sarah rose and went to put an arm around Miss Barnes's ample waist. "There now, ma'am, do calm yourself," she said. "There is no reason for anyone but the two of us to know what you have just told me."

"But Evan already knows of the notes! You did ask him to help you, didn't you? I was that startled to see them in his room one morning when I brought his shaving water."

"Yes, I asked him. I felt he was the only one in Sutton Cross I could trust," Sarah said. "But you stopped writing to me. He will forget them. And if he does not, I will only have to tell him it must remain a mystery. Since it is over, we can forget it."

"You are too good, and I do not deserve it at all," Miss Barnes said weakly.

"I would ask a favor in return, ma'am," Sarah said carefully. She was feeling so much better just from knowing who had sent the notes that it amazed her. Not that she thought she could ever come to love Miss Barnes now, remembering some of her words, her threats. And she admitted she had been delighted to hear that the woman did not like living on the farm, and was eager to leave it. She wanted to be alone with Evan, just the two of them. She did not want to have to share him with a single soul. Not for a long time, anyway.

"I will do anything," Evan's aunt said fervently, and Sarah led her back to her seat, sat down herself, and leaned forward to explain the plan she had just concocted.

After Evan had seen Sarah safely home, he returned to the farm to pack a few necessities for a journey. There was no help for it, he told himself. He could not stay here near her, not after that kiss. She was too tempting. And since he knew that his decision not to ask her to marry him was the only one possible, best he remove himself from temptation. He had always considered himself a man of strong character, but where Sarah Jennings Lacey was concerned, he realized he was nothing but a weak fool.

Evan rode first to the woodcutter's cottage where he had found Sarah. There was no smoke coming from the chimney when he arrived there, but as he tied his horse to a post, he saw a team of horses in a lean-to with a cart nearby, and he nodded in satisfaction, his hazel eyes grim.

Good! he thought as he strode to the door. Jaspar Howland was still here, and now he would have the satisfaction of beating the man royally, inflicting pain, to punish him for what he had done to Sarah.

He knocked on the door. Inside, he could hear the scrape of a chair as it was pushed back, then hurrying footsteps. "Sarah? Have you come back, darling? If you knew how depressed I've been feeling, you—"

The door was flung open, and as the earl stared at an angry Evan Lancaster, saw his clenched fists, he looked stunned.

He dropped his welcoming arms, and a look of such abject misery came over his face that Evan was taken aback.

"What do you want?" the earl asked in a dull voice.

Evan hesitated. Howland looked terrible, so young and yet so despairing with the growth of dark beard he sported, and his sad eyes. Suddenly he had no desire to beat him. It appeared he was being punished quite adequately without that. Then, too, Evan remembered he had felt the same despair five years ago when Sarah had wed another, and the coincidence caused him to feel a sense of camaraderie he would never have expected. Not where Earl Castleton was concerned, at any rate.

"I came to teach you a lesson, m'lord, but I see that is not necessary," he made himself say. "However, what you did, kidnapping Sarah Lacey, was wrong. Very wrong, no matter your motive."

He paused, but the earl only continued to stare at him. "You know that, I'm sure," Evan went on. "It is obvious you love her, which excuses a great deal. However, you must put her from your mind now. She does not love you in return, and she will never marry you. And no one, not even you, my fine lord, can compel another to love. It is either there, or it is not. It cannot be forced.

"Now I must have your word that you will not bother her again. If you do not give it to me, I'll see that news of what you have done gets out, and you will be scorned and ridiculed."

"Where is she?" Howland asked, his voice tortured. "Is she safe?"

"Aye, she's safe. I found her here and took her back to Three Oaks. I expect she will be leaving the area soon.

"Your promise, m'lord?"

Howland put his hands over his face, his shoulders slumping. Evan waited patiently.

"Very well. You have it," the earl said in a muffled voice, sounding sad but resigned. "I see I have little choice."

"None at all," Evan agreed, his own voice hard. "Give you good day."

He turned and walked back to his horse, aware Howland was staring at him, his eyes bleak with disappointment. Poor lad, he thought as he mounted. But he's young. He'll get over it. It's as Sarah said, he is merely infatuated, and those fires burn out quickly. And, I suspect, this is the first time in his life he has ever been denied something he wanted. It was a good lesson for him, albeit a painful one.

Evan spent the night in Biddenden, and he was up early and on the road to Tunbridge Wells at dawn. Once arrived there, he called on his sister, admired the new baby, and stayed for supper. But nothing Janet or her husband could say would persuade him to sleep at their cottage. It was too painful for him, seeing their happiness together, too hard to watch his sister cuddle the baby, kiss her little son and laugh with him.

Instead, Evan put up at an inn. The town was not overcrowded now in November. He fell into conversation with the innkeeper over a pint of ale, and learned from him of some of the notables in town. But his mind was only half on what the man said, and eventually the innkeeper went away, leaving Evan to his thoughts.

How sad it is, he mused. To have loved Sarah so much, and for such a length of time, and then to have to put her aside because she had become a viscountess. As he stared into the depths of his mug, he saw her face, those wonderful brown eyes of hers that turned almost golden in passion or anger; remembered how she had felt in his arms, her lips under his. He groaned a little, knowing that no matter how long he lived, he would never forget her.

He spent another two days at the spa town, trying to find things to do to distract him from his sad thoughts. On the third morning, he woke early as every farmer does, and lay in bed wondering at the futility of what he was doing, and the waste of it. Suddenly he came to a decision and nodded. And he smiled for the first time in days.

He would go back. He loved Sarah, and he would not try to do without her anymore. He would ask her to marry him, honestly explaining what her life with him would be like, and he would not try to make his description of farm life any more idyllic than it really was. Then the decision would be hers.

But he knew he would do his very best to persuade her. No doubt it was selfish of him—he found he did not care. He needed her, loved her, too much.

He did not leave the spa town until early afternoon. There was an important purchase to be made first, and a special call on a dignitary who was visiting here that the innkeeper had told him about.

As he rode east at last, Evan's spirits lifted, for every mile brought Sarah closer to him again. He felt he had been away from her for weeks, instead of days, and he pressed his horse hard, eager for their reunion.

It was evening when he reached his farm two days later. Evan stabled his weary horse, rubbed him down, and gave him a measure of oats before he walked up to the house. Then he heard barking, and he frowned. Was that Ruff? he wondered. But what was she doing *inside*?

He hurried to the door. The dog's barking was frantic now. Aunt Hetty must be going out of her mind, he thought as he fumbled with the latch. But why had she let the dog in the house?

When he stepped into the hall, Ruff leapt up on him, whining her pleasure and trying to lick his face. Evan bent down to pat her, smiling as he did so.

A slight movement near the parlor door made him look up. His breath caught in his throat when he saw Sarah standing there. She was smiling at him, and he shook his head as if he did not believe what he was seeing.

"Sarah?" he asked. "Is it really you? What are you doing here?"

"I've come to live here," she told him, her eyes glowing golden with her pleasure at the sight of him.

Evan put the dog inside and walked toward her. When he was only a foot away, he stopped, as if he still didn't believe she was real. Sarah was having none of that. She came to him to pull his face down so she could kiss him. At the first touch of her lips, Evan caught her in his arms, kissing her back as if he were starved for her.

It was a long time before the two of them drew a little apart, although Evan kept her captive in his arms. Ruff danced around them, still barking, but they ignored her.

"I don't understand any of this, yet I don't care how you came to be here, or why. It's enough for me that you are. And let me warn you, Sarah, I've no intention of letting you go."

"Oh good," she sighed. "I hoped you'd say that."

"Ruff, down. Be quiet!" Evan ordered. The dog subsided, sitting at their feet staring up at them with such a quizzical expression that Sarah laughed.

Evan picked Sarah up then and carried her to his favorite chair in the parlor. "Tell me," he said quietly when they were seated there, Sarah on his lap, and his arms around her as if he feared she might escape him even now.

She told him everything: her banishment from Three Oaks, her decision to come here and tell him how much she loved him, how she and his aunt had devised the plan to surprise him when he returned. The only thing she did not tell him was the identity of the mysterious letter writer. She was glad he seemed to have forgotten all about that.

"Where is Aunt Hetty?" he asked. "I still find it hard to believe that she let Ruff in the house."

"*I* let her in, and she's been a perfect lady, haven't you, girl?

"As for your aunt, she's gone back to Tunbridge Wells by stage. She left this morning, after showing me how you liked things done in the house."

"Good," he murmured, his voice husky. "I love her, of course, but I want to be alone with you now."

"I hope I haven't offended you by my boldness, sir," Sarah said softly. "Assumed too much?"

He kissed her throat, and she closed her eyes. "Well, you did nip in before me," he admitted with a wry grin. "But who cares? Not I! I love you too much.

"But to be fair, I want you to be very sure you know what you are doing," he went on, sterner now. "When we are married, you'll not be m'lady anymore, but plain Mrs. Lancaster. Not that *you* could ever be plain, my darling."

"I shall adore being Mrs. Lancaster," she said firmly.

"And you'll not be received by Lady Willoughby, perhaps not even by some members of the gentry. Miss Farnsworth and Miss Withers, for example, are very proper, and—"

Sarah chuckled as she reached up to caress his face. "Goose!" she said. "Do you really think I'll feel deprived by their loss? It is absurd! Besides, Mrs. Denton will stand my friend."

"Then there's farm life. It can be hard. And it's isolated here. And although you will never want, it won't be a luxurious existence," he continued, frowning a little now in his determination to lay everything before her honestly.

She kissed his frown away, and he captured her lips again with his own. When he let her go, she said breathlessly, "That kiss reassures me. For a moment there, I thought you were having second thoughts about the wisdom of marrying me.

"As for life here, you forget I grew up surrounded by farms. I'm used to them. And as for isolation, I look forward to it, for I, like you, want us to be alone. Together."

Quite a long time later, he said, "I do seem to remember you telling me once that you would never marry again. Why this sudden reversal?"

"Are you teasing me, Evan? To tell truth, I didn't think I ever would, but somehow the thought of marriage with you is different. I feel I could still be my own person then, as well as your wife. That we would be partners, sharing everything, and you wouldn't treat me as a child, or a beautiful object. And with you, I feel safe. Safe, and loved, and needed, too.

"As for the money I bring with me—"

"Yes, the money," he interrupted, his voice hardening. "I'll not touch it, you know."

"Very well," she said. "I won't touch it either. We'll keep it for our children."

"Children?" he asked, sounding amused.

"Lots of them," she told him. "Boys to help you on the farm, and little girls for me. What a shame that we must wait three weeks for the banns to be called before we can begin doing something about that."

"You are a hussy, ma'am," he said. "I wonder I never noticed it before. But there'll be no more waiting for us, even without this," he added, reaching into his pocket. "See, I've a special license that I acquired from a bishop who was visiting Tunbridge Wells to drink the waters. Thank heavens for the man's dyspepsia! And here's your wedding ring. I hope it fits tomorrow morning."

"Oh, Evan!" she cried. "You did come home planning to ask me to marry you, didn't you?"

He took her face between his hands and stared at her for a long, solemn moment before he said, "The very first minute I could manage it. Now, why does that make you cry, love?"

"Because I'm so happy!" she said, smiling through her tears.

Ruff got up from the hearth rug then and came over to them to rest her head on Evan's leg and look at both of them with her dark, trusting eyes.

"It's a good thing you like Sarah so much, Ruff," Evan told her as he patted her head. "Because you are definitely going to have to take second place in my life from now on!"

Epilogue

July 1810

Mɪss Hᴀɴɴᴀʜ Fᴀʀɴsᴡᴏʀᴛʜ broke precedent by calling on her friend Miss Eloise Withers only a day after their weekly tea party. This was so unusual that Miss Withers told her maid to bring her guest to the parlor at once, and not keep the lady standing about in the hall.

She saw from Hannah's pink cheeks and barely suppressed excitement that she had news indeed. Barely waiting to be seated, Miss Farnsworth exclaimed, "The most exciting thing, my dear!"

"What is it?" Miss Withers asked, not at all pleased that Hannah had gleaned some gossip that she herself had not heard.

"Well, as you know, Helene Holmes was kind enough to take me up in her carriage today, for she knew I had to visit the dentist in Wye, and she had some small shopping to do there."

Miss Withers nodded, her face sour. *She* had not been asked to go, and it had rankled all day.

"As I was leaving the dentist, you'll never guess who I saw!" Miss Farnsworth told her, delighted to be first with the news for once, and not at all loath to string out the telling of it if she could.

When her friend had no comment, she went on, "It was Mr. and Mrs. Lancaster. Oh, Eloise, it was so affecting to see the way they looked at each other, the tenderness with which Mr. Lancaster helped his wife from the carriage. How he bent to kiss her cheek before he took her arm. Oh, the look in his eyes, Eloise! I was almost overcome! And they are so in love, they did not even notice me!"

As she sighed, Miss Withers sniffed. "Touching, I'm sure," she said a little tartly to try and stop her friend's romanticizing. "I've been wondering how Sarah was doing. She was so little seen in the village this past winter."

"Well, she's a bride, and that is such a *delicate* time, isn't it?" Miss Farnsworth reminded her, blushing as she did so. "But I suspect she had another reason, too, for she was wearing a pelisse today."

"So?" Miss Withers asked, her dark brows upraised. What on earth was Hannah getting at, she wondered, and why is she so embarrassed? Was age beginning to make her dithery?

"But surely it is a very warm summer day for a pelisse, wouldn't you say?" Miss Farnsworth asked coyly. "When the breeze blew the garment open a little, however, I could see why she had worn it."

Miss Withers leaned forward. "Never say she is with child!" she exclaimed.

Her friend nodded, turning a fiery red as she whispered, "It appeared confinement cannot be far away. I would say no later than August."

She paused then to allow Eloise to count the months since the surprise wedding, before she went on, "What a shame it is that her family disowned her like that. I was never so shocked. And I do think *we* have been amiss, dear. Sarah is a lovely girl, and Mr. Lancaster, quite the gentleman, for all he's a farmer. I expect he'll be an important landowner one of these days. And I've never seen a couple so happy. Perhaps, after the baby is born, we could call at the farm? Take some small gift? Do tell me what you think."

Miss Withers considered. "Yes, we might do that," she agreed. "Let's have a glass of sherry while we discuss it."

As she went to the decanter, she added, "I hear Sarah has quite transformed that old farmhouse. Mrs. Denton was telling me she had a lot of lovely furniture and carpets, china and silver, sent on from the dower house in Oxfordshire. Oh, and some paintings as well. I'd dearly love to see it all, wouldn't you? And we don't want to be the last to do so. That would never do!"

"I wonder how the earl will take it when he learns she's had a child. But we probably won't find out," Miss Farnsworth said sadly. "He's not been at the Hall since last November, and when I saw his aunt a week ago, she told me she had no idea when he would return. Poor boy! I'm sure he was distraught when Sarah chose Mr. Lancaster instead of him."

"It will be the making of Jaspar Howland," Miss Withers said firmly as she handed her guest a brimming glass. "Besides, now we still have his courting and wedding to look forward to, isn't that so?"

Miss Farnsworth tittered and nodded. "I can hardly wait," she breathed.

"To the future, my dear," Miss Withers said as she raised her glass. "To the future!"

More Romance from Regency

Available at your bookstore or use this coupon.

___**THE BERINGER HEIRESS,** Jan Constant	22137	**$3.99**
___**TIME'S FOOL,** Patricia Veryan	22077	**$3.99**
___**GRAND DECEPTION,** Rebecca Ward	22110	**$3.99**
___**THE WILD ROSE,** Rebecca Ward	22164	**$3.99**
___**THE DUKE'S DECEIT,** Leslie Lynn	21969	**$3.99**
___**MISS WITH A PURPOSE,**		
Rebecca Ashley	22088	**$3.99**

FAWCETT MAIL SALES
400 Hahn Road, Westminster, MD 21157

Please send me the FAWCETT BOOKS I have checked above. I am
enclosing $ ...... (add $2.00 to cover postage and handling for the first
book and 50¢ each additional book. Please include appropriate state
sales tax.) Send check or money order—no cash or C.O.D.'s please. To
order by phone, call 1-800-733-3000. Prices are subject to change
without notice. Valid in U.S. only. All orders are subject to availability of
books.

Name_____

Address _____

City_____State_____Zip Code_____

Allow at least four weeks for delivery.

14   3/93 TAF-205